Paperback ISBN 978-1-83889-523-5

Large Print ISBN 978-1-83889-519-8

Ebook ISBN 978-1-83889-517-4

Kindle ISBN 978-1-83889-518-1

Audio CD ISBN 978-1-83889-524-2

MP3 CD ISBN 978-1-83889-521-1

Digital audio download ISBN 978-1-83889-516-7

Boldwood Books Ltd
23 Bowerdean Street
London SW6 3TN
www.boldwoodbooks.com

For my parents

Neere unto the place where Lug and Wy meet together, Eastward, a hill which they call Marcley hill, in the yeere of our redemption 1571 (as though it had wakened upon the sodaine out of a deepe sleepe) roused it selfe up, and for the space of three daies togither mooving and shewing it selfe (as mighty and huge an heape as it was) with roring noise in a fearefull sort, and overturning all things that stood in the way, advanced it selfe forward to the wonderous astonishment of the beholders...

— WILLIAM CAMDEN, *BRITANNIA*, 1610

1

MARCLE RIDGE, 1570

We would sit on the ridge, Sunday afternoons. On bright days, the shadows of the clouds sauntered over the fields bigger than churches, with no weight or noise at all, making their way wherever they wished and no one to stop them, not night nor hunger. 'Look, Owen,' I would say, 'there's the whole world lapping at our feet,' and he would believe me.

Often the men would be at the butts by the chapel, practising with their bows, and sometimes in the summer there'd be dancing, though like as not we'd be down with them then, watching the boys vie to dance with Aggie. They passed me by

– spiky Martha Dynely, skulking by the hedge – but that was no matter, Owen was as handy for a partner. Once in the set you take what hand is offered you.

I loved to dance. I loved the whirl and the stamp of it, especially in the open air, with the line of the hill steady above and around you like a mother's arm. The boys could go hang. They laughed at me because I had a way of closing my eyes to my partner, of being alone with the fiddle and the steps. One time Jacob Spicer put out his foot to trip me as we weaved the Black Nag. The grass bounced me back and I laughed in his face, then I grabbed Owen's hand and we ran off towards the slopes. We didn't look back till we were out of breath, till the crowd was none of them bigger than my thumb. How close we dance to the graves, I remember thinking, and I did not like the thought, so I turned away to the hill that sat heavy and still like the frame in one of the paintings at the Hall, bounding the scene and fixing it for ever. If I close my eyes I see the picture: folk around the chapel at their jigs and talk, me and Owen running up the slopes, with the ridge and fields piled about us.

It was all I had known since I was a tenderling, when my grieving father had brought us here. Every day I trotted after my grandmother and she taught me the names of plants and how to use them. It was only after we had laid her in the earth that I began to notice the world and our footing in the village. I was unhappy, but my unhappiness felt as familiar as the red soil that lined our nails and stained the hems of our garments brown as old blood. I dreamed of escaping the fields and flitting over the horizon; I had no sense that the horizon itself would fall. That I might bring it down.

When I think back I don't know where to begin. The slip did not happen all at once; there was some pulling at the stitches before the cloth gave way. One night in the last month of the year I lay down in my bed and called on my dead mother and woke to the noise of a terrible rending. I threw on my cloak while my father lit a lantern, then we hurried outside. The noise had gone as if it had never been, but through our feet we felt the earth softly shudder. The wind blew out the lantern and we saw it: the road ripped open. The earth itself had come undone. I felt in my heart at that moment that I was answerable for this undoing of the earth. I had picked at the threads and they had come loose.

A curse unpicks God's work. That's the truth of it. Words pelt out of our mouths and we think they are gone when the sound dies, but they are not. They hang in the air, or puddle at our feet, biding till they can start their cankering. Some trickle into the earth itself, joining whatever evil lingers there; some flow back to the sayer, smiling as they sour the blood. That autumn was full of rain and cursing. My father's cursing as he blundered drunk through the workshop, marring his work, and my curses that I threw at the air and at my neighbours. The curses I called out in the chapel.

* * *

It was November, Accession Day, the twelfth since our queen had come to the throne. Owen and I had gone up to the ridge to watch the world and get away from our fathers. The chapel bell rang out the holiday, but there was no chance of dancing. The ground was too wet. Besides, Father Paul did not like it. Owen pointed him out below us, hopping between the men.

'Ain't the Father like a great black fly, Martha, like a fly on an apple?' And he pulled himself tall and straight and put on a grim face like the priest and began to ape the sermon.

'There is a worm, mark you.'

'I mark you, Father Owen.'

'Mark me, there is a worm. It curls around your heart, it creeps through your veins, it is eating away your flesh.'

'You've got him, Owen, word for word.'

'Silence! Do you think yourself handsome? Do you think yourself fine? I tell you, the worm is within you. You are riddled with decay.' He raised his arms just as Father Paul did and lifted his eyes to heaven.

'Oh, Owen, Owen, the devil will have you,' but I could not stop laughing. I did not like the priest, though Aggie and the other girls called him handsome, with his fine hair and his beautiful clean hands. It was true that his voice was like music. It mixed itself with your own breath, with the rise and fall of your chest. The words of the Bible tasted rich as sweet pastry when he spoke them. *'By the waters of Babylon,'* he said, and I repeated it, over and over. It did not matter what it meant. The words had melodies in them that promised like a dream of gold. If I had been bolder I should have liked to talk to him about the verses. If I had been somebody else's daughter he might have looked kindly on me, but I could tell he didn't think much of my soul.

My father wanted none of him. He scoffed at the priest's flapping arms and declared that he fed off the rottenness he railed at. He said it low, of course, but I feared how his tongue might work loose in the alehouse.

When I'd done laughing at Owen I looked down for my father amongst the men, though there was little point. He'd have been on his way to the tavern by the Cockshoot an hour or more since, intent on losing all his wages on slidethrift and dice. No doubt Father Paul would have nosed out Walter Dynely's absence and noted it on the tables of account that lurked behind his pale eyes. I took Owen's hand and pulled him further along the top of the ridge.

Winter was not here yet, but it was gathering, giving a thickness to the clouds. The land was brown and grey, clagged with the recent rains. Come St Agnes' Day there would not be enough food. We sat down on Green Hill and Owen huddled close to me to keep from the bite of the wind. He stood as high as my shoulder now, but he was nothing but bones. It struck me that, at eight, he was the age I had been when he was born. My grandmother had helped at the birth. I had stayed below with Aggie. We held hands when her mother screamed and we tried not to catch her father's eye, for he scowled at the fire as though he wished to beat it with his fists. 'My baby brother,' Aggie said when the women shouted that a boy was born. My brother too, I thought, when they let us see the baby and he reached out his tiny hand and grasped my finger. We recognised each other, even then.

'Look, there's my father,' Owen said now,

pointing down at the archers, though they were too far off to make out clearly. Sure enough, one of the figures would be Richard Simons, doing his duty. No cursing at the tavern for him. He'd be straining at his bow, his mouth a thin grim line. He was a worthy man, everyone said so, but his wife was with child again and likely to lose it, as they had lost all the others save Owen and Aggie, and it was a miracle Ann Simons had not gone too, her body wrung out with bearing and nursing and the line of small graves in the litten.

Below us lay the straggle of the village and the lane that led to the Hall where Sir William lived with his grown-up daughter. Most of the land belonged to them, most of the people too. We could make out the lines of Miss Elizabeth's beautiful garden, with its patterns of clipped hedges that in the summer were filled in with roses. It seemed only a jump to those paths, to where the gentry walked between the blooms with little steps, stooping to breathe the scent on summer nights. Owen said that if he didn't get sent to school he should like to be a gardener at the Hall. He'd bring me a rose every day, he said. He'd tuck it under his doublet so they wouldn't see.

'You'd get pricked by the thorns,' I said. 'You couldn't bear it.'

'I could too. You don't know what I could bear, Martha.' He was put out, so I smiled, patting his hand, but then I looked at his thin, delicate face and felt afraid, and turned my gaze away.

Past the Hall, the land stumbled on to the great straight road that the Romans had built. The road that leads to Gloucester, where a vast cathedral lifts itself up to heaven and tall-masted ships jostle at the docks. One day I was going to follow the road all the way there, just as my mother did. She was sent for to be a servant in a great house. My father said she was dark like me, but beautiful. When I got to the city I would find the house where she worked and the lady would open her door to me for the love she had borne my mother. In spring, just as soon as the days grew long again, I would do it, and the red clay would fall off my boots with every step. When I was rich I would send for Owen and together we would buy or-

anges. The vision was so strong it was a while before I noticed him tugging at my sleeve.

'Martha, quick, there's Harry Stolley coming
up, with two of the others. They said after the service as they were looking for you. Harry said you'd
put a curse on him.'

'It was a scrap of nothing, Owen. All I did was
pass a note to him on the way to chapel. That's all.
Don't look at me like that with your big ninny
eyes. He deserved it. He said my father plucked
my mother from the stews—'

'You should have let it pass.'

'—and that she died of a pox from an Irish
sailor.'

'But what if he shows Father Paul your cursing, writ in your own hand like that?'

'Ha. Let him. It was nothing. Sanctified words
– I took them from the Bible. *The leprosy therefore
of Naaman shall cleave unto thee, and unto thy seed
for ever.* Leprosy can't look worse than Harry's
pocky face. If they beat me for a line of scripture
they strike the word of God.'

Owen got to his feet. 'I'll stand with you,

Martha. Three against two: that's not so bad. I'll not desert you.'

Owen, I thought, they could floor you with a finger; you're as spindly as the barley beneath that shock of barley hair. They could snap you.

'I know you'd never desert me, ninny,' I said, 'and I'll never desert you neither, but go on home. I'll be quicker running without you, and your father will forbid you from school if you mar your clothes.'

He would have argued, but he knew I talked sense and so he left me. The boys were hidden for a moment passing Little Hill. I might avoid them yet. I paused a moment while Owen scampered off down the side of the hill and then I picked up my skirts. The sun had come out for the first time in days and shone hard and yellow to outdo the clouds that ran along with me, buffeted by the same wind that smacked at my cheeks. The path flung itself down, knobs and stones, knolls and slitherdowns. My breath caught in my chest but I could not stop; I could outdo anything and anyone by running. Yet how far away the village seemed, pegged in its mire.

Along by Little Puckmore they spied me. Lucky for me they didn't come up quiet. I heard their whooping and took to my heels again, skittered and slid through the slurry from Nuttal Farm down to the Noggin. Each time I glanced back they were there, three of them, holding out the bit of paper as though the marks on it would burn them. The marks I'd made. Their sheep had more chance of reading it than they.

I would have outrun them if the thrill of it hadn't made me bold. I clambered a bank where the hedge snicks and it felt so good to be looking down that I turned full to face them. That stopped them dead for a minute, all in a thrumble below me, like yapping pups. I looked at the mud on their breeches and their panting cheeks and I laughed.

'How are you feeling, Harry? Takes a while to come on, you know. You better not go to sleep. Little by little you'll feel it. Like goblin nails scrit-scratching at your skinny legs, reaching up till they get your skinny throat.'

'Damn you, Martha Dynely, damn you and your devil's marks,' he shouted back, pop-eyed, pointing at me so that I stepped back in spite of myself, till I felt the hawthorn pricking at my neck. He took heart, then, seeing me bayed into the hedge. 'I 'ent afraid of you. Your mother got you in a ditch. You 'ent nothing but run-off. You take this paper back, or else we'll stick it down your throat. Maybe I'll have myself a look if you're just as brown underneath that kirtle.'

That set them all grinning. Gorrel-bellied striplings – their chins were as hairless as a plucked turkey's arse. My mother was a white dove; nothing of their filth could touch her.

'I've got a little doll of each of you,' I said, as I edged sideways towards the gap, heedless of the thorns snagging my cloak. 'I made them out of tallow and straw. You say that again about my mother and I'll put a flame to them tonight.'

Harry blinked at that all right. The other two tugged at him. I had no call to be afraid of them I thought. They were clowns, no different from the clay that caked them. They'd never dream higher than a hedge. I sucked up, leaned over and spat.

All at once they went for me, scrambling up the bank. But I was through, into the field. The turf was sodden, water-logged. More than once I was near sent sprawling, but I knew the chapel was not far. Every step brought me closer. I was a good half-chain clear when I reached it. They came up as I wrestled with the great oak door, but they daren't grab me, not there. I turned to grin as the door swung open and a great dollop of mud hit my hair, and slid slowly down my cheek.

'Lady Muck!' they shouted. 'Your mother kissed the warts off pedlars. You'll be going down on your back in the dykes soon enough. Ain't none of your writing will help you then.'

Then I was the other side of the door, held safely by the thick stone and the silence.

2

THE CHAPEL

My heart was pounding. I told myself I should not have run. The year before I would not have. The year before I'd have turned and fought, but now my skirts felt too long for fighting. And there was something else. I didn't like a beating – no one did – though I had known plenty of them. But for the first time I felt a different kind of fear: that they might not stop at beating, quite.

Some of the sludge had dribbled into my mouth, so that my tongue rubbed on grit and earth. I could have retched, it was so bitter. No amount of spitting cleared the taste of it. Before me, still and solid in its holiness, stood the cross of Our Lord. Wherever I stood it reproached me, so I came and kneeled before it. I closed my eyes.

It was in play, I argued. They had no business to speak of my mother so. She could not defend herself. Next time I would copy them out a prayer. They would not know the difference anyway. All letters were magical to them and I'd laugh to see them shake and holler at a blessing. Forgive me, I said, and opened my eyes. There were the arms of the cross. I could not be forgiven, they said. How could I be, when my prayer was filthy with plotting?

It would soon be night. The pretty colours thrown by the west window began to fade and shrink back into the glass. I wished that I could hold them, reds and blues and yellows, take them back across the wet grey fields to the dirty lane, where the rain and the thatch dripped into the raw November filth. All along the lane the shutters would be closing. It made little difference: the windows let in small light and there was no colour to look at anyway, except in my father's face. My own eyes were brown and green like the hawthorn, or the chapel yew, but my father's eyes were blue, bright as the Virgin's robe in the window. They made folk think of empty sky, of tales of the seas, of distance. They made them restless. I think that's why they liked it when he clouded them in drink.

My father said women were not let on the ships, that a woman on board was held to be unlucky. I should never have been a girl. If I'd been a boy I could become a mariner and learn the stars and sail till the ocean and the heavens were one bright blue bowl, and maybe I could've brought the vision back to him.

It was time to be going home, but I wanted to be sure the boys had gone so I lingered. The chapel walls were plain. I stroked the plaster for its knags and hollows. To the eye it was smooth, but not to the hand. Not so long ago it was painted. Sometimes I'd hear people talking of the old religion, back when the carved angels still had faces and the walls were alive with bright, bright pictures. If Father Paul got wind of talk like that he'd hiss and shout about papists and plots. To his lights, crossing yourself was halfway to murdering the Queen. But people were careful how they were overheard. I didn't remember Queen Mary, let alone King Henry's time. To me it all sounded like another country, full of saints and incense and Latin enchantments, the air so thick with spirits you could breathe them in.

The whiteness of the walls soothed me. Here and there, where the coat was thin, I could make out the shapes of the old paintings underneath the whitewash. Perhaps it was the slant of the light, for I had not seen them before so well. I traced the outline of a creature, running. It was a hare, I thought, long ears pressed back in fear and speed. Just behind it were the hounds, open jawed, tongues lolling. Poor hare, was it glad when they came to paint it away? It must have been so tired with running. Or it may be that the hunt had never stopped, and this was why it was coming back now, through the white. The hare hoped it might still be free. Was the whiteness freedom? It was very pure, but it offered nowhere for the hare to hide itself. The walls were full of ghosts.

I glanced around. There was no one to see me if I stepped up to where the Bible lay and touched it. I laid my hand on the open page and traced the letters with my fingers. They thrilled me. My grandmother told me a story once, of a door in a mountain that opened into fairyland, and when she told it my father laughed and said it was a story about reading. I didn't understand him till he taught me letters, and felt how it was to step through the lines, into a different world, one I could walk freely in. The boys were right: there was a magic in the letters. They were like the colours that the chapel window sent dancing across the floor. The Bible was open at Hosea. It was getting too dim to read, but I made out the words, just.

The high places of Aven, where Israel doth sin,
shall be destroyed: thistles and thorns shall
grow upon their altars: then shall they say to
the mountains, Cover us,
    and to the hills, Fall upon us.

How strange it was that all of our past and our future, the running hare and the hills themselves, should be clear and known in a blink of the Lord's eye and that they should be gone again as quickly. I saw it clear as day: the hills tumbling down like the walls of Jericho. Yes, I thought, there's not one I would miss, barring my father and Owen, and Owen's sister, Aggie, I suppose. As to the rest, their minds are earth already; they might as well have done with it. I traced my finger over the text. *'Cover us,'* I repeated aloud, *'Fall upon us.'*

The words echoed into and around the dark recesses of the chancel. I had not noticed how fast the night had come in. There was something moving in the shadows of the apse. A bat perhaps, or a bird thinking to roost. Then a light was struck and I gasped, for it was no bird, but Father Paul advancing towards me, holding a candle that sent his shadow craning over the walls. He paused while I stepped quickly down, but he did not take his eyes off mine. The flame lit up the thin line of his mouth and glittered in his eyes. For a while he said nothing, then he pressed the candle towards me till I could see nothing else.

'Look how the fire likes you, Martha. You and he will spend time together by and by, is that not so?' There was a singsong in his voice that frightened me. It sounded gentle but I felt that it was not. 'Whom do you call on, Martha? Did you come here to pray?'

I found my voice at last. 'Yes, Father,' I whispered.

He put the candle down and peered at me, resting his hands on my shoulders. I'd rather have faced any number of boys than him.

'Did you, Martha, did you in truth?'

'No, Father.'

'But you need to pray, Martha. The devil is looking into your soul and he thinks he might find a home there. Ha!' And with a strange smile he jerked his long thin nose this way and that in the half-dark around my head. 'Do you smell it, Martha, do you smell it?'

'What should I smell, Father?' He was performing, but I felt no temptation to laugh. I could feel the mist of his breath on my cheek. He stood for a moment regarding me, then all at once his face twisted in disgust. He picked up the candle and yanked my head towards it until my hair singed and stank.

'It is the smell of burning flesh, girl, it is a little

wisp of hell. You must cast it from you, Martha. You must ask mercy of our Redeemer.'

Just as I was sure he meant to burn my scalp he pulled my head away and tilted it so that I had to look directly up at him. His eyes peered right down into my soul. All was laid bare to him, I was sure of it: all my blackest thoughts. He glowed in the candlelight, but beyond the light the dark pressed close and I stood in that darkness. When at last he let me go I was unable to step away. I was all confusion. He began to trace his free hand slowly down my forehead. He still said nothing, just stared at his fingers as he drew them down across my lips, my neck, my bosom.

'So much sin,' he said in a queer, thin voice. 'How I have prayed for your soul, Martha Dynely!' His fingers pressed like a burning rod against my breast. Then he was at the door, opening it, ushering me out, his voice brisk, normal. 'Tell your father, when he is conscious, he must come to church next Sunday or be fined. I will brook no more excuses.'

The message had to wait, for it was hours later that my father reeled in, chuckling as he flung himself into his cot. He reeked of the alehouse. We had little bread, but it seemed he had money enough for ale. Three days his tools had sat idle in the workshop, though there was a carriage out at Hellens waiting for its wheels to be mended. 'He's finishing work over at Checkley,' I had told their man, 'he'll be over as soon as he's back.' They would not wait much longer. The Clutterbucks at Putley would take on the work, if they hadn't already. They'd do it quick, too; turn it around in a sneeze. What were we to eat if my father did no work?

He talked as he slept. By day it was hard to eke words out of him – a week could go by without his saying barely a word to me – but night unstoppered him and he'd converse with the darkness for hours. When I was younger I'd creep over to listen to mutterings like these. Occasionally words rose up out of the early life he would never speak of. 'Oh, but she's fine, Johnny, fine as a swan,' he'd cry out, 'for all that she leans to starboard.' And I'd picture the docks and the great river pouring out into the world; my father free of muck and bitterness. There'd been times when he'd suddenly speak of my mother, so that my heart yearned in jealousy and longing for them both. 'We two, Bessie,' he'd say, 'we two...' Or else he'd say things I didn't understand and knew I could never ask him: 'I'll not let them, Bessie. By God, I'll plant a chisel in his head.'

From habit now, I strained to listen. 'Damn your eyes,' he was saying. 'Damn your eyes, William Nesbitt, you tinker's whoreson.'

I turned to the wall and tried to think about the lights that had washed over my hands in the chapel – red, blue, yellow, pink. Above me, rain trickled from the eaves.

3

IN THE SCHOOLROOM

Next morning I got up before dawn. My father had given over mumbling and was snoring instead. He'd be out a good while yet unless I roused him. I picked up the blanket that had fallen off his back and made gruel for us both, but when it came to it I did not wake him. The truth was I didn't feel like facing either his glowering or his remorse. So I let him be and sat and sipped my breakfast by the light of the candle stub, while my eyes wandered through the shadows and the light on the familiar walls, and I wondered why I was so full of choler.

My belly was knotted up with fury. It wasn't

only my cupshotten father snoring in his bed, though that had a part in it. I woke and it was there in the darkness, waiting for me. Every day of your life, it said, will be clutter. I performed my chores, spoke politely to neighbours, went about my work, and all the while hot thoughts and words knocked about my head. Lately I had appeased them with small acts of recklessness, like dropping a curse in Harry Stolley's lap. There was a demon in me, and no amount of praying would seem to shift it. I reasoned with myself, counted my luck. If I was not pretty I was learned; I had my grandmother's understanding of simples and my father's knowledge of letters. We had the favour of the Hall and a good cottage. There were quite a few ready to say it was too big for one man and his daughter, with a workshop where only the dust moved for days at a time. Our neighbour, Widow Spicer, was crammed into two small rooms with her son grown nearly a man and her penniless sister newly arrived to live with her. I should have been glad of what I had, I knew, but I was not.

I stared at the stain on the wall left by the evening candle, which would not come off, but only seemed to get worse with rubbing. How was it, I wondered, that light left a smear of the dark behind? Perhaps darkness left its mark in us, too, when we stood in the sunshine. Perhaps behind the borrowed light our spirits were black with tar and grime. How could anything be pure and good?

From out the back a cock crowed. The day was getting on; there were already people in the lane. I collected my things, nudged my father on the shoulder and quickly stepped out before he could halt me.

For two hours every morning, bar the Sabbath, I taught the village boys to read. Miss Elizabeth had had benches laid out in the room above the stables at the Hall. The Bible was Christ's bread, she declared one harvest, and no boy in her parish should have his soul starved of salvation. At first she couldn't find a teacher. Father Paul tutored the yeoman sons and not a soul else that knew their letters wanted to give up the time – feeding souls did not pay well. She'd tried to persuade my father, but he'd convinced her that he did not have the temperament. 'Why not Martha?'

he had said. 'She can read as well as a grammar school boy.' Miss Elizabeth had turned in surprise and beckoned me over from the corner where I skulked. 'Can you?' she'd asked. 'Should you like to be a schoolmistress?' I'd burned redder than her velvet gown.

For days after I could scarcely see the ground I walked on.

'Aggie,' I'd said – we were gleaning and the yolk-yellow sun burned our stooping necks – 'what do you think the boys should call me as their teacher?'

She'd grinned and poked me in the ribs. 'They will call you a saucy cocket wench, and worse than that. Stop your strutting, Martha. Folks won't think it decent.'

She was right, of course, the village did not like it. They said as much to my father, which pleased him no end. Miss Elizabeth cared nothing for their grumbles. 'Why not a girl?' she said. 'Aren't we ruled by a learned Queen?' She insisted on the boys coming to her school, said she'd fine the parents if they denied them. People shifted their feet a little but they could not argue. As soon as harvest was done they sent them, for as many days as they could be spared, until something more pressing arose. The Queen herself couldn't have stopped their fathers calling them to work when the fields began to quicken in the spring.

It had been two years now, and if it didn't set me preening as it had done, I still cherished the dignity. It felt to me a feather from the peacock's breast, all shimmering blue, had been woven into my kirtle.

'You'll not have dirt under your nails for long, Martha wench,' my father would say. 'You'll not stay here long.'

And I agreed, for Miss Elizabeth Mortimer had drawn me out of the corner and smiled while I read to her. She had inclined her head and said to my father, 'Walter, what a gem you have been hiding. Let us see if we might not let her shine a bit more brightly.' How I wished just then that my grandmother had been alive to hear her say that! Or then again perhaps not: Grandam had always looked sideways at gentry, even the Mortimers themselves. 'We go on foot and they ride,' she'd say, 'and no matter how good they are they won't have us riding along with them; they'll leave us in the dirt sooner than slip out of the saddle.' She had taught me how to read plants, but she had barely been further than Hereford. It was my father's reading that could open up the world.

Somewhere or other the sun had risen, for it was light enough when I turned into the lane to walk the half-mile to the Hall. The cold was a coagulate grey, heavy as jelly. There would be snow very soon that was pretty clear. I prayed it would not come too fast, and prevent my father's going to Marcle, and that he would get the animals housed. The puddles in the cart ruts were heavy and grey as iron pots, and many as deep, too, so I stepped with care. The thought of the winter frightened me. What if the snow gripped us for months and there was no work? We'd precious little stored up and nothing much to trade. Even wood was scarce.

Perhaps my father would wake up sober and walk to Hellens to fix the wheels. Tomorrow he would be back with silver in his pocket. It was likely enough, though there was a tavern on the Ledbury Road he'd have to walk past. I shrugged the thought off and tried to look about me. The track climbed slowly towards the park and the trees either side were thick with birdsong. Birds sing louder when the snow is coming. I think the notes echo against the quietness that's about to fall. A blackbird eyed me from the field's edge. One had flown through our window yesterday morning – this very same bird most probably – and I had fallen to my knees to pray, to ward off the evil that was coming, even though my father laughed and said I was a goose to mind such things. The bird looked at me now with its black bead eyes and cocked its head to the side. When I did the same the air whispered colder on my up-turned ear, but I still saw only what lay just before me. The blackbird could hear the slow winding of the worm beneath the grass; it saw two different worlds all the time – the world of the left eye and the world of the right. Who's to say that all that is to befall us isn't threaded through what a black-bird sees and hears? I was looking at the blackbird as though he might tell, but then a familiar voice accosted me and he startled and flew off. Widow Spicer had come up behind me; I forced a smile and bobbed.

'Good morning to you, Martha. Whyever are you mopping and mowing like a mad thing? You certainly look well pleased with yourself, although I don't know what there is to smile about with the sky so heavy, unless it's a piece of wickedness. And how is your father this morning, my girl?'

'Well, in God's mercy, thank you kindly,' I lied. The Widow took in washing for the Hall, but her tongue found and spread whatever dirt it could far quicker than her hands could scrub and launder.

She looked at me slowly and drew in her breath. 'I am glad to hear it, glad to hear it indeed. He was certainly well last night – the whole village could swear to it – although God's mercy had little to do with the song he was singing. It's lucky for you Sir William lends Walter Dynely his protection, or it's likely come Lady Day you'd be asked to skip. You'd best tell him be careful. There's quiet decent folks enough, natives of this village, too, who'd make good use of that house of yourn.'

Meaning your son, of course, I thought, though I did not say it. A pretty cottage for that oaf, Jacob, when he came to marry, just next door so her meddling fingers wouldn't have far to stretch. Give me a life elsewhere, I thought, and I'll leave tomorrow. At least my father was not like her, all scrawn and cunning, not an ounce of softness on her.

'I am sorry, neighbour,' I said. 'It must grieve you to see us so well provided for when you have both your son and your sister in so small a place. There's not many could count on a sister's generosity as Goody Reynolds has done. I am sure she must prize your kindness very much. I heard Miss Elizabeth herself say so.'

'Did she? What did she say?' the Widow eagerly leaned forward, touching my arm like a friendly aunt.

'That it was a Christian deed to take your sister in. She was talking to Father Paul in the stables,' I lied. 'May I help you with your bundle?'

'Yes, well,' the Widow smiled, passing me the sack of sheets, 'you're a mite too sharp sometimes, Martha, and you're a funny dark little thing, but as

I said to my sister the other day, Jane, I said, she's a soul worth saving, in despite of everything.'

I was pleased with myself then, for handling her so well. It was only later that I wondered what she meant. No doubt it was my father's wildness, but I couldn't help thinking there was something else, some new shift in her manner, and that of others, too. We were not liked – my father saw to that – but lately I had felt there was more. Harry Stolley had played free with my mother's name, there in the street where people heard, and no one had stopped to cuff him. Something had changed, but what it was I did not know.

When I reached the schoolroom there was no wood stack. I sent a couple of boys to filch some scraps but they came back empty-handed, with a stable-hand cursing at their backs. The timber was being watched, they said. It had got to such a price and scarcity that Sir William himself had sworn he'd bring down the law on anyone snapping off so much as a twig from his woods.

'It's true an' all,' Ben Ladding piped up. 'My pa has always had what he wanted from Hoar Wood and welcome, but last week he was beat off. Sir

William's had enough of thieving, they told him. Said he should be thankful he wasn't taken to the pillory.'

'My father says there's not been November rain like this since King Henry's time, even longer. Pentaloe Brook is become a river.'

'The bridges over by Sollers Hope have gone.'

I set them to working then, or I tried to, chalking out letters on the slate. Most of them fidgeted or ignored me, however much I cajoled or threatened. They had no use for letters and no fear of the rod, either. They were used to that. Miss Elizabeth would come and test them, and for each that could read the Bible verse she showed them she promised to pay me an Angel. An Angel for a saved soul, she would say, with a small laugh, because it was as close as she ever came to a joke. Near two years of teaching and I'd only held the silver Angel in my hand the once. It felt good, but my Owen was worth more. He spoke the verses clearer than a priest, eight years old or no.

From the first day he had worked at his writing sternly, as though it were a hound he had to train. And now he was master of it. Often

I would let the others play at bones and Owen and I would sit together reading from the books Miss Elizabeth lent to us. We copied lines and songs to scare away the nightmares that came to visit him at night. Miss Elizabeth called him gifted. She wanted to send him to the Cathedral School in Hereford, but her father would not pay and no one else had been found to offer. I told myself I wanted him to go, and I did, too, but there was a part in me that could not bear the thought of it.

Halfway through the morning and the boys were snarling through the alphabet. I couldn't blame them: the cold had taken our feet and hands. They could barely feel the birch on their palms when I struck them. It was unbearable to be so still. They would have run off if they'd dared. Instead they looked at me with stupid resentment, stubborn as the donkey Goody Reynolds had brought with her when she came to live with her sister, though it did no work.

A shadow fell across the doorway and the boys looked up. Jacob Spicer walked in, hesitantly, holding his cap.

'Mistress Elizabeth has given me leave to come to the lessons, Martha, days when work's not so heavy, seeing as I'd like to learn myself.'

'Very well,' I said, and pointed to the back bench, next to Ned Stolley, who if he got to the end of the Lord's Prayer would be doing better than a Stolley ever should.

He looked confused for a minute, but there was nowhere else to sit so he had to perch on the low bench, knees almost up to his ears. The boys laughed, and I couldn't help smiling too, as I stood over him with a slate. Jacob Spicer, who'd stood with the other boys all last year and curled his lip if I passed him on the road. I remembered the dance two years back, when he'd put out his leg and tripped me, while his mother looked on and said nothing.

'Well, Jacob,' I said, handing him Miss Elizabeth's book, 'I am sure you can't have grown so tall without learning something, so why don't you show us what you know?'

I pointed to the passage that Owen and I had been reading, 'The chief element of happiness is this: to want to be what you are.' Jacob took it and stared at it a long while. The boys began to nudge each other.

'Here, Robbie,' I said, poking a boy on the next row, 'help Jacob with this first word.'

'I know that,' said Robbie. 'That one's easy. It's "the".'

Jacob reddened and bent down further over the book.

'You're supposed to read it,' I laughed, 'not wipe your great red nose upon it. Do you not know anything at all?'

He sprang up and kicked the ridiculous bench, sending Ned reeling in the dust. For a moment he loomed over me, furious, and I stepped back a little, in case he turned and swung a clout at me. But then he straightened himself and narrowed his eyes, thrusting the book back into my hands. 'I beg your pardon then, Martha,' he said. 'It was a foolish wish.' And he turned and left.

The boys went quiet and did not need me to shout at them as I did. Clowns are there to be laughed at, I said to myself, but I didn't believe it. Through the open window slit I watched him walk out into the yard. I thought to call him back, and ran down the ladder after him, but by the time I reached the doorway he was the other side of the yard and striding off towards the warrens. He might be the dolt next door, as Father called him, but I had no right to talk to him as I had. I had forgotten how he had grown into a man.

As I turned to climb back up I noticed a box of apples I'd not observed earlier. There was nobody about and so I took some up in my skirts. They were wizened, red little things, sweet to taste.

'Here,' I said, handing them out to the boys. One by one they solemnly returned them.

'I beg your pardon, Martha,' Ned Stolley said, 'but we're not taking apples off of you.'

'Don't be daft,' I said. 'There's no one to see, and I'm hardly likely to tell, since I took them myself.'

The boys glanced at one another awkwardly.

'It's not that,' Ben Ladding said at last. 'Who caused them apples to be there? I didn't see no apples this morning.'

The others nodded. Ned Stolley muttered something to the boy in front.

'What's that?' I said. 'What's that you said?' I had to rap him on the neck before he'd answer.

'My mother said we was to be careful around you, that's all,' he muttered. 'Apples is the devil's own fruit. Everyone knows that. And yesterday you slipped a curse onto my cousin.'

'Your cousin is an idiot and so are you,' I said, and took a bite of my apple.

'You wrote out a curse on him,' Ned went on.

'Your Harry can hardly put on his boots for fear of treading on a fairy,' I said. 'Tell me, if I were at the devil's work would I have run into God's own house? The paper I gave him had nothing but holy words upon it. Your cousin took fright at a line of scripture.'

'You told him you made a doll of tallow and straw,' Ben Ladding put in. 'That weren't out the Bible.'

Then Owen got up from his bench and came to me and took an apple and stood in front of the class and ate it. 'Martha's no witch,' he said. 'I'd lay my life on it.'

'The life of a Simons child ain't worth that

much, though, is it?' Ned muttered loud enough for all to hear.

'If I was a witch,' I said, 'I wouldn't be stuck here, schooling the straw-brained sons of men who'd piss on their own mothers' heads for a penny. I'd be dressed in silks with brilliants in my hair, and pies and cakes for dinner. While all of you are lying grunting in your beds I'd be careening through the night, turning cartwheels over the stars themselves.'

I think I said all that. I would have said it, too, if I hadn't just then looked out to the yard and seen an old tinker woman crossing. She'd come round before with her bundle of knives and pans. Last time I saw her she'd been spreading them out on a cloth for a group of gossips, smiling and nodding as they'd picked up one blade after another. Oh, she could see they had good eyes: they could pick out the best and no mistake. And when they'd put one down her hand had darted out to seize it and she'd stroked the shiny blade, while she carried on nodding and smiling, nodding and smiling. Where she came from or where she went I did not know, or what she thought of the housewives she fawned on. No doubt she slept in ditches and barns and went without food as often as not. It was late in the year now for her to be tramping, that's for certain.

She was not in luck. A servant bustled out of the house and shouted at her to be gone. When she lingered he pushed her by the shoulders and stood there watching her go. She took each step slowly, as if her feet were bleeding.

To my surprise the servant didn't turn back to the house but began purposefully striding towards us. A moment later he was calling from the foot of the ladder.

'Martha Dynely,' he shouted. 'You're to wait on Miss Elizabeth directly after the lesson. Directly, and remember to scrub the filth from your boots.'

'There now,' Ned Stolley said, 'she's heard about your cursing and your goings-on. Happen you're for it, happen—' but I cut off his jibing with a sharp crack of the birch.

4

AT THE HALL

There had once been a moat all around the Hall, so my father told me, but now it only stretched around three sides, and a little more. Handsome steps at the back of the house led down into Miss Elizabeth's garden, but I took the path that snicked from the stableyard to the servants' door. The man who'd brought the message opened the door to me; he stood for a moment on the threshold regarding me without a word before finally he let me in.

'You'd better have scraped your boots.'

I followed him across the entrance hall and

down a corridor to the scullery. He pointed to a stool.

'Wait here,' he said, smoothing himself down. 'And don't touch anything.'

I peered across into the kitchen. It was clear that great preparations were afoot. Only a yard the other side of the kitchen door was a long table, with tray after tray of tarts upon it. I could not see the cook or his boy, although I could hear voices from the dairy.

The tarts gleamed. The smell alone made me tickle-headed. Butter and almonds. The tops were decorated with little leaves and stems of pastry. I had never seen anything so fine. Tonight, at the feast, the ladies and gentlemen would hold them between their delicate fingers and take a nibble. They'd pat their stomachers and refuse a second: 'Oh, you must excuse me, I couldn't possibly.' There were at least fifty on the trays. I glanced around. Nobody was about. I stuffed one in my shift and sat back down. And just in time, for a second later a door along the corridor opened and the servant reappeared. He beckoned to me to follow.

It was not the first time I had been inside the Hall. Once, last year, Miss Elizabeth had taken it into her head to give me a tour of the house 'like a lady', and I had followed her from room to room, as she reeled out information about the house and the furniture. There was such brightness! Colours I had only seen in flowers and the sky. I should have liked to stroke every hanging, every chair, every piece of silver, but Miss Elizabeth caught at my hands with a dart of her nervous fingers when I reached out to touch some brocade.

There was one room, in particular, that had thrilled me: the great chamber at the top of the main staircase. All the treasures in the world were gathered in that room. The walls were hung with painted cloths. Miss Elizabeth had told me the stories. Not Christian ones at all, they were from the ancient world of the Greeks, who saw gods in the winds and the water. The king of the gods made himself into a swan to take a girl; and a boy saw a goddess naked and was drowned for it. There was a low table on which, Miss Elizabeth explained, Sir William played chess. Tiny carved figures were laid out on its chequered board. It

was a game of the court and everyone manoeu-
vred and might be killed or changed, but not the
king. He stayed the king; when he died all was
lost. The pieces, she said, were made in Turkey,
where it was always warm and the air was sweet
with spices, but the people did not know God.

It was into this room that the servant led me.
Nothing had changed except that the light from
the windows was weak and grey and a bright fire
burned in the grate. Miss Elizabeth was seated at
a writing table. Father said she could not be more
than seven-and-twenty, but I thought she looked
more than halfway old. Today her gown was of
buttercup yellow, which paled her little face and
made ashes of the piled hair that I usually
thought so pretty. There was always something of
a bird about the way she perched. I could see that
now she was more than usually anxious. Her grey
eyes continually flitted to the window and the
door as she talked.

'So you've come, Martha. Good. I have a letter
to write and I have hurt my wrist.' I noticed that
she was holding her arm carefully, drawing her
fingers back and forth over her right wrist. There

was a cut, too, just below her hairline, heavily covered in powder. 'You can write it for me. Come, sit down here. You have eaten, have you?'

I glanced up. 'I would be grateful—' I began, but she cut me off, talking in that quick way she had, glancing hither and thither. 'Nonsense, child, you are doing me a service. Your father is well, I presume? And your students, I hope they are making good progress?'

'He is tolerable well, ma'am, and—'

'That's very good, very good. I shall visit one of these mornings, I certainly shall. You are ready? You see the quill is sharpened for you. There is so much to do today, I feel quite distracted. One of our visitors is riding to Shrewsbury tomorrow so you see it's essential, quite essential, that I write to Mary now.'

I sat myself down on the stool she pointed to, with the quill poised over the ink, endeavouring to appear less baffled than I felt.

'"My dear Mary" – write exactly what I say, Martha dear, Mary is my cousin... Stop, stop, I am explaining. Only write what is intended for the letter. Really, child, I had not thought you stupid.'

I bowed my head. She paced around the room for a while, then went on, 'Mary is my cousin... more to me than a cousin. After my mother died I lived with her under my aunt's care, in Ludlow, more than I lived here.' She smiled and paused in her fretful pacing. 'We swore we would never be parted. We were like David and Jonathan. Have you ever known such friendship, Martha?'

'Well, ma'am,' I said, 'I believe so. I am very fond of Owen.'

'Yes, he's a gifted child, but that's not really the same.' She put a hand to her head, pressing gently at the cut. 'I feel a need to talk, and I know you will be discreet.' She paused again and after a moment I realised that an answer was expected.

'Of course, ma'am.'

'Of course. And I am aware that you and your father stand a little by yourselves. We have had to speak on your behalf more than once...'

'We are very grateful.'

'Yes, yes, I know.' She laid a hand on my shoulder. 'You are a clever girl, Martha. I doubt things have been easy for you. Since your grandmother died I fear you have lacked advice. You are nearly grown. You must leave off scuttling over the fields like a fox. And the godless baiting of other souls.' She gave me a sharp glance and I did not dare ask what she had heard. 'You must learn to use your gifts to further God's plans, not to thwart them. I speak this as your protector, Martha. I feel I have earned some right to counsel you – as your poor mother might have done.'

'Miss Elizabeth,' I ventured, 'did you know my mother?'

'No, of course not. She died before you came here.'

'I thought, perhaps, seeing as Sir William knew my father in Gloucester, that you might have met her when she worked in a lady's house.'

'No, I knew nothing about her, nothing at all.' Her voice had grown sharp, but then she softened and patted my head. 'Do not dwell on such things, child. It was all a very long time ago.' She gave herself a little shake. 'To the matter in hand.' She leaned over me and looked at the blank paper, chewing at her lip.

My dearest Mary,

Forgive my long silence. My eagerness to give you news is proven by the strange hand in which this is written. I have engaged a village girl as I can scarcely sign my name. What a month I have had! It rains so much I believe the air has turned to water. My father rants about bridges lost and roads near past repair. He cannot spare a man to ride with me, and quite forbids me to stir abroad. I spend days walking the gallery, watching as the rain pelts the last leaves from the trees. All my comfort is in prayer and in reading. But you don't need me to write of that. You ask for news. Where should I begin? Which of all my nothings should I share first? The new minister, he shall be my burden.

He is a university man, very ambitious, I believe, a protégé of Bishop John. I have seen him several times and he talks earnestly of the souls in his care. He is shocked at the lingering of superstition hereabouts. I fear there will be battles with Papa. Oh, Mary, he has the voice of an angel.

I glanced up. Miss Elizabeth had started her pacing again and when she turned towards me her face was flushed. 'How is Father Paul regarded in the village, Martha? How do you find him?'

'Well...' I said, not sure how to answer, seeing as we all saw him so different, 'Richard Simons and the other wardens speak very highly of him. He is a God-fearing man and no timeserver. For myself, I am rather afraid of him.'

'Yes, that is as it should be, Martha. He has explained to me how he seeks to inspire a proper fear of God's justice. The parishes hereabouts have grown lax. I'm afraid my father is to blame. He has ever been a friend to custom and carousing. Pick up the quill, we must return to the letter. I was describing Father Paul... Begin.

He is quite a young man, about our own age, tall and lean, with a searching look in his eyes. When he reads the scriptures the holy words flame into the world; it feels as though you are quite opened up before him, that he sees into every byway of your heart. But yet he is gracious in company. He talked for an hour

together with silly Margaret Beauchamp about
her sister's wedding. There is a restraint about
him I believe is gentleness. He let slip one day
that his father was a ruthless man who would
beat him bloody for a trifle and that it trained
him to be vigilant to contain his own excess
and that of others. He works his fingers
earnestly together as he speaks, as though the
faith in him urgently presses to be released
into the world.'

She stopped talking and I turned to her. She
had lost her fretfulness and stood quite still, and
distant. For the first time I thought her handsome.
When she caught me looking she smiled quickly.
    'Continue, Martha.

Father, of course, refuses to admire him. You,
my dear, and I, rejoice in all that my father
likes to deplore. He is civil to the vicar but no
more, and when I ask his reasons he merely
snorts that the dogs don't like the man. Of
course not. Father Paul is a town man, not used
to baying and licking. My father needs to make

peace with the bishop, but he will not see it. Rather he flouts him at every turn, and sets on his men to do so, too. Poor Father Paul cannot but do his duty and report back to his patron. He has confessed to me that he finds his position difficult, to say the least.'

Miss Elizabeth turned suddenly. There were voices in the hall below.

'Oh, this will never do. Both of them, in the hall, just when I thought myself alone. Quick, Martha, place the blotting sheet over it. I shall round it off as best I can in a moment. Tidy the desk up and then go your way down the back stairs. I shall recompense you later. Goodbye.'

Before I could say a word she was on the stairs, hailing the gentlemen. I crept to the door to look down the grand staircase. Sir William had advanced to the fire and was bending and fondling one of the dogs as a servant tried to lift his cloak from his shoulders. A little way off stood Father Paul, as though keeping aloof from the warmth. With one hand he flicked a servant away, with the other he warded off a muzzle. As Miss Elizabeth approached he stepped forward and bowed, keeping his eyes full upon her.

Sir William watched them for a moment, frowning. 'Bill Tranter was asking for you, Elizabeth. Some business about the posies. And there are the gypsies come. They'll need some accommodation sorting if they are to play for our guests tonight. Come, Father, share a cup of wine with me. I believe you bear a message?'

I ran back to put away the writing things, covering Miss Elizabeth's letter carefully. I had barely finished when they entered.

'What's this? Who are you, girl, in the family quarters?'

'It is Martha Dynely, Sir William, a girl from the village, although why she should be loitering among your precious things I can't explain. It might be wise to ask her to empty her pockets.' Father Paul smiled coldly. I thought of the tart in my kirtle and blushed.

'Miss Elizabeth, sire, she asked me to write a letter for her. I am just leaving.'

'Yes, yes, Dynely's girl, are you?' Sir William looked at me closely. 'None of your father's looks,

I see, but you're a strong-looking wench. Now Father Paul wants me to search all your pleats and your pockets. What do you think, eh? Should you like that? Or might it be better if the Father took a look? He's got good long fingers; he could search out all your hiding places. Look, Father, the girl's turned redder than a Lancaster rose. Get along now, ask the cook for some pie on your way out.'

I was halfway down the gallery that led to the servants' stairs, when he called me back with a change of heart. 'Wait, girl. I've a message for your father. That's it, stand there a moment. I shan't take too long.'

I loitered, and watched them.

He turned back to the vicar. 'Mark that sleet. There'll be snow too, or I'm no judge of the weather in my own land and I have lived here long enough for that. Can't recall when we've had such dreadful weather. Not a day since October without rain. And look, there's two trees down: good big elms, mark you, brought down by last month's winds. It's trees you've come about, Father, if I'm not mistaken. Or is this merely a pastoral visit? I know you saw the bishop last week. Come on, man, out with it.'

Even from the gallery I could see Father Paul shifting awkwardly. 'My lord, Bishop John sends his blessing and begs to remind you of the matter of Hoar Wood. There has been some felling there of late.'

'I knew it! He sent that keeper to spy. My men saw to him, and no mistake. God's blood, the wood is mine and I have told his Grace so myself. I tell you, Father, I don't take kindly to his sending you here to wheedle for him.'

Father Paul coughed 'His Grace begs to remind you, my lord, that the late earl conferred the woods on the Church as security for certain debts.'

'And as I explained to his Grace, they were not the earl's to promise or to confer. He should let the matter drop. There is no doubt at all about the case. It is clear cut, solid, transparent as glass, not an ounce of ambiguity. I'd be obliged if you'd not mention it again. You'll be joining the company tonight? Of course you will, Father, no excuses.

My daughter can only digest food in the presence of holy men. I'll see you out.'

'There is another – small – matter, my lord.'

'Yes, well, what is it? Anything I can help with, you know, but keep it brief. It's past two o'clock and I've got visitors arriving. And a horse in the yard threatening to go lame on me.'

'It is a little *delicate*.' Father Paul's strong voice had shrunk to a thin treble.

'What is it? Not got a girl in trouble, have you? Don't look so shocked. You wouldn't be the first in a frock coat to lose your footing, so to speak,' and Sir William let out a great laugh.

'Sire, no, never! I am God's servant here. No, his Grace has been made aware of some, *ahem*, rumours, about your lordship. He knows better than to credit them, of course. Your loyalty to our noble Queen could never be in doubt. After last year's terrible events in the North...'

'The rebellion, you mean? The traitors Northumberland and Westmorland? God's truth, man, what has that to do with me?'

'His Grace wishes you to know that he holds

you in great esteem and pays no heed to evil reports.'

'What the devil does that mean, Father? No, don't hem and haw at me, what reports? Exactly who has said what about me?'

'Please your lordship, I think we both know the kinds of things...'

'No, Father Paul, I don't know. You tell me. You tell me exactly what *kinds of things*.'

'Some say the papist traitor Nicholas Craddock has returned, and that he has been spotted hereabouts. Nonsense, I am sure. No one would think of harbouring such a renegade.'

A long silence followed. They had wandered to the other side of the great chamber, where I could no longer see them. I wondered if they had gone down. Then Sir William spoke again, in a more subdued voice, which carried, nonetheless.

'I will not honour that last remark with a reply. I'll wish you good day, Father Paul. The afternoon draws on. I'll see you out.'

I listened to their footsteps on the stairs. Should I leave too? But Sir William had told me to stay. I stared out at the sleet on the gardens and broke off bits of the tart. It was sweet and rich in my mouth. I closed my eyes, the better to savour it. When I opened them I saw the sleet had changed to snow. Flakes were whipping at the glass, beginning to settle on the ground below. Even in this light the gallery felt bright. I had never seen any building with as much glass as they had at the Hall, not even a church. Each diamond pane framed a view of the garden. I leaned back and looked. Father Paul thought I must be a thief. Perhaps I was, and of more than the tart in my belly. I stole the feel of the fine things: beeswax and varnish, silk and brocade and china. I stole the light and the colour and the stories on the walls. Who's to say, if a box of gold had been open before me I should not have crammed some of that, too, into my pockets? Could it be wrong to want to possess all this beauty, to step into the beautiful world?

When I had come the first time there had been a stack of paper on a low table, sheets and sheets of it, smooth and white, with a unicorn imprinted into it in one corner. I had quickly rolled up some sheets and stuffed them in my skirts. That night I'd lain awake thinking of the words I could write on them. Beautiful words, lines that would feel like sunlight when I read them back. But I couldn't bear to mark the page. Months went by. In the end I'd torn a scrap off for a curse. All that was fine turned to dirt in my hands.

Now I kissed the glass where a snowflake rested. I could see all its detail, finer than lace. The bishop thought Sir William himself a thief. He would not notice a snowflake – why should the lace belong to him and not to me?

If I were a witch, like the boys said, maybe I could make myself disappear, become one of those little birds depicted in the hangings and stay for the feast. I would sing on a branch, watching the gentry come and go before me. And they'd talk and chatter and maybe sometimes one of them would look right at me, but all they would see was a painted bird.

Sir William had told me to wait, but he had not come back. I began to be afraid of the message he had for my father. Perhaps we were to be thrown out. The Widow would be sweeping our step and smiling before a cock crowed twice. Where would we go...?

At last I heard Sir William stamping up the stairs again. I started forward, even began to bob, although his face looked murderous. He did not see me. Instead he ducked into a chamber that led off the gallery. I sunk back into the wall, unsure whether to wait or go. I had waited this long and, after all, he had told me to wait. I edged closer to the chamber door, so that I could catch his eye just as soon as he emerged.

Loud grunts came from the room. He was evidently trying to lift something. I leaned into the chamber. Oh, it was such a pretty room, with flowers painted on the walls and a bed with bright blue curtains threaded with gold. It must be like waking up in summer every day. Sir William was in the corner shoving at a high chest. Something told me he did not wish to be observed. I drew back and listened.

Once the chest was pushed aside he knocked on the wall, one, two, three, four times. Then he waited and knocked again, using the same rhythm: quick, quick, slow, slow.

'Nicholas, it's safe. The fellow's gone, but you must be, too. He's back soon and he sent a warning from the bishop.'

A door swung open and another, quieter voice spoke, with the accent of the North.

'I can leave now?'

'Yes, yes, I'm afraid you'd better. There's snow falling and your tracks will be covered if you go soon. But you must eat first. I feel hungry myself. It's watching that pinch-faced vicar. You have everything you need? I tell you, Nicholas, I haven't the stomach for this work.'

'It is the Lord's work, sire.'

'Yes, yes, quite right, but I want to die fat and rich in my own bed and leave my lands to my grandchildren. Come, come, the house is empty. You must be off very soon, before the company arrives, before the snow lets up. There's food made up for you. We can go down the main stairs; there's no one to see you.'

As they came out of the blue chamber I retreated, praying none of the boards would betray me, but the two men turned towards the great chamber and did not look round.

5

CONCEALMENT: SNOW

Sir William had clearly forgotten me completely.
He would not want a witness to what I had seen. I
knew little enough of such things, less than anyone, but it was clear enough even to me. My foot
was on the back stairs when, to my horror, I heard
the voices of women coming up. What to do? I
had no choice. I turned back and ducked into the
blue chamber. Under the bed, perhaps? The
women were in the corridor already.

'Oh, it is good of you, Judith,' one was saying,
'to help me with the beds. There's two gentlemen
here already and both needing chambers, and

nothing drying in this weather. We left his lord-ship's till last in case any of them came early.'

'I don't mind, Mary, not at all,' Widow Spicer's voice rang out. 'It's good to have a bit of a chat with you all at the Hall and I know you'll re-member me if there's an extra bit of mending or such like needing doing.'

Not the bed then. I glanced around in a panic and saw the strange door in the wall. It was a little ajar. I did not like to go in after the priest – it did not feel right to me – but there was no choice. I crept in and pulled the door shut, just as they bundled into the room.

It was pitch-black. I felt around me. There was a seat built into the wall and beside it a deep shelf. A slight wind brushed my cheek. I could hear the women in the room as they bustled about making up the bed and setting things to rights. As soon as they left I would make a run for it, come what may.

'Met Walter Dynely's girl on the way here.' It was the Widow. 'She's still learning lads their let-ters. Been nigh on two years now.'

My ears burned. I pressed my head to the

door.

'Miss Elizabeth's idea. She wants everyone a-reading of the Bible.'

'What does his lordship say to a girl learning boys like that? Does he think it's proper?'

'Well, I couldn't say as to that, though the parents don't like it, nor the stable men. I think Father Paul calls it pious of her, and he's not about to give up his time to ploughboys. There's no gainsaying Miss Elizabeth, not about scripture.'

'It's not good to raise her up like that. Martha, I mean. No good will come of that poor girl,' the Widow said. 'The way she looks at you. Like she's gentry. I wonder if she's safe around young souls, that I do, with her charms and potions. Her father is doing his best to go to the devil.'

'And to think you thought of him once, Judith,' Mary giggled.

'Well, that's as may be,' the Widow replied. 'You can't deny, Mary, that he is still a fine-looking man, and him widowed so young. Best wheelwright in the country when he's sober.'

'*When* he's sober.'

'You can't blame him for the girl. Not entirely.

Not natural for a man to bring up a girl by himself, drunk or sober. But she's turned out wild.'

'The spit of her mother, your sister calls her. Says she was brown as a nut, too.'

'Yes, well, I don't like to talk about *that*, seeing as most folks don't know, even now. And to think I could have married him, and had to be a mother to such a thing. And my Jacob would have had her for his sister!'

They both had a good laugh at that. I sat in the dark and listened, imagining her waving her great red meddling launderer's hands. My heart knocked at my ribs so hard it was a wonder they did not hear it. What did Goody Reynolds know of my mother; what business had she to talk of her?

'Makes you think,' Mary went on after a while. 'You never know the truth of strangers. You show a little kindness and you're taken advantage of. That's the truth of it.'

'Very true, Mary. He turned up vouched for by Sir William himself.'

'Praise Lord Jesus that bad secrets are bubbles that burst in the good fresh air. They are lucky his lordship took pity on them. Right, that's done. Don't forget the pot, Judith.'

'I don't think I could forget it. It's ripe enough.'

I thought they would leave then, and I started to nudge at the door, but I heard a large sigh and pulled back in time. The Widow started up again, close by this time. I heard a great creaking.

'This, whatever it is of his lordship's, is askew, Mary. I'll help you put it back.'

Mary must have been leaving, for I heard her rush back. Her voice was high and flurried.

'Oh, leave that to me, Judith. He can't abide outside people touching his things. It must have been one of the men, after rats. We'd better rush. Yes, well, it is a little heavy. If you take the other end of it we can put it back against the wall.'

And with pants and sighs the chest was scraped back against my door. I held my breath; what should I do? Reveal myself - and have the Widow march me to Sir William as a thief – worse, a betrayer of his secrets? But to be walled in and left? I heard Mary hurrying the Widow out and raised my fist to bang at the wood – but I could not bring myself to do it. A terrible silence fell; I stared into the dark. Surely the chest was not so big. I could just heave it forward a little and work the door open. I started with little shoves. Nothing. I put my shoulder to it, careful at first, then stronger, then with all my force. Not so much as a creak. I leaned back and put my legs to the door. My back, my fists. My belly snaked up in panic.

It could have been worse. There was a cushion on the seat and fresh air whistled down the shelf. I put my arm out to feel the extent of the space and lighted on a box. In it was good fresh bread and ham, a book and a candle. I felt further. A full pitcher of water and an empty pot. I held the bread in my fingers and breathed in the smell. I chewed each mouthful till the sourness turned sweet. For a long time I ate and thought about nothing but the bread. A kind of dizziness took me as I finished it and I put my head back. I must have gone to sleep for I fell into a strange kind of dreaming...

Dogs bayed all around me and the men flung banter over the heads of the horses. Somewhere someone was playing a lute, and sometimes there was singing and much laughter and clapping. When I glanced back, I noticed that the gentlemen were clerics to a man, with Father Paul leaning forward in the saddle, a wide white grin on his face. So I bent my head and ran with all my strength, and kept running. And the laughter gave way to grunts of effort. They were close, all around me, whinnies and snorts. 'Come, girl,' said a braying voice, and I followed the line of his arm. There was the hare, the hare from the chapel, and she was white as snow, and the dogs were almost at her throat, and I was with them, and in my hand a knife.

My head jolted against the board and I woke and remembered; a strange kind of shame unsettled me all over and I did not like to think of the blade in my hand and who I had found myself standing with. Just beyond my door the panting rhythm of the hunt went on. There are thin walls enough in the village. I knew what it was. But Sir William!

'Come, girl!' he wheezed, and she whinnied.

My neck was cricked and I was stiff with hours of sitting. I had no idea what to do. The noises from the bed subsided, but I did not know how deep they slept, or if Sir William's companion would be staying. Any sudden movement might bang the door and all would be lost. Perhaps Father would be missing me, calling out my absence even now, turning our neighbours reluctantly out of their beds for a girl none cared much to lose. The draught from the shelf blew cold on my chest and I touched the worsted of my bodice. It was wet through. I must have been sobbing in my sleep. The draught! Of course, it must be coming from outside. Maybe the hole wasn't just a seat and a shelf, but a passageway. I'd heard stories of such houses, with warrens behind the panelling, and the priests like rabbits hiding there.

Very slowly, very gently, I moved the box of food to the seat, tucking the ham into my shift and taking a good long drink from the pitcher. I needed to piss, too, but I dared not do it so close. I climbed up into the shelf. It was made for lean papists. Even I, little as I was, had to stretch out and shuffle, reaching my fingers before me, fearing to meet a rat, or worse. After a short while they closed on nothing but the dark and a great rush of air. It was a kind of hatch but there was, I soon re-alised, a ladder reaching upwards. The rungs were slick. I did not want to be found a crumpled heap at the foot of the great chimney, for that of course was where I was, but I had no choice but to clamber up. At least it was not so dark here, for some light filtered in, with a biting cold that numbed my clutching hands.

At length there was a wide opening and I felt my way out. I realised I was in the tower that must have been the beginnings of the Hall, before Sir William's ancestors put aside their armour. Or that is how Miss Elizabeth liked to tell the story. This top room was used only for storage now. I groped my way in the dark around the walls, and soon came to a door. It was locked. I had escaped one prison to find myself in another. It was too much. I sank to the floor and hugged my knees and moaned like the lonely wind that whined through the flues and the dead stone hearth. But then I gathered myself and continued around the room, crawling over great piles of furniture. At last, on the far wall, I found another door, and on this one I could undo the bolts.

Outside was a high, clear moon and that kind of silent glow that snow gives off in the night. There must have been a heavy fall, for the land was all smoothed over with hollows and dimples. Even the trees were white and laden. And all was still, as though the world were waiting to begin. I was free, with a great lump of ham to boot. It felt good to be raised up above the country, all the fields beneath me and the cottages and the sleeping people. An owl shrieked and far off I saw it slide across the night. The moon was bright and hard and the stars were brilliants. I gave off a shriek like the owl and flung out my arms. How good it would be to sweep over the ignorant land with the eye of an owl that could see a mouse moving in the thatch and all the secrets beneath it.

Then a man stepped out from the stableyard and paused and looked up. He must have heard my foolish shrieking. I shrank back into the stone. The whole world rolled back into silence and waited while he stood stock-still and looked up towards me. Even the owl had stopped its haunting. I could not tell what the man saw. Finally he crossed himself and carried on. Getting down was not so hard. I was light and quick; I had scaled trees far more troublesome than Sir William's house.

I kept to the hedges, thinking to avoid any night wanderers. I quite forgot that there'd be men out checking the sheep in the snow. I was singing quietly to keep me from feeling the cold, and watching my footing, when a man loomed up before me.

'Begone, fiend, I'll none of you,' he shouted, lunging at me with his staff.

> Blackthorn bark and poppy seed,
> Thistledown and water weed
> Send the witches off full speed.

'For the love of the Lord Jesus, William Leigh, leave off with your stick and your charms. It is only I, Martha.'

He cocked his head slowly and peered at me in the half-light, frowning. 'Martha, Martha Dynely?'

'Do you know another?'

'And you are not a demon, or a witch?'

'Can you not tell a girl from a fairy? Would a demon leave such tracks in the snow, or have such cold fingers as I have?' I reached out and touched his hand. He flinched a little, but let me touch him. Poor Will, he was still not sure. He rubbed at his eyes, which were set too close together. People said his brain had been squeezed when he came into the world, and that was why he was never quick.

'You look a sight, girl, all soot like one of the devil's own. You'd best be careful,' and he flicked his head back towards the village.

I thought he meant my father, but it was worse than that. He was not the only one abroad before dawn. I scrambled back down to the track and through the hedge. Directly into the narrow black shape of Father Paul.

I curtsied and tried to step around him, but he grabbed my wrist.

'So,' he said. 'I called on your father last night, to remind him of his duty in the law. He was not civil and you were not there.' He pulled me closer to him. In the glimmer of the night his face was all shadows but his breath made a white cloud. It smelled of meat and sour wine. I tugged a little at his arm and he drew me closer still, till I looked up at him. He was peering intently into me as though looking for something, his tongue pushing at his lower lip. I don't know if he found what he was looking for, but he suddenly threw me off so that I fell into the snow at his feet.

'Miss Elizabeth has a simple trusting heart, and Sir William might be content to let you loiter around his house, but know this: I am watching you.' He pointed at my heart. '*Get thee behind me, Satan: for it is written: Thou shalt worship the Lord thy God and Him only shalt thou serve.*'

I was afraid, for it seemed he could see into my heart itself and knew all my thoughts of thievery and flying. I got to my knees in the snow and lowered my head. 'Father, forgive me and bless me, make me humble before the Lord.'

For minutes I stared at his skirts in the snow, not daring to lift up my face. Then suddenly my head was seized and thrust down into the snow and the ice and mud beneath it.

'Fetch out the dirt within you, Martha.' I felt

the ice and stones cutting at my face, and his fingers clenching and unclenching in my hair. 'Martha, while there is time.' His voice was strange, choked. And then just as suddenly I was released. I heard the soft pad of his footsteps in the snow. He was gone.

Nothing was more welcome to me than my bed that night and the oblivion of sleep. When I awoke a short while later my father was by my cot staring down at me. I was afraid to speak. He stood as still as the man in the stableyard and stared. How I wished again to be gone, to hurl myself free. Even in the half-light I could see the grim set of his mouth, the fury tightening his eyes. I forced myself to meet his gaze. For a minute we defied one another, while his fists clenched and unclenched. Then he shook his head and left.

6

ASHES

I was sullen with the boys and they were sullen with me, throwing glances at the soot on my dress and the cuts on my face. I suppose they thought I had been beaten. I remembered Miss Elizabeth's promises to visit the class and shuddered, but she did not come. At the end of the morning Owen sidled up to me and lingered while the others ran off. As the last one left he took my hand in both of his, pressing bread into my palm. I stuffed it into my pocket and hugged him. He felt so slight he might have been a fairy.

There had been no one in the yard when I had come that morning, but I feared now to step into it. One of the men had looked up at the tower in the moonlight and had crossed himself in fear. Any one of them might look at me more sharply than the boys had done and craft a tale about what they saw and store it up for telling. I sent Owen a little ahead to scout who was there, but as I hovered in the doorway he ran back calling me.

'Martha, Aggie's here.'

I looked, there was Aggie, with her back to me, over the other side of the yard. I watched her twine a golden plait in her fingers. Even Miss Elizabeth's gown could not have dulled her hair. She was talking to Jacob, who leaned up against a wall and smiled as she talked and twisted her hair. He saw me before I was even out of the doorway. He frowned as he took in my stained cloak, and no doubt my cut-about face too. He muttered something to Aggie and slunk off, hands deep in his pockets.

Aggie turned, and started at the sight of me. There were a couple of other men, who paused and chuckled. She pursed her lips and came and put an arm around Owen and greeted me coldly.

'You are needed at home, Owen. You must come along with me.'

We had been close as peas, Aggie and I, but as we grew older she grew more at ease with folk and I did not, till she said I was a sloe and my tongue was sour. But there had not been this coldness between us before.

'I can walk along with you, Aggie. I should like to see your mother – is she doing well? She wanted some herbs off me.'

'No, Martha, that's quite all right. You must be busy here,' and her glance travelled down the length of my dirty cloak.

'Don't be silly, Aggie,' Owen put in. 'Of course Martha can come with us. Mother would like to see her. She just had a fall in the lane is all.'

'No, Owen,' I said, 'go home with your sister. I have to put the room in order.'

Aggie pressed her mouth into a thin hard line and turned, pulling Owen with her. I watched them for a moment and then I couldn't help blurting out, 'It's not what you think, Aggie, it isn't. Please.'

She turned. 'Then what is it? A fall in the

lane? There's old Will Leigh. Father was out checking sheep and met him at first light. He said he'd seen you flighting over the snow, scarce leaving tracks, all lit up by the moon, like you were the devil's own sprite.'

'And you believe that?'

'He's an addled old fool, but look at you, ragged and sooted. What were you about? Did you go with the gypsy fiddlers Sir William brought over for the feast?'

'Aggie, no, I wouldn't. Please...'

She was pulling to go and Owen was resisting. 'You've got to say sorry, Aggie,' he said.

'You're a baby, Owen – what do you know?' She looked me full in the face, and some of the stiffness went out of her. 'You have always been my friend, Martha, but sometimes I think I scarcely know you.'

I watched them leave, Owen turning and grinning anxiously as he was yanked away. The yard was empty. Slush dripped from the eaves and puddled at my feet. It hadn't long stayed white, the world.

There was so little chance of passing unobserved that I did not wish to risk walking back along the lane. I climbed up the slopes instead, muddying my cloak still further with snow melt. They had sown the winter wheat already in the low fields and snow bones lingered in the furrows. Up on the ridge, the branches dripped and plopped. Meltwater stung the cuts on my cheek. I had thought myself so lucky to escape uncaught last night; I had thought myself unscathed. As girls Aggie and I had made one another crowns of buttercups and wild garlic, pinching the stems with a nail and threading the stalks through. Buttercups for her because her hair was golden, spike-flowered garlic for me because she said my hair was night and belonged to the moon. We'd play round the lane till Grandam called me home. How I missed my grandmother.

It was a while since I had sat at her grave. I dropped down by Hooper's Oak and headed for the chapel. She was buried not far from the great yew that towered over the dead, protecting them from witches. Some of the boys had thought me a witch before. Now they believed me a whore to boot. There was nobody in the graveyard. Snow lingered in scraps and patches and the ground was sodden, but I kneeled anyway, and rested my head against the stone. If she was alive she would have scolded and soothed me. She would have mixed me up a poultice to heal my cuts and helped me clean my clothes. Then when they were drying she would have sat by the fire with me and spun me stories with the wool rippling into thread before her. Some of the stories were about my mother. I liked those the best.

There was a winter, when my mother was very young, my grandmother had told me, when it had snowed for weeks. Their cottage was a mile or two outside Moccas. There was no road and the drifts got so bad my grandfather could not get back to the cottage. One night brought a blizzard that banked up the door so heavy they couldn't get out but by the window. 'Your mother jumped up and down with delight', Grandam said, 'then sat and stared out at the folds and the billows for hours, called the snowfall the kiss of the north wind.' A robin came and lived in the hollows underneath the thatch. They fed it oatcakes till it was tame, but then one morning they woke to the sound of water dripping and a new yellow sun. The robin flew out the opened door.

My grandmother had been full of such stories. A few remained with me, but, more and more, when I tried to hold them they melted away.

My knees were numb. I clambered stiffly to my feet. As I raised my eyes, I saw him, Father Paul, sitting on a bench my father had made. It should not have been a surprise, of course – this was his church – but it hit me as unjust that I should encounter him again so soon. He gestured to me to sit beside him. I could not civilly refuse.

'I have been watching you. It is good to pray. There's a simple piety in coming to your grandmother's grave at such a time. But you must not make an idol of the dead.'

I said nothing. It seemed that nothing was required of me. It was hard to reconcile the terrible figure who had ground my face into the stones with this quiet man. My head ached. I slipped my fingers beneath my legs to warm them and let him talk.

'I fear I was harsh with you last night. You appeared in the moonlight ragged and filthy, as though you had been belched from hell. I had been thinking of you. The Lord Jesus challenges me with you, throws you into my way, your whole body charged with blackness. There is meaning in it. I pushed you into the snow to redeem you, do you see? Do you see? How could you thrust such sin before me?'

He got up and stepped back a little, regarding me solemnly. There, only a few feet behind him, my grandmother lay, as dead as my mother. I barely followed his words, but they wrapped me in loneliness. Without thinking, I reached my hand up to my cheek.

He was still talking. 'I didn't mean to cut your face. Never before I came here have I felt how much the world is riddled with death.'

I looked up. He was no longer looking at me, but somewhere out into the fields. He seemed half to have forgotten I was there.

'Last night I ate with the company at the Hall. It was snowing thickly as I walked there and in the darkness I caught sight of a sheep in the ditch. I thought to move it out of the drifts, which would no doubt soon come, but as I approached I saw it was long dead. More than that, the carcass was crawling with maggots. I cannot get them out of my mind. This is what we are. A foul act begins us; we end in the procreation of rottenness. The sun itself is a breeder of maggots. And all the time the flesh calls to us with its appetites. I looked at the meat on my plate and I was appalled. It sickened me. It was such a relief to leave the company, to be in the cold clean snow and the moonlight. Then the devil flushed you out before me, breathless with degradation.'

His voice was almost pleading. I wished I was anywhere else.

'I am not what you think me,' I began, for the second time that day.

He started when I spoke and I felt I should have stayed silent. His tone changed abruptly. It was friendly now, almost conversational. 'No, in the light of morning it came to me that you must have been helping his lordship with his chimneys. He has some very large chimneys at the Hall.'

I nodded uneasily.

He went on, 'Perhaps there might even be tunnels or some such, connecting old parts of the house. Did they have you cleaning them, perhaps?'

'Yes,' I said eagerly, 'yes, I was cleaning, in the cinders.' If Father Paul himself cleared me, nobody would dare so much as mutter.

He was smiling down at me. 'Cleaning tunnels, strange old spaces in the house?'

I felt the heaviness return. 'No,' I said firmly, 'nothing like that, just the cinders and the brassing in the kitchens.'

His smile wound itself back in. 'Are you very sure? Think about it, Martha. Count up your friends.'

It was both an offer and a threat. .

7

PLANS

As soon as I was home I scrubbed and mended my cloak and gown and set them by the fire to dry, and I teased out my hair with the comb my father had made me for my last birthday, all carved with pretty flowers. Then I set about the broth, dropping in pieces of the ham I'd taken from the Hall. I did not hear my father come in. His voice startled me.

'Where were you?'

I opened my mouth. It occurred to me that I had not thought what story to tell him. He leaned down over me; the light from the flames played over his face. His voice was low and angry.

'I got work, up at the Hall...' I began, and then faltered, for he had raised his hand to slap me.

'Don't lie to me! Not me, you hear? You can lie to the others – yes, and I know you do. It's all the same to me if you damn them to hell, but don't try it with me. I came back last afternoon and found you not returned. So yes, I thought you were working up at the Hall.'

'It's true, Father. Miss Elizabeth—'

'*I* am speaking!' he shouted, grabbing my shoulders, his face an inch from mine. 'Late on, Widow Spicer came nosing round to borrow a flint, or some such tale, and said she was surprised you had not lingered up there yesterday as there was that much work, with all the fine people coming, and were you not back yet, indeed? You'd best be careful, she said, what with the gypsies staying to entertain at the gathering.'

'Why, how dare she—'

'Oh, she dares, all right – what's to stop her? She's a soul as spotted as an eel and as slippery; she wants us in the mud so she can wriggle out and claim more light. And you help her.' He let me go and paused as though the words were

stopped in his throat. I watched his hands, clenching, unclenching. I hoped he was done, but in a
breath he'd turned full at me again. 'You come
crawling back, ripped and cindered, scaring up
old Bill like a dark spirit or some kinchin harlot
out of her ditch. You want that? You want every
lumbering oaf and his wife to snigger as you go
by? By God, I should beat some sense into you.'

'Do you think they don't snigger already?' I
shouted. 'Do you think they don't hear you when
you come back roaring, Father?'

I took a step back as I said it; he was sure to hit
me now; his face grew twisted and ugly and he
raised his right arm. For a second he hovered and
I thought he would stride right through the
hearth to knock me down. But then his hands fell
to his sides and he spat on the floor.

'Curse this life,' he said. 'Curse this wretched
hole and all its vermin.'

We stood like that for a while, either side of
the stew, neither speaking, bleak as the weather,
with the promise that the snow made gone and
nothing left but the grey and straggling thaw.
Slowly the smell of the ham drifted through the

misery in the room. It is the best smell in the world when you are hungry and we were both very hungry. He reached out and took my hand.

'Come here, Martha. I'm not going to beat you. I was afraid. You did not come home. How did your face get so cut about? You are grown so big and wayward. I think I would go mad if I lost you, child. I have not been a good man, Martha, or a good father to you, especially these last years. I know it. It's strange how fortune plays out. I was my father's darling. No one could touch me. I wrote a better hand than any of your university men. My father was a freeman of the city. And here we are. There's not much left for me in this life, nor any other, I suspect, but do you have to set about undoing yours so quick?'

It was as gentle a speech from him as any I could remember. We sat and ate and I told him the truth. Or some of the truth. Miss Elizabeth's writing about Father Paul I left out because it did not seem right to mention what was private to Miss Elizabeth. Also, Father Paul accosting me in the lane, because there was bad blood enough already between my father and he. I was shy of telling Father of the priest and his hole. I even lowered my voice, though only a mouse could have heard us. To my astonishment, I saw that he was smiling.

'So,' he said, 'well built, is it not? Ingenious, even?'

'You know of it?'

'I built it, child.'

I nearly spilled my broth. He patted my wrist. 'I am not of Sir William's persuasion. I'll pray whatever prayer I'm given, so long as I'm left alone, but his lordship knows me to be close with secrets and reckless of my life and I owe him a debt. Why are you so surprised? You must have heard the talk, the mutterings, even if no one would dare say much aloud.'

'But to harbour a priest!'

'It's a dangerous game, I'll grant you that, but he plays the bluff country fool pretty well. He keeps away from the great families; he doesn't go looking for enemies. And Walsingham himself could not doubt Miss Elizabeth.'

'And Father Paul?'

'Ha! Him. He suspects, I dare say. It may well

be why the bishop placed him here. He's the bishop's man and he'll be reporting back to his master. The more he knows, the more power it gives him over Sir William. Who's to know when he might want to ask for something Sir William is reluctant to give?'

We sat until only the light of the fire lit the room and I was more happy than I had been for a long time, with the taste of the ham in my mouth and my father talking to me frankly and the shutters drawn against the night.

'Tell me again,' I said, 'about growing up in the city.'

He let his gaze rest on a flame and go far off. 'I had a friend. Johnny. We'd set off for school together before dawn and in the afternoon when the gates closed behind us we'd slink off to the docks where the ships laid at anchor. Castles in the water, with pinnaces gold, green, red in the sun; beetle-brown sailors who smelled of the oil they rubbed into their hair. You could hear all the languages of the world in the dockyards. Even the English was strange, studded with ship talk and far-off places. We'd set ourselves down outside the taverns and listen to their yarning; Spanish galleons, raging storms, eerie calms when the wind dropped and the sun was a vengeful eye. Calms that could last for weeks. Weevils in the meal and the barrels bitter, but the sea like a bright blue jewel around you. Once they told us of a boy, just the spit of you two, they said, who sat atop the rigging in the full sun of a terrible calm for hours on end, searching the sky for the great white bird the sailors knew brought luck. The blazing light must have turned him, for though the ship hadn't moved a whisper he fell down. His foot caught in the rigging. Lucky? Maybe. Some of the sailors thought it a good joke, the boy dangling on the rope, his white smock bagging above the crosstrees: "Best start praying, lad. Swinging's saved you now; it'll do for you another time." All of a sudden a breeze shook up. It was an hour before they got him down and when they did his wits were all gone. He cursed the rope that'd snagged him. Said he'd seen sea-girls singing to him in the water, reaching out their white arms. First chance he got he was overboard; by then the wind had picked up lively and he was lost in the wake.' He chuckled. 'No doubt they meant to warn us off the sea. Much good it did. Might as well spit in the dust to water your corn.

'Not that my father would have let me go. We were rich. Our house was big: three floors, it had; room for two servants or more along with the family. There was a horse in the stable and meat every day. I and my sister lacked for nothing.' He was quiet for a while. 'And then it was gone. All gone. I was thirteen years old. There'd been crowds in the streets revelling that Queen Anne was put to death. We were all asleep. The flames took hold in the kitchen. Old Adam got me and my sister out, but it was too late for my mother, my father. Too late for the warehouse, too. But you know this story.' His voice grew bitter. 'All my life I've been riding Fortune's wheel. The fall comes and knocks the breath out of my body. Just when I have learned to breathe again I am thrown down, harder than before.'

I knew the story. How he'd had to leave school, how he'd been apprenticed to a wheelwright and, not long after, his sister married off to a widower near twice her age, with children who resented the gown on her back and were barely civil to her relations. This kind of talk led to the tavern. I took his thick working man's hand in mine. How strange to think he was born to dress in velvet, with a servant to cook him roast meat every day.

'Father,' I said at last, 'does my aunt still live in the city?'

He looked at me, puzzled. 'Should you like to see her? She's alive, if she has not died since summer.'

'Could we not go? Not for a visit, but altogether. Leave the village? You are still strong. You could show me the fine people's houses and we could sit in the Cathedral and listen to the choir. You could ask Sir William for work with the people he does business with. Oh, Father, how I should love to go to the city. What is to keep us? My grandmother is dead. You have said yourself, there is nothing here but mud.'

It was not the first time in the last two years or so that I had urged it. He railed against the village but would not leave. He was threaded into his life here, and even if the threads were of contempt and anger he seemed to fear to snap them. Sometimes, when I pressed him, he grew angry; sometimes he patted my chin and smiled, as you might to a child who said a pretty but a silly thing. This time – perhaps it was a memory of the courage he'd felt in patching Sir William's house with holes, or perhaps he felt too that things had changed, that there was a murmuring, like the rustle of a wind before a storm breaks – whatever it was, he neither scolded nor scoffed, but caught my eye and held it.

He said nothing for a long while. I waited. Still he said nothing, so I got up and began to set the place tidy. Only when I had half forgotten I was waiting did he speak.

'It could be done,' he said. I turned in surprise. His eyes were shining, as though he were gazing at the streets and the crowds already. 'You would have a chance of meeting some fine fellow, not one of these country idiots. It could be done. I could... I will write to my sister. Sir William will know people. Don't pester me. It'll take time, but I'll set about it. Ask me again in the spring, Martha. In the spring.'

8

THE ROAD RIPS

It was not many nights later. I dreamed I was walking over a high level plain, pulling a small wagon with all my things piled high. Now and again the cloud dropped so low the road before me was hidden. I knew my father had gone on ahead a little way. It was a lonely place, with the cloud drifting across me and not a soul around. The only birds to be heard were crows that wheeled in and out of the mist. I came at last to a crossroads. The mist cleared and I saw right in front of me the ruin of a gibbet. With the strangeness of dreams I knew I should wait here to meet my mother, though it made me shudder to sit so near the scaffold. 'Mother!' I shouted and the wind and cloud threw my call back to me. Why did she not come? I shouted again, 'Mother!' This time a voice answered, but it was harsh, not my mother's voice at all. It seemed it was the ground itself that called me, over and over, and then it was my father's voice. He was standing over my bed, shaking me awake. He shoved my cloak at me and pulled me towards the door. The bed itself was rocking; dust fell from the thatch, from the walls. There was a terrible sound, a tearing, coughing sound, like a monster puking. Just as we stepped outside, the cottage juddered and the noise abruptly stopped.

A bone-bright moon picked out the lane like a woodcut. People huddled in doorways. Crows cawed around the trees and the branches swayed a little, but the rest of the lane was still, and seemed just as it always was, clearer than by day, if anything, for the moon silvered the damp thatch and the mud and threw long inked shadows from the elms. We stood there unsteady and afraid. Had we all of us merely dreamed a monster? I glanced at my father; it was not a dream. He would not entertain such a fancy. He was frowning, glancing at the huts, then back up towards the hill. A sharp breeze blew out our lantern and we became part of the darkness.

Then Goody Reynolds let out a scream and pointed. We none of us had seen what was at our feet. One of the long shadows was no shadow at all, but a great black hole. The road had wrenched itself open. There was a gash along it, deep as a horse and more than a perch long. We stepped as near as we dared to the edge and stood close together, staring into nothing. Looking could make no sense of it. People turned to Rob Tanner's father, old George, who must have been near eighty, and had lived in the village all his life. He'd heard of such like happenings, he said. Over Leominster way, back before King Henry died, for example, there was a drover who'd dined well across two counties on a tale of how he'd been sleeping out by Kimbolton one night with his animals when he was woken by a monstrous gulping noise. The beasts had been near dead with fright. And no wonder. Scarce three yards off, the grass had torn wide open, with a pit so big it had taken a whole

steer. The drover swore it was the fairies, on account of how he'd scorned to pay them passage.
But folks said as how he'd had a gill too many at
the Stockton Cross. I felt better listening to
George, sucking his three teeth and grinning at
his own story, but Rob snorted the old man aside
and turned to my father.

'You, Walter, with all your learning, what's
done this?'

My father paced out the length of the hole,
then picked up a long branch and probed the
sides and the depth of it as far as he could. People
shuffled back for him to pass by and leaned in to
watch his expression. There was a monk of
Poland, he told them at last, who died during King
Henry's time, and this monk showed that the
earth we live on is forever moving, turning and
circling round the sun. And the rocks and soil are
moving too, and jostling and shifting. This is what
that is, he said, a bit of earth has slipped out of
kilter with its neighbour.

There was a murmuring at this, and more
than one glanced up to check if the stars had wandered. I think I did so myself. There were clouds

gathering, but the stars were in their places. My father looked serious, but it was hard to know at times when he was taking you for a fool. He talked in his own patterns and would not bend to the grooves of people's thinking, and this offended. Here, now, he turned to the hole, kneeling to rub some earth between his fingers, oblivious to the frowning at his back. I walked round behind him. In despite of his words I did not feel it could be explained so easily. It drew my eyes like a horror in a dream.

'More ale talk,' Robert Tanner burst out. 'If you can't talk sense, you'd best put a stopper in that mouth of yourn, Walter. I've heard it before, that story, the earth gallivanting all around the sky like a child's ball, and the sun, that we see moving every day, standing still as a post. You might get away with that with papists and atheists, but what does the Bible have to say, eh? That's what we want to know.'

My father turned back, with a countenance of strained patience and spread his hands, as though he were fitting a wheel to test if it was true. His hands were large and strong, but I noticed that they shook a little. They did not use to do this, I was sure. Perhaps he needed the wood, the perfect circle of the wheel, to steady them.

'The Bible is not an almanac,' he said. 'You'd be better looking to the weather and the hills to seek out your answers.'

Robert Tanner spat into the dark, but another voice rang out in rich, familiar tones.

'I will tell you what the Bible says.' It was Father Paul. We had not seen him approach, long and thin and black, like the trench before him. He was silent for a moment, letting his eye fall on each one of us in turn. We felt ourselves gathered in his gaze, wrapped around and held by it. When he spoke his voice was so soft we had to crane to hear, just at first, but bit by bit it grew till it rang out like a knell. 'Hear the Gospel of Luke: *And great earthquakes shall be in divers places, and hunger, and pestilence; and fearful things and great signs shall there be from heaven.*' He stared at my father as he spoke and my father stared back, unstooping in the gloom of the early light.

I understood, as clearly as if they had had swords in their hands, that this was a duel, although my father said nothing for a long time, but just stood there, facing the minister, with everybody watching him and the trench and Father Paul.

At last Father spoke, turning away from the minister to our neighbours. '*Hold fast your souls with patience,*' he said, and turned away and ducked into our cottage. I lingered after him, gazing at where he had stood as though that might explain his words.

Father Paul looked around the knots of people triumphantly and his voice rang out.

'Look into this darkness – surely you can see that it is a sign? Take it, take it into your hearts, and root out evil. *For these be the days of vengeance, that all things that are written may be fulfilled.* There is sin among you and heresy among you, and I have seen the devil and his kind walking on the highways and the pathways and the fields. Even now God wounds the earth of the parish as a sign. Which of you will heed it?'

There was a general murmur and nodding. Father Paul smiled and opened his arms wide. I dropped my gaze to the ground. When I raised my eyes he was gone.

Across from me, on the other side of the trench, Goody Reynolds lifted up her stick and squawked, 'It is coming, it is coming, the judgment of the Lord.'

She was pointing her stick right at me! I looked around. No one else much marked her; the daylight was coming and it was time to be moving, the end of the world or no.

'Come, sister,' the Widow Spicer said, taking her arm, 'I think we should go home and pray. Come, Jacob.'

The two women moved off and the other groups did too, till the lane was all but deserted again. A soft rain began to fall. I was glad of it, because it flowed down my cheeks so gently. Father Paul and then the Widow's sister; they both believed a devil had entered my soul. A worm of fear stirred in my belly. Why were my eyes so drawn to the hole, to the dark rip in the earth, wide enough to lie down in? I had no doubt that if I were to fall, just to lean a little more and topple, it would take me and cover me over. I could close my eyes in the cold clay and the rain would fall and wash me till I ran like water into the earth. I edged a little forward.

Under the elm tree opposite someone moved. It was Jacob. I had thought him gone in with the others. The surprise made me start. I teetered at the edge and felt a prick of panic, then took a good step back. I could not but be mindful of our last meeting in the stableyard, but there was no avoiding him. He was almost in front of my door and I on the far side of the hole; I could hardly walk round the village, half dressed beneath my cloak, with day near full upon us. It struck me we were stood exactly as my father and Father Paul had stood, him on one side, me on the other. I swallowed and met his gaze.

'I must apologise to you, Jacob. I did not talk like a Christian to you in the class. I beg you will stop nursing the grievance.'

To my surprise he smiled. 'Very like you, Martha, to say sorry and then take it half back, but in truth I barely remember the occasion.'

'Very like you, Jacob Spicer, to pretend it is of no consequence. You have not forgotten it at all.

Truly, I am sorry.' I paused and tried to offer a smile, but he looked as serious as ever and my patience failed. What good was it abasing myself to such as him if he played the prelate? 'Just as you should be sorry for tripping me at the dance two years back and laughing.'

'Did I? Oh, yes, I remember. You snarled like a vixen and looked like you would tear me with your nails. I've half a mind to trip you up again to make you more polite to your elders.'

He grinned and there was such a warmth in it I could not help grinning back. The little shame I had been carrying sloughed off; the little resentment, too, seemed suddenly a paltry thing. I felt lighter towards him than I had for a long while. We stood a while, smiling, with the rain running down our hair. 'Trip me then, I challenge you. But I think you daren't jump the trench, for if you slip the devil will have you in the pit.'

'Daren't I?' he said, and without a pause or a run he took a leap over it, straight to my feet, where he slid in the mud and went down on his knees. It made me laugh after his vaunting, and as I bent over to help him up I saw that he was laughing too. There was a great slap of mud across his cheek. I would have wiped it off with the corner of my cloak, but he had not let go of my hands, even though he was up now and looking at me and not laughing any longer. His hands were warm, calloused, a man's hands, not a boy's. His breath made a mist in the cold air. I pulled my hands away and faced him, but my voice came out knotted.

'Come back to the class, Jacob. I will teach you. I should like to.'

He threw his head back a little and regarded me, then all at once his eyes grew colder and he stuffed his hands in his pockets. 'What were you doing the other night, Martha? Why were you walking the fields so late? How did your face get cut?'

It was like a thump. No, not so much a thump, a sick weight of shame fell back on my shoulders, into my guts. So he, too, thought that I'd tumbled with a gypsy in the ashes of his fire, or else been caught and cut a little, but taken nonetheless. Lost my jewel for a snatch of ham, or a few pieces of silver.

'You already know, don't you? I'm a dirty slut who'd turn a trick for a piece of pie.' Without thinking I slapped him, and he near stumbled with the surprise of it, standing on the edge of the hole as he was. 'Fall,' I said. 'It's where you belong, you and the rest of this midden. You live in filth.'

'Aye, I live here, Martha. You live here, too,' he said, leaning in so close it was barely more than a hard whisper. A minute, more, passed. Somewhere close by a cock crowed. Then there was the Widow calling him. She cast me a sharp look.

As he joined her I recovered myself and called after them, 'Yes, I live here, and I think we are all damned. I hope this whole benighted place is swallowed up and carried down to hell.'

9

EXPLANATIONS

At first the hole, as we began to call it, was all that was talked of in the village and beyond. Indeed, several gentry rode up on the days that followed to view it, some had come all the way from Hereford; carriages, too, with fine ladies in them, till Tom, the miller, said he was bored of the sight of satin, but that the hole should be the making of us all, what with the pies and cakes and ale that the rich seemed to have need of at every turn. We stepped gingerly by it and glanced at it nervously for fear it might have grown. Mary Tucker, whose cottage was closest, was up several times a night till her husband forbade it; she was convinced that the hole might grow in the night and gobble up her children. We all had troubled nights. There was nothing like the roar the night the hole had come, but there were new noises, like sighs or light moans from the hill. They were so slight that in the day you might take it for the wind, or the cows lowing at the Hall, but at night we lay awake in our beds, afraid of our own rocks and soil.

My father fell into conversation with one of the gentlemen observers, who, astonished at the learning of this country wheelwright, introduced him to others. The learned men pointed to the puddles and the heavy rain and nodded. My father led them up the track to Little Hill where the lie of the land was clearer and the hole looked like a tear in a seam. After these discussions he was happy for days, explaining what the old Greeks said about earth movements. Aristotle was wrong on this one, he declared; he was all for Democritus and his gases. All I could see was the way they condescended, making a show of him before they went off to drink their wine and laugh at the country philosopher. It did him no favours with his neighbours. Rob Tanner wasn't the only one muttering about godlessness and pride, though he and the rest helped drink the Angels the gentlemen gave my father as a guide fee.

It doesn't take long for a monster to become a familiar. The visitors dropped off and we began to forget our fear of the hole. Boards were fixed across and people dumped their rubbish; one morning we found the stinking body of a horse had been tipped in. Soon there was barely any hole at all; a scar and a long line of water in the track was all that showed. We marked the edges with rocks to warn travellers, but they kept washing away. More than once my father got work because a cart did not know the road or wasn't careful. Tom was right: there's money in disasters. We grew used to the hill moaning. It's the dragon turning, we'd say, and laugh because we didn't believe it. Only Goody Reynolds and the Widow liked to shake their heads and mutter about omens. 'There's more coming,' Goody Reynolds would say to anyone who'd listen. 'Mark my words, this is only a beginning.'

She was waiting for me one late afternoon as I returned from the Hall, laden with good blocks of wood Miss Elizabeth had given me and pastries too, in my pocket.

'Fling yourself down and ask for His forgiveness, Martha,' she said. 'Hell's door opened a crack with that hole. The Lord has given you another chance.' She stood before me so that I could not pass and began to poke me with her finger.

'Go your ways,' I said. 'I'm nothing to do with you.'

'No, don't doubt it, and you won't be. This is a good family.'

'And what does that mean?' I asked, setting down my sack. She stepped back and just stared, chewing at her lips, nodding and saying nothing till I could not stand it. I darted forward and tweaked out a couple of dirty grey hairs. That made her shudder all right. Christ forgive me, but it felt good to play the witch. 'Tell me what you mean,' I said, as she began to back away, muttering, 'or I'll light my fire and feed it with these and the devil will come and tell me himself.'

'You,' she said, and glanced from side to side. There was no one about. 'You and your mother, both. She did it and you helped her. She's trying to find her way back from hell.'

I grabbed her shoulders. I think I meant to shake her till her last few teeth fell out, but her shoulders were so little and her cloak so thin that my anger failed me and in its place I felt weary and sad. She was a frail thing next to her sister; a sparrow, pecking around for rumour and talk. She had half lost her wits – everyone saw it from the moment she arrived; it would be a wonder if she lasted the winter. No doubt the Widow let her know she was a burden. I took out the pastries and held one out.

'Here, neighbour,' I said. 'I'll thank you not to speak ill of my mother.'

She looked a little nervous, then put out a scrawny hand and snatched it and concealed it in her gown, as though afraid I'd take it back. 'I will pray for you, girl, that you be brought back to the Lord Jesus.'

'You had better do it quietly,' I said, 'so your sister does not hear.'

When I reached home there was my father, cheerful, with food he had bought from the Hereford market. He had fallen to talking, he said, with some tradesmen of the city. They were of a mind that there was work enough there, for capping was strong again, thanks to her Majesty and there were always carts needing mending for the fulling mills along the river. Hereford, then, not Gloucester. We would be gone before Lady Day he said. We would leave this dismal valley and never come back.

'I'll make you a fine lady yet Martha,' he said. 'Oh, I can't forgive myself for the years I've wasted. There are pigs with more conversation than the oafs in the alehouse. I thought it was right for you to be in your mother's country and maybe it was the best thing while your grandmother lived. You're almost a young woman now. You're educated, after a fashion; I'll not have you getting a swineherd for a husband.'

For the first time in all my life I believed it would happen. We would move to the city. I could not speak for joy. All week it bubbled in us, and we grinned when we caught one another's eye as though people would stop us if they knew. As if anybody would stop us! Miss Elizabeth would smile graciously and say she would do whatever she could, and when she came to the city perhaps once in a while she would bend her graceful head to come into our rooms where she would pull off her gloves carefully, finger by finger, and exclaim how cosy we had made the space. But I thought with a pang of Owen. What would he do and who would speak for him when his father called for him to leave off books and work? Perhaps, I thought with a jolt of delight, he could come with us. That was it! He could lodge with us and continue his schooling and Miss Elizabeth could enter him into the grammar school.

And why should I think of Jacob, who thought me a trollop; why should I think of him at all? I blushed to remember how he had stood so close and blushed again because I could not rid the picture from my mind of his face as he bent towards me. When we moved I would leave Jacob behind and that was good.

I think I have never been so happy as I was in those days of December. We had more food than we had had for months, and Father barely drank at all, or not to notice. Many evenings we sat close by the fire and made plans, and cared nothing for the cold outside and the frosts, which set in so strong that the world of mud became a world of stone. Little by little it seemed to me that our neighbours were forgetting to regard me with suspicion. Even Goody Reynolds, I fancied, glanced less sidelong at me as she picked her scrawny way along the edges of the lane.

I should not have grown so easy. I should have listened to how the hill kept up its unquiet moaning.

One evening we were sitting either side of the fire, contentedly enough, watching the yellow flames lick the ash in the grate. A low hum came from the ridge, but we were used to this. I paid it little mind at first, until I realised that it had changed its tone and dropped to a coughing growl. My father stood up and went to the door.

'I think the dragon's belly rumbles,' I said, to make him smile.

He turned to me, with a frown. 'Don't indulge that silly talk,' he said. 'There are no dragons.'

'Will Leigh says it is a wyvern, like the one little Maud found in the legend, and it is waking in anger at the thirst for timber that is causing so much felling of the old woods.'

'Ssh, girl, let me listen.'

'And there's some who hint it is the driving out of the old customs.'

'Ssh, I told you.'

'And there are some who say – but they say it very quiet – that it is punishment for them as harbours papists in their walls.'

'For God's sake, still your tongue!' Though he spoke quiet enough Father's voice was harsh and angry. 'Damn their stories and their superstitions. The noise has changed, do you hear it? The hole won't be the last of this. It may be we shall have to move before spring after all. If we get more rain... Stay here, I'll be back presently. I'll climb up past the Noggin to listen.'

After he left I stared into the embers and prayed that he did not turn into the inn. Perhaps there was no dragon, but I could not but think that there must be a reason for this wailing, for the hole. There was one explanation, of course, that I had not told him. Goody Reynolds' words came back to me. I had made the hole to bring my mother back from hell. Mad old crone. But I was uneasy. The fear nagged at me that I was indeed to blame, that I was stained with evil. Why would my father never talk to me of her death? Had he come back here to work away the guilt that stuck to us? When I thought of my mother she was dressed in white, in a white shift in the glow of dawn; she was a white dove, with a collar of black, singing in a tree.

That night Father passed the alehouse and though the door was open he did not go in.

10

CHRISTMAS EVE

The days before Christmas were washed away in a cold rain that did not stop. Day after day it puddled in the fields and the tracks, found its way through thatch, leaked down the walls. Wood hissed and steamed on the hearth and the fire would not set. The worst of it was the sense that things were losing their proper shape, the lane and the field a sticking mess of mud, the sky and the land dribbling into one another, grey, and brown and grey. Even our faces sagged and grew pallid as the clouds. When ice came again at last we welcomed it, for it let us find our footing and gave the world some definition.

On Christmas Eve I gathered holly and mistletoe and threaded it through the cottage and the workshop, through my spinning wheel and all my father's tools. He held no holy days dear, not even Christmas Day itself, but I would not have him working, not this year when I was determined we should have no strife between us, nor with our neighbours. He had been away two days, fixing the wheels of a brewer's cart in Ledbury. He would be back, he promised me, by Christmas morning, but not before. There was a man he intended to seek out who owned lodgings in the city. I spent hours scrubbing up the cottage, rubbing the wood with lavender and rosemary so that it should welcome him home.

Most years I went with Owen and Aggie to fetch the great yule log, but since she had been so high with me, hauling Owen off as though I would harm him, I had not courted Aggie's company. A nod, a brief good morning was all we'd exchanged, I as haughty as she, but since the hole, and over the last few days especially, I fancied the affront was wearing thin; we'd both managed a curt smile. Still, I was surprised to find her with

Owen when he rootled me out to go along to the Hall.

Sir William had done himself proud. It was a huge piece of oak, and four men straining to pull it now it was off the wagon. Even the hearth of the great Hall would scarce accommodate it. At the edge of the park we caught up with the crowd that had gathered to bring it. There was already a fiddle or two to aid the singing. Owen was delighted, and ran to join the other children scrambling up for the ride, till the men turned and clipped them. Ned Stolley bounded up and turned a cartwheel, and some of the adults cheered. Aggie and I had not spoken much as we walked. She had asked after my father and I had wished her mother well but now she turned to me and smiled. It was the music, it caught at our spirits and made them jig. I took her hand and squeezed it and we fell in behind the log, hand in hand like that all the way to the barns. There was a cold buffeting wind that smacked us cheerfully. 'Adam Lay Ybounden' Tom sang, and the fiddle picked it up. 'All was for an apple...' the song rang out from man and woman and child, and before us the Hall was lighted up with candles, and nearby the doors of one of the barns were flung open. Later the log would be taken into the Hall itself, but before that we'd all make merry in the barn.

When we were young Miss Elizabeth herself would pass among us handing out ribbons to pin to the log, but she had reserved herself from village customs the last few years. It may be she had grown a mite too refined, or perhaps she wasn't sure of the sanctity of decking the oak with gaudy stuff. It was her chambermaid, Mary, who oversaw the decoration, but Sir William himself handed out ale to the men as they undid the ropes, clapping them on the back till beer sloshed over the jugs.

'Well done, men, that's a fine log. Bishop John won't have a better, I dare say. Drink up and there'll be pies and the wassail cup a little later. Very good, very good, what better than a fiddle and such pretty girls...' catching Aggie round the waist and swinging her round.

She bounced back into me blushing and I handed her my ribbons to pin. Across at the back of the barn I had noticed Jacob putting up tables, and now, to my consternation, I saw that he was looking back at us. He smiled. Well, who wouldn't smile at Aggie, flushed and happy, her fingers full of ribbons? I shot a glance at her, but she hadn't noticed him. She was taking direction from Sir William, who was gallantly helping her to press in the pins.

Soon the wassail singing began and the whole place felt warm and jolly, with holly and mistletoe on the walls and the glow of candles. I felt a hand slide into mine.

'Look, Martha,' Owen said, 'they are bringing pies and the wassail cup, and Jacob says we'll have dancing.'

I followed where he pointed and there indeed the cup was already going around from hand to hand and mouth to mouth, Sir William, in great high spirits, urging it on. Goody Reynolds took a peck at it, like a biddy hen, but Tom put back his head and drained the cup. Owen threw back so much he fell to coughing. I allowed myself a good gulp. It was sweet and rich. The ripple of the cup passing from hand to hand warmed and loosened us till neighbours who an hour before could not abide each other linked arm in arm. All the world seemed good and happy.

Sir William took Aggie's hand and led off the dancing, and her gold hair outshone the candles. Jacob had been hovering, but he'd have to wait, for he could hardly step in before his lordship. I grabbed Owen and when it came to threading down the line we whirled and laughed till I felt as silly and young as he. The candles swum before me and the faces were yellow moons. I left Owen to sneak more pies and took my ale outside to let the cold air and the pricked stars settle me. Perhaps my father was even now walking home. He hardly ever came to dances and some years forbade me, too, but I thought how this time, this last time, perhaps he might like it. It felt odd to me to think that I should never spend another Christmas here, nor perhaps dance with my neighbours again or drink the wassail cup. Not that I wasn't glad to be leaving, but it was odd, nonetheless.

Someone nudged my elbow. 'I'll partner you for the next round, Martha.' It was Jacob. I was so surprised that I assented before I thought what my response should be.

'But what shall we talk of to avoid falling out?'

'I think you'd best decide that,' he said.

'Then we'd best say nothing at all to any purpose,' I replied, 'or I'll vex you and then you're like to trip me up again. But where's Aggie? You've not danced with her yet.'

'No,' he said, 'I've not.'

I didn't know what to make of his tone at all for he turned to his ale and drank it off and looked away. Then the music stopped and he took my elbow, almost roughly. 'Come,' he said, 'it's time.'

Just as he did so Owen appeared before us. 'Martha...' he said. 'Oh, good evening, Jacob. Look, I've got a pocket full of pies—'

He was cut off by Sir William, with Aggie breathless and laughing a step behind him. 'Here he is. A fine young swain for a pretty maiden. That's it, that's it, take her hand. Don't be shy, boy. For goodness' sake, anyone would think you'd taken vows. You know her well enough.' And he seized Jacob's hand and joined it with Aggie's. 'Go and dance, go and dance. I must be off, but I'm not such a blackguard that I'd leave a lady standing with nothing but her curls for company.'

Jacob frowned and threw me a glance and a slight shrug, but Aggie was leading him back into the barn and I watched as he put on a better face and smiled down at her and handed her into the set. Sir William was right, they looked fine together.

I turned to Owen. 'Let's see those pies you pilfered,' I said.

There was more dancing later, but not with Jacob. I saw him approach before the next set, but I turned to Tom who happened to be by, and he gave me a grin and ducked me a bow. Tom had always been a friend to us. He'd been a drinking man, but it did not turn him sour. Many's the time he'd lugged my father home and helped me lay him on his bed. Then a year or so ago he'd stopped going to the alehouse. I think he and my father had had words, for he did not come by any more either. But he was always friendly to me. He was older than my father – there was as much grey as black in his beard –

but he was no less strong for that. He swung me around as though I were a half-peck of corn and he threaded through the line more dainty than a courtier. I had a great desire to tell him our plans, but I had promised Father I would breathe a word to nobody.

'You must dance with the young folk, Martha,' he said as we finished.

'Oh, I do, some,' I said, 'but there's many that don't like me.'

'Don't like you? Oh, you kimet child, they'd like you well enough if you let them. Anne Boleyn was little and dark; that turned King Henry's head.'

It was very pleasing to hear him say so, though we were all of us warm with ale. The night and the dancing and the fine rich food gifted everyone with beauty. I had never been pretty. The Widow had said so bluntly enough, and the boys found me too plain or too fierce to want me as a partner. My father was a handsome man, or had been, but I did not look like him and though I was dark like my mother I knew by the way he stared at me sometimes and sighed that he looked for her in me and could not find her. Still, I felt myself glow with pleasure.

'You look happy, Martha,' Jacob said when he swung me in the four; he sounded surprised. 'You were content enough to dance with Tom, I see.' He began to say something else, but my arm was taken by Ezekiel Tucker, who trod on my toe, for he'd grown a little tipsy, despite his Mary seizing the cup off him whenever she could.

Soon I sought Aggie out to walk home, for the hour was late. There could be no dancing on Christmas Day. We could not find Owen anywhere in the barn, although most folks had wandered home and the fiddles were sawing out carols. We stood outside in the yard and made him out over by the barn opposite, where the plough oxen were housed against the winter. As we approached Aggie got ready to scold, but Owen put his fingers to his lips and we noticed Jacob behind him, swaying a little. 'Jacob said we could come and watch the oxen to see them kneel in prayer for the birth of our Lord. He says there's ever so many have seen them Christmas night. Some say they can talk.'

We glanced at one another. I could see Aggie hesitate between duty and curiosity. 'I don't think —' she began.

But Jacob butted in, 'Come, Aggie, it is holy, I swear it is. Yes, a kind of worship, God's Holy Hiwacle.'

I knew that kind of talking, although Jacob slurred with a smile dancing on his lips.

'Martha,' he turned to me, 'you'll come.' He grasped my hand and I caught Aggie's and we ducked into the barn. It was dark inside, with a soft musky animal darkness, but Jacob had a lantern and he led us to a corner piled with fresh straw where we could make out the sleeping beasts. They stomped and snorted at our coming in, but Jacob spoke gently to them and they settled. We sank down in the straw and watched. In the distance we heard the bells ring out midnight: Christmas morning. Owen squatted up on his haunches, eagerly leaning forward, but Aggie and I sat down with our backs to the wall, Jacob between the two of us. He kept hold of our hands. We breathed the rich heady smell of the straw and the beasts; I was aware of my body in an easeful way, and of Jacob's warmth beside me, but it did not feel lewd or wrong. We were brothers and sisters in the darkness and the oxen blinked at the lamplight and seemed to recognise us. We stayed stock-still, not speaking, not counting the minutes. All of us, all four, it seemed to me, had stepped from the meddle of ordinary time. It was the hour between night and morning, on the holiest of nights. The oxen looked right at me.

'We should kneel,' I whispered, and Owen nodded and got down on his knees. I glanced across at Jacob and Aggie. Jacob's head leaned back against the wall, Aggie's leaned on his shoulder. Both were quite asleep. I love each of them, I told myself, as I endeavoured to kneel without disturbing them, why shouldn't they love one another? Owen smiled and pointed, before he bowed his head. One of the beasts had dropped down too. A thrill went through me: it was kneeling, at this hour of His birth; it had dropped to its knees! Its eyes were as deep as Pentaloe Wells, where the water descends into blackness. I edged forward under the rail and laid a palm on its blood-brown neck. I could feel the pulse of its life beneath my fingers. Such power and stillness, and the hot moist breath clouding my face. Somewhere far off folk were bidding each other good night and merry Christmas; the fiddles had fallen silent. All that was left of the lantern was a soft yellow glow. I leaned my forehead against the shaggy brow and let myself sink into the darkness and the understanding of the ox. There was a holy magic around us. He spoke to me of strength and the pull of clay and the fiery flower that bloomed and died each day, and of labour and rain, and my own heart spoke and he understood that too.

I don't know how long I stayed like that – seconds, perhaps; perhaps minutes – but then there was a hand on each of my shoulders pulling me back. Jacob had woken, sober enough now. Quietly he ushered us out to the cold starlit night with all its hard clarity.

'What in God's name were you doing, Martha? Are you mad? Did you fancy a goring? I should not have taken you, any of you. Entering the stall of an ox like that!'

'It spoke.' I said, smiling round at them. 'It spoke.'

Jacob raised his brows and gave a low whistle. Then he shook his head. 'To no one but you, Martha, no one but you. It was a foolish venture. Come, I'm stopping here tonight, I'll wish you all a merry Christmas. You should get on home.'

We set off. Aggie giggled. 'Not but what I do believe it does happen,' she said, 'but, Martha, do you think it might be the wassail cup and the ale?'

'I wish it'd spoken to me,' Owen said.

Oh, Owen... I could scarce look at him without shame. How could I leave him, how could I? I hugged him close. 'You don't need beasts,' I said. 'All God's angels will speak to you.'

11

THE SIMONS' BABY

Two days after Christmas, well before dawn, Aggie was banging at our door, hollow-eyed and drawn. Their mother had given birth the evening before to a baby girl. Neither mother nor baby were well. Richard Simons was praying and Father Paul had been called. There was a mixture I had given Mary Tucker when she was sick after her Thomas was born. It was not so special, but after she got better so quickly people talked about my preparations as though I had an uncommon gift with herbs. Could I make it now, Aggie asked, could I help?

It took me all morning to assemble it, for I ran

out of yarrow and had to walk over to Putley to beg some off an old woman I knew there. When I reached the Simons' house Father Paul was there again. Agnes was praying beside him. The winter light fell across her as she kneeled and she looked like a lady cut in alabaster kneeling at a tomb, except that her nose was red with weeping. I thought of the chiselled saints in the chapel, with their smashed-up faces. It made me shudder. Owen glanced up at me and smiled, but Father Paul carefully did not. I was grateful for that. One of the gossips put water on to boil and let me up. Owen's mother looked like all the blood had been drained from her body.

She had been doing well, one said, for one with so little strength in her, till the fever came and she began raving. Now she was bleeding again. The baby, they said, when I asked, seemed to be out of danger, although she could not be cured of being a girl, and old Simons would not get over that.

I took Ann Simons' hand. I did not think she could see me, but after a few minutes she smiled.

'You've been a good friend to Owen, Martha. Look after him.'

'You'll pull through, neighbour,' I said. 'You'll be baking by Candlemas and dancing in May.'

I gave the women instructions for the herbs to be added to the caudle and I gave them the preparation I'd brought for the baby, too. It looked a weak little thing to me, and so it proved, for Ann Simons grew stronger day by day, but the child did not. Only a few days later Father Paul was summoned again to the house, this time to christen the child before she died. Ann named the baby Martha, for me. She was convinced that it was I who had saved her, that my herbs had brought her back to life, even though I could not save little Martha.

The bundle looked pitiful, as it was lowered into the earth. There were few mourners. Father Paul scowled as he looked around and saw how few. The villagers would be preparing for Plough Monday. Another idolatrous superstition, he declared, that had no place in a good Christian life. I held Owen's hand.

'*All is vanity,*' Father Paul intoned. '*All go unto*

one place, all are of the dust and all turn to dust again.' The rain fell down as he spoke until he seemed only a pillar of black. Or perhaps I was weeping.

'She barely cried,' Ann whispered to me. 'She took one look at this sinful world and turned again to God. It was a mercy.' She was very pious, Ann. For my part, I could not see how the poor child's miserable life could be held a blessing. But I said nothing.

Widow Spicer, never one to miss a funeral, was more forthcoming. She leaned forward. 'Yes, Ann,' she said. 'She will be better off with Him. I often praise God for giving me just one child, so that I could feed and clothe him decently and bring him up to be a strapping lad. Perhaps, having been spared, it will teach your husband to leave you alone at last.'

I pressed Owen's hand harder and looked down. 'I do not doubt that she means well,' Ann said to me later, 'but her words have a bite to them.'

'Forget her,' I said. 'She has no teeth at all.'

I was wrong, of course. She had teeth. She was

a dragon, or she knew how to wake one up. In the end who was the greater witch? I watched her leave the funeral with Jacob and wondered at her being his mother. It struck me I had very little understanding of him. It was no doubt because of Aggie that he took pains to be my friend. We were not alike, at all. We were forever at odds. The warrens and the horses compassed his world about and he was happy for them to. Why did he unsettle me so? But we would soon be gone; in Hereford it would be easy to pry my thoughts free.

12

PLOUGH MONDAY AND THE FOXHEAD FOOL

There were six crowded onto the plough. They whooped and hollered as people threw their coins, and their teeth looked white and strange against the blacking. Before them, the Bessy and the Fool mopped and mowed around the bells and the flute and the fiddle. The rain let off and a weak sun smiled a little. I found that I was smiling too, at the young men jostling and pushing at the plough and the Bessy holding up her bosom.

I remembered how I liked it. The men with their blacked-up faces, the Bessy, the Fool, nobody themselves and the world topsy-turvy. When I was a little girl, I followed the plough. There was always a rabble of children behind it, hoping to catch a ha'penny at Wall House or Cockyard Farm. None of that for me any more: now I made sure that *I* had put aside a coin to pay them. The Widow was already at her door, looking pleased with herself, as always. I saw her sister, Goody Reynolds, was with her. Hags, both. One of the young men would be their Jacob, though at this distance I couldn't tell which. Well, so be it, I could not forever avoid him.

The Fool had a fox's head, rich and red. You could not see his face at all. It was usually old Will Leigh, loon that he was, but he'd been taken ill. Father said that they'd even come to *him* to ask him to play it, but I think that must have been in jest, for there was nothing more unlikely. 'As if I'd don old skins,' he scoffed, 'and prance through the village to humour their swinish practices.'

The Fool laid down the sticks to dance before our house and they set to, even though the mud was thick and slick and they looked to lurch onto their backsides every moment. The Bessy was too bothered with her bosom to kick out as she should, but the Fool jumped high, and every time he approached me he clacked his sticks close. I could smell the skins he wore as they flapped and the thick cloud of his breath in the cold air hung before my face. He grew faster and the fiddle raced to keep up with him; the crowd clapped. The long line of his fox teeth grinned and his fox eyes glinted. And each time he turned to me, I curled my fingers on the coin till it hurt, for my heart raced and it felt I was falling into his quick, hot rhythm. The fiddle caught my breathing, fast and sharp, fast and sharp and there was a wild joy in it; the sticks flew around my head, nearer and nearer; I was alone in the white day, wrapped round by his dance. I squeezed the hard coin in my hand, and I felt giddy, giddy...

But then the door broke open behind me and there was my father, haggard with morning and shouting through the music till he shattered the spell.

'Go on, begone, the lot of you. I'll not be paying you. Pass on,' he shouted, yanking me to him, for the Fool had stopped so close to me I felt the air lifting the bright red hairs of his pelt. He shook his bells in my father's face and stepped lightly back. It seemed to me his yellow fox jaws were laughing. I glanced at my father and felt ashamed. Often enough folks had seen him a singing drunk; now he was a parson.

The boys with the plough surged forward. 'Stand aside, Walter, skinflint, hardpenny, if you mock the plough you'll be hungry in the harvest. Stand aside, you'd better grow corn in your doorway.'

My father tried to stop them, grabbed the plough itself and half wrestled it over, but they were six to his one, and the crowd laughing and jeering them on. It did not take long for them to push him into the mud. The Bessy came and plonked herself on his chest, waggling a finger at him as he lay there swearing and spluttering whilst they carved up the earth before our door. I leaned back and watched it all go, all the planting I'd put in over years. Rosemary and marjoram and thyme and bay. My little path, too, buckled and gone, all gone. How could he put his stupid pride before my garden? For a moment I saw my father as I suppose the others saw him: flailing like a beetle on its back, all its fine shell useless and misplaced. Then I looked back to the youths on the plough, laughing to each other as they dragged the blade and the clods flew. The Fool stood askance and watched me.

I found my voice then. 'Shame on you. You do not have to ruin it all.'

They paused as if they had just noticed me.

'Hark at you,' one said. It was Davey Yapp. I knew him even through his blacking. 'Not so proud now? Tramping the fields in the crook of the moon. And right after that the devil came and dug us a hole. Ain't no coincidence, if you asks me. And what did you do to old Will Leigh? He's scarce been out of his bed since you frighted him.'

'That's no fault of mine,' I said, clutching at the plough to stop it. 'I've no quarrel with Will, and you know it. There's plenty have got comfort from those herbs you're busy wrecking.'

I was going to go on. I had plenty of insults ready, but they closed around me in a circle, me and the plough together. The handles dug in my back, and my insults died in my throat. I could not see over their shoulders. I knew Davey and one or two of the others, but three of them I did not know. They were sneering at me, and each time I tried to step through they moved together and did not let me pass.

'Let me go,' I said. 'Why don't you let me go?' I could hear a silly panic rising in my voice. They heard it too, and smiled.

'You're a bit too high and mighty, aren't you?' Davey said, and pushed me, just a little, so I stumbled over the iron against his neighbour, who grabbed me by my arms and spun me round, then passed me on and another took me and hooted at the game. Yellow teeth and flecks of spittle on my face and I couldn't wipe it off for they were shoving me, flinging me from one to the other around the plough, reaching out their big hands to grab at me and throw me on.

Perhaps it was only a minute – I don't know – I heard my father in the crowd. Then the circle was breaking, the Fool was pushing through and as I turned to him the arm of the plough caught my skirts so that I fell headlong into the welling soil. There was a gasp. Next to me, a thumb's width away from my head, sat the sharpened blades, sticky with mud and clay.

I closed my eyes to the day and shrugged off the hands that tried to pull me up. The same hands, no doubt, that had gripped my shoulders, my arms, my waist as they shoved me from one to the other, like a dog before the fight. I willed myself to think only of the wet earth and the rain. The rain was soft and cold; it fell so kindly.

By the time I had clambered to my knees, the flute and the fiddle had started up again. The plough and ploughmen were gone. Only the Fool lingered. He bent his fox head to glance down at me as he turned to go and in the angle of his head I knew him. I opened my palm and let the coin fall to the ground.

13

A RECOGNITION

It was all over. The procession cheerfully progressed down the lane, leaving my father and me stuck with clay before our door, and the Widow and her sister enjoying the sight.

'Go on now, there's nothing to see,' my father barked at them as he pulled me up. I took his outstretched hand. It was only a short time ago that he had talked so joyfully of rolling up our possessions and stepping out onto the road. All up until Christmas, and even after, his eyes were alight with planning. Why, he'd spoken to a man about taking lodgings and to another about work. In the spring, he'd said. But in the days since the year began the earth had eased itself into weeping once again; and the alehouse had seen far more of him than I. As he helped me to my feet I felt a terrible sense that he had shrunk. For a moment I had seen him as a stranger, pitted by years of drinking and rage. It was worse than being flung in the dirt myself. I felt that if we were alone, I was not sure that we were alone together any longer. I could not bear to look at him, though I knew he wanted me to.

'Well, what a mess they've made,' the Widow said, making no sign of moving on.

'This is how the Good Lord humbles pride,' Goody Reynolds added. 'I might be new here, Walter Dynely, but I know how to respect folks. You've no business flouting the plough like that. There's no good will come of it, you mark my words.'

I pressed his hand to urge him not to answer.

'Now come, sister, show a little kindness,' the Widow put in, then bent her head to me. 'Don't you fret about the rumours, dear.'

I looked at her. 'About Will Leigh? That's a cold story. You know as well as I do that his wife says he got soaked digging out the ditches in the Sling and came down with a chill from it.'

'Not Will Leigh, dear, though Heaven alone knows what possessed you to wander the red field under the moon last November, sooted like a demon, scaring up the old man.' She turned to my father. 'Forgive me, neighbour, but we have lived so close I feel like an – auntie – to your poor motherless girl, and it's my duty to look out for her. As soon as I heard the tittle-tattle I said, "For shame, the Dynelys have their strange ways, but that girl would not cause harm to an old man who has a lairy way about him but has never hurt a soul in all his life..."'

'Of course I would not, even if I could.'

'And so I said, "If she would not harm an old man, why then would she want to harm a baby?"'

My father started forward. 'What do you mean?'

She stepped back a little under his gaze and enjoyed a pause. We must have looked a sight, the pair of us, shivering and mud-caked, though at the time I barely thought of that. I was shaken by the morning's events, but on the watch as always to curb my father's raging. It would not do to make a public enemy of the Widow today.

'What do you mean?' he said again. I glanced at him, surprised, for his voice was low with worry.

She flustered a little as though she'd gone too far. 'I am just telling you what I've heard, as it's my duty to do, because I am your neighbour and a friend. There are those who've been saying Martha traded the mother for the baby. That the baby was well enough until she came.'

'Who is saying this? Who?'

The Widow gave a little nervous laugh and glanced at the grimy hand he'd outstretched. Her sister pulled at her sleeve.

'We'd best be getting along, Judith. We're expected, you know.'

'Goody Reynolds,' my father said, 'I was not addressing you, who has barely unpacked her bags and has no business telling me my business in this place or any other. Give your sister leave to speak and hold your tongue.'

'Oh, you don't mark me, Walter Dynely,' Goody Reynolds went on, 'but I marked you. Soon as I came here, I marked you. Blood don't wash away, do it?'

It was the Widow's turn to pull. 'Oh, it's something and nothing, no doubt,' she said to my father, pushing her sister aside. 'Just an idle word dropped by a gossip. Pay it no heed, sir. I wish I had not mentioned it, I'm sure. You'd best warm yourselves or you'll catch cold.'

But my father was staring at Goody Reynolds. All the colour had drained from his face and a look of horror or hatred or fury, or all three, was gathering. His fists were clenched. He looked on the old crone as if he would wring her neck. I stepped between them, afraid that the drink and the shame of the morning had fogged his wits or sent him a devil. It seemed a while before he shook himself and ducked into the house. Goody Reynolds, who'd been stepping back anxiously, paused and gave me a satisfied little smile.

'Look to the Lord Jesus, girl. Only He can restore you.'

'What does that mean, Goodwife Reynolds? What do you mean, restore me?'

She stopped and fixed me with her squinty

eyes. 'Pray, girl. Get down on your knees in the mud and pray to the Lord Jesus, lest the bad seed bears foul fruit.'

I stood in the ripped earth and watched them go, while the clouds grew heavy and rain began to fall in earnest.

14

RAIN, MORE RUMOURS

All January we walked through the rain to the chapel and walked through the rain back to our houses, and in between we sat on our benches in the nave, whilst Father Paul talked to us of the flood. He leaned forward and tapped the Bible as he spoke and thrust a long arm out to point at every one of us.

'*I, even I, do bring a flood of waters upon the earth, to destroy all flesh, wherein is the breath of life under heaven, and everything that is in the earth shall perish.*'

We barely dared look at one another, but glanced at the floor nervously, afraid of his shining eyes. As he spoke rain pelted the high windows. We had been undone by pride, he said, and by desire. There were those among us who had forgotten the commandments and who indulged the sins of the flesh. People glanced around eagerly in hopes of a scandal. We were corrupt, Father Paul went on, we were worms' meat, the meanest things alive would crawl over our graves. Nay, they would crawl in us and through us, they would be our brethren, closer than a husband to his wife. There had been no king on earth, no mighty warrior, but the worm was his Fortune.

'I look about me,' he said casting his gaze this way and that, 'and I see those among us who are not content with the lot the Good Lord has granted them, who seek wickedly to take His powers, even the power of life and death unto themselves.'

He paused and held us all in his silence. I prayed for my face not to redden; he was speaking to me, directly to me. Surely all eyes were upon me. I did not know – perhaps they were not – I hadn't the courage to look. When I did, Father

Paul had raised his eyes to heaven and lifted his arms; all that could be heard was the patter of the rain and the gurgle of an infant. Then he crashed his two fists down and his voice came worse than thunder.

'BEWARE THE VENGEANCE OF THE LORD. Yes, I say it again. Beware the vengeance of the Lord and remember His power. Listen to the rain. It gathers in the fields and washes away the roads. It seeps through your thatch and your clothing; it wets your skin. It is your wickedness made manifest. The earth itself is sodden with your sin, it is revolted, you are soaked through with the filth of it. And only the flame of faith can save you. Remember His words: *And I will rain upon the earth forty days and forty nights: and all substance that I have made will I destroy from the upper face of the earth.*'

I looked up at him. His whole body thrilled with the words and his face was in rapture. That is how I had felt, I thought, when I'd thrilled with the wild dance of the Fool. But that was not faith, it did not feel Christian at all; it was curling in my stomach, as though my belly was grinning. And there, in that holy place, with the threat of damnation in my ears, I suddenly knew I had wanted to rip his fox's head back and kiss his lips. I blushed at the thought of it. It was fitting that I was cast down into the mud. I looked at my hands and felt yet more confusion. Were they wicked? When I rubbed and dried the herbs my hands felt powerful. It was like reading. I could read letters and see the meaning in them, and I could read the plants, too, and see the meaning they held and how I could use them. I had thought it innocent. But now I was afraid of what was in me, what was working through me.

Everywhere I went now I felt I heard a murmuring, constant as the rain. It would be starting as soon as we left the service. I was impatient for Owen's mother to be churched for I felt sure that if she stood by me at the chapel door it would put an end to the slander. I glanced at my father, who sat with lowered lids, but whether half asleep or ironical, I was not sure. He had little patience with ministers, though he knew the Bible better than most of them, and knew the devil too, and feared him. I dared not tell him how I had become afraid of my own soul. Perhaps I should have done. Perhaps it would have roused him from that long slow stupor of despair and ale, and saved us both.

That night I stayed a long time praying, till my knees ached and all the village was quiet around me. The rain ceased at nightfall, and I leaned out to look at the stars, which were glistening as though fresh washed. The line of the hill was solid and black, and the moon was as crooked as it had been the night I'd been stuck at the Hall. I could not free my mind of the words from Genesis: *'and all substance that I have made will I destroy from the upper face of the earth.'* But looking at the stars comforted me. They were such a long way off. They looked down on all of the countries of the world. Even now an Indian girl would be looking up like me and seeing the same stars. One day I might walk over the hills all the way to India, where the air was scented with spices. I would be a servant to a princess and help her thread her hair with gold.

How did the stars hang there without falling? When I was very small, my father used to crouch down beside me and tell me their names. I remember the rough feel of his face, level with mine as he pointed.

'That long bright arrow,' he said, 'that's named for a princess who was chained to a rock, food for a sea monster.'

'Did the monster eat her up?' I asked.

'No,' he answered, 'a prince called Perseus saved her.'

Then he pointed to a single star, the brightest of all, that marked the princess's head. 'Look. That's where your mother is, in that white light. She's waiting for us, ever so patiently, and she's watching over us, too. Look for her just before winter. She loved the weeks when the fields were still warm with summer and the orchards full of apples; that's when she's brightest in the sky. Wave at her, Martha. See how she blinks and twinkles? She's waving back.'

This was a strange way to talk about heaven, but it felt very safe, standing between his arms and looking at my mother's star, though I knew it made him sad. I told myself it was because he wished he had been like Perseus and freed my mother when they chained her, but instead she had been eaten by the monster.

It was years since I'd searched out my mother's constellation, and now when I looked I could not see it. Had it gone from the sky? Had I forgotten how to find her? It worried me that I could not find her. It seemed to me an ill omen, so much so that I thought of waking my father to help me, but I did not want to seem foolish and he had a long walk in the morning to fix a wheel at Caplor farm. I pulled the shutters close and lay down, humming softly to push aside my unquietness.

15

CANDLEMAS

At Candlemas, Judas is let out of hell. He goes to soothe his burns in the sea and even the whales flee his howls when the saltwater finds out his wounds. But still the cold water comforts him. How must it feel, I wondered, to be Judas, hated by God and the whole world, with only cold salt-water for a nurse and hell your only fortune? For days I walked the fields and lanes, saying goodbye in my head to all the places of my childhood, but I could not rid my fancy of the thought of hell. Sometimes when I closed my eyes I half saw – or thought I saw – a goblin laughing; for the first time in my life I felt sick with dread that I was not saved.

The weather was fine at last. There were bright cold days with the sun slanting towards spring. I knew it was a false hope. Good weather at Candlemas is a sure sign of more cold to come, and yet I was glad of the break in the clouds and the glancing light on the snowdrops in the woods. My fingers were cracked and sore, though I rubbed them with butter each morning. When Miss Elizabeth visited the schoolroom she wore gloves of red leather, and while she talked about knowing the word of God I could not help staring at them and nor, I noticed, could the boys. I wished that she would take them off and carelessly drop one so I could pick it up and hand it to her, saying, 'Here is your glove, Miss Elizabeth,' crumpling the leather in my hands so that the smell of it lingered.

There were no stragglers at the Candlemas service. Even the sick dragged themselves out for Mass. The late growlings from the hillside had reawakened our fears and all were eager with hope that the procession would purify the village.

I think we were the only parish hereabouts to cling to it: Rushall did not, nor Marcle. I dare say Father Paul would have put it down, but for the particular wish of Sir William. As I kneeled to say the five prayers I felt very light, almost dizzy, as though I could feel the power in the spoken words. I clutched my candle, with its flickering light. If the devil has touched me, I thought, this candle will banish him back to hell. We walked around the chapel, each with their own light, and the dozens of little flames against the bare branches and the desolate sky were beautiful. I held up my hand to protect my flame and my heart felt full of love towards the world. The procession paused and I was bumped into a man who had come up beside me. I turned to smile at him with apology, but then I started with surprise, because the eyes I met were Jacob's. He opened his mouth to speak, but just at that moment his mother gasped and pointed. Hot wax had dripped across my fingers onto the damp grass. She did not dare cry out, for it would have disturbed the singing, but she grabbed the elbow of the woman next to her and whispered in her ear. They both turned round and looked at me and at the ground. There in the clear print of her foot on the grass lay drops of candlewax, quite as though I sought to lame her.

'It is nothing,' I said. 'It was an accident. This is the light of Our Lord – how could it harm you?' Both women looked at me and turned away. 'It is nothing,' I said again, this time to Jacob, but he had leaned forward to talk to his mother, patting her shoulder in comfort.

'Please,' I said, grabbing at his sleeve, 'believe me. I wished her no harm.' He turned then briefly, and raised his brows, but just as he did so his mother gave a little cry and clutched at her leg and he jumped back to take her arm. Already I could feel the rumour rippling through the crowd, with only my grim-faced father oblivious to it. Martha dropped wax into the Widow's footprints, the rumour said, and see how Judith Spicer squeals already. She'll soon be limping.

I set my face against caring and continued in the shuffling, slow progress round the chapel.

It was in vain for Father Paul to tell us not to take the candles home. 'Do not worship wax,' he proclaimed, 'only your prayer will deliver you. The evil that is stirring will be vanquished by righteousness and faith in the Lord. I will write down the names of those who burn the candle against the coming storm.'

Even as he said it he knew well enough that every house in the village would light the blest flames tonight and every night that we heard the dragon stirring in the hill.

Everywhere I looked there were sidelong glances and pursed lips. It frightened me. I wondered if I should approach Miss Elizabeth as she lingered in the graveyard, dispensing kindness in her lovely leather gloves. At the last I walked up to her, but by then she was turning to get into the waiting carriage and my nerve failed. I glanced at my father. He would laugh at me for minding such idle superstitious chatter. I recognised the grim set of his jaw, which meant he had decided once again on the alehouse. Sure enough, when we had returned home he bade me leave him food enough and not wait up.

'Don't go,' I dared to say. 'Please, Father, stay

here with me. What of our plans, what of Hereford?'

He gave me a shallow smile. 'Today I need to go. No amount of little flames will banish the demon in me, Martha, not today. Ale alone can do it. This month is sick with death.'

'You hate the men you drink with.'

'Quiet, girl. Not quite. It's true they are ignorant brutes, but we are all brutish at some time or other, even the daintiest lady in the land. That's the call of the tavern. I drain my pot of double beer in the hope it will find my knot of pain and loosen it. And with each pot it is so nearly found, but just not quite, and it is only by unravelling myself utterly, till I don't know day from night or friend from foe, that I will be free. Don't look so scared, girl. The demon must be fed, is all. But not for long. See if I don't slay him outright. I think I will leave him behind when *we* leave. We will be rid of this whole place soon enough.'

He turned to go. 'Soon, Martha,' he said, as he ducked out of the door.

I sat amazed at this talk of his drinking. It frightened me a little, but there was nothing I could do. I swallowed down hard and turned my thoughts to the events of the day. I must appease the Widow for the accident with the candle wax. I poured out a quart of milk, which we could ill afford to spare, and walked the few steps to her cottage. For several minutes I was left standing on the step, till I was afraid I would not be let in and the whole village would witness the refusal, but after I had called again that I brought something, her greed got the better of her play of hurt and she opened the door. She did not ask me in, but stood there, proud as marble, waiting for me to humble myself, Goody Reynolds fidgeting behind her like a shadow. Jacob was in the corner of the room, his back to us, busying himself with some ropes or suchlike. He said nothing to me, nor I to him. My resolve wavered. I can flounce as well as you, I thought, you eel-faced crone, and I was near to turning on my heel and leaving, but I called to mind the muttering round the chapel. Even though we were surely leaving in a month or two it would not do to let this spread, especially after the other talk of Ann Simons and her baby.

'I am heartily sorry, neighbour, that I grieved

you today,' I said. 'I swear to God that I did not in-
tend the wax to fall in your footprint and I laid no
words on it. May the Good Lord strike me down if
I lie. I have brought you the cream of our milk as a
pledge of my good faith.'

'Well, Martha, I am sure I never did anything
in my life to cause you to hate me. I have ever
been good to you, you being a poor motherless
child with precious little kin. Perhaps there was
no ill will. I will accept your apology, but I warn
you, girl, you had better stop these games of
yours. There are those who are not as forgiving or
as generous hearted as I. There's been plenty of
talk against you.'

I hung my head a little. 'Then I am grateful to
you for speaking up against such talk. I know you
will have been a good friend to me against such
idle rumour.' I would have gone on, but I noticed
Jacob in the corner, his head thrown back a little
and half a smile on his face. It would not do to go
too far, I told myself; she would not take kindly to
being laughed at.

The Widow preened herself a little. 'And so I
have, Martha. She can be wayward, I've said, but

there's no harm in the girl, whatever her family. Think, I've said, of the damage false report can do, and her with no one to defend her.'

'My father will defend me.'

'Well, yes, child. And where is he tonight?'

I bridled, but I let it go, congratulating myself on my restraint. She was watching me closely though, for she went on, 'And don't think Miss Elizabeth will step in for you. They've their own troubles at the Hall, and no one will defend a witch.'

'There, you've said it,' I said. 'I am no witch.'

The two women stared at me. 'It's time she knew,' Goody Reynolds put in.

'Knew what?' I said.

She went on as though I could not hear. 'It's time she knew about her mother.' She turned to me. 'How did she die, Martha?'

'She had a fever,' I said, 'when I was two years old. It was in Gloucester, before we came here, just at this time of the year.'

Goody Reynolds put out a finger and jabbed me in the chest.

'No fever,' she said. 'Ask your father when he

comes home, if he's up to talking. Ask him to-morrow if he's not.'

And they threw one another a knowing glance. It was almost a smile. I felt tears prick at my eyes. I did not know what to say, but I felt I could not leave them holding the milk and their victory. I had a good mind to fling them out a curse, but fortunately Jacob came forward and asked his mother impatiently if he should have to wait all night for his meal.

'Good evening to you,' I said, turning for home and pulling the door shut behind me.

'You'd better heat that milk through,' I heard the Widow say as I lingered a moment on the step. 'Get it good and hot. That will take any of the girl's malice out of it.'

If you listen hard enough you can hear the frost. There is a tautening of the air as it takes hold. I stood in the dark and listened. The ruts and the puddles had grown a skin of ice and the thatch glistened in the moonlight. An owl swooped by, but it did not hoot. The shutters were closed, but behind them the blest candles would be lit against the dragon in the hill. It was silent tonight. Perhaps the prayers had worked and the dragon had been banished, like Judas, back to hell.

16

THE CREEPING FROST

I let the fire go out as the woodpile was low, but I could not sleep. It was often enough my father had gone to the tavern and not come home till dawn, but that was before we had resolved to leave. I could understand him drinking before, when his life was comprised only of tramping the lanes between the farms and the soaking dreams of the ale cup. Now it was different. Perhaps that was why I felt a foreboding as the minutes dragged into hours and he did not come.

I had resolved to ask him Goody Reynolds' question if he was not too bad, for he was looser tongued in drink than ever he was sober, though as likely to storm as to talk. I sat there thinking how to phrase it, anxious that he was not coming through the door, dreading the moment that he did, lest he told me when I asked. I had pictured so often the scene of my mother's death. In it, he sat by her bedside, clasping her hands in his. Sometimes in the picture I sat on his knee, or happily next to my mother in the bed. Her head lay back on the pillows with her beautiful hair framing her face. The air was scented with herbs – rosemary, thyme and lavender. She opened her eyes and he bent forward to hear the words of comfort and love that she whispered, and then she closed her eyes and died. But I knew, as I stared into the ashes where the fire had been, that none of this was true and had never been true, and that there was another story with another picture I had hidden, which was waiting to be found.

At last I could wait no longer. I gathered my cloak about me and went outside. The moon was high and the lane was deserted. The skin of ice had thickened and the mud bore my weight without shifting. If need be, I decided, I would walk to the alehouse at the Cockshoot, wake him from his stupor and drag him home. I did not meet a soul on the road, but when I reached the tavern, through the shutters I could see that a light still burned. I banged on the doors and set the dogs barking.

'Who's there?' said a woman's voice presently. 'What kind of hour do you call this? We're closed, can't you see? Be off, you'll get nothing here, be you a bishop or a prince. I'll set the dogs on you, so I will.'

'Meg,' I said, 'it's Martha, Walter Dynely's daughter. Is he there? I need him home.'

She opened the door a crack and two of the dogs wriggled out. They would have gone for me if she'd not grabbed them and given them a blow on their snouts.

'Whatever are you doing, girl, walking the lanes at this hour and at a time like this, with who knows what stirring? Your father is not here, and he's not welcome back, neither, till he pays what he owes.'

'Please,' I said, 'he's not come home. Who did he leave with?'

'Left on his own, three hours since. Me and my Peter kicked him out. Proper addled, he was, and loud with it, lurching and swearing. We told him it was time to go, and he would not budge, but kept hollering on, blaspheming till old Nick would have blushed to hear it. A couple of the lads tried to talk some sense into him but he wouldn't have it; even took a swing at poor Dick Loader. I'm not having none of that, I said. Not in my establishment. Out on his arse he went, and he's lucky we didn't get the constables.'

'He's not come home,' I said, frightened now.

'Well? I'm not his nursemaid. Maybe Jack Frost will talk some sense into him. You'd best get on home, girl. You've heard that hill – there's bad spirits about. If I were you I'd lock the door against him, though he is your father, for like as not he'll be in a beating mood.'

'He doesn't beat me.' I said, but it was to myself, for she had already shut the door. I could hear the big bolts being dragged across.

The cloud had thickened and rolled down till

it hung like wool from the trees and pushed its way between houses, thick and silent as dread itself. I could barely see the ground at my feet, and all the time the air was freezing. Morning would not bring light for hours. From the Cockshoot to our cottage was not so far – a mile and a half at most – but he could be anywhere. I called out, quietly at first and then louder, setting the dogs barking and the pigs shuffling. More than once I thought I saw a man's shape ahead on the lane and ran towards it, reaching out as though I could push the fog aside. But the figure drifted into nothing as I approached. All the phantoms of the world might have been with me in the fog and I should not have seen them, though I peered till my eyes hurt. I should not have cared, either; would have taken their hands and laughed, if they had led me to my living father.

There were many different ways. It struck me that with the ground so hard he might have walked the fields: Goosefoot Meadow, Hungry Croft. I tried the lanes first, calling and calling, trying not to think of the ditches: that he could be lying there, with the ale freezing his blood. When it was light surely I should be able to see, even if only a few feet, but by then he might be dead. I needed others' help. At the Fosbury the black wall of the Young's farmhouse defied the drifts of cloud. Farmer Young was no friend of my father's, not after last summer when he'd gone on a drunk leaving a cart half done, but other years he'd done good work for them; they'd four or five hands at least who could be roused to help me search. I steeled myself and knocked up the house. Edward Young came to the door with a cudgel, his wife at his shoulder. When I told them my father had been at the Cockshoot, they laughed in my face. Pleading made no difference, though I sank to my knees. I'd forgot how high they held themselves. Damn them, I thought, as I got back up and turned to the lane. I said it too out loud.

'Damn you both, you turd-teethed, stink-breathed wretches.'

'Fie on you, little Martha Dynely,' they called back. 'Your father can go to hell and join your mother. You won't feel so strong for curses when you're a walking mort and earning your bread on your back. Be off before we set the dogs on you.'

I moved further off, shouting all the same, 'May you waste like the dew against the sun, all of you. All of you.' I would have given a piece of myself, then, for the power to make it happen.

The air was so thick I near missed the gap into the Goosefoot, but as I climbed across Hungry Croft to Little Hill it grew thinner. Shreds of the fog drifted past me, white and aloof like the wraiths of horses. I stood still for some time with the mist about me, listening. The world felt very empty and quiet. If he should die, what would there be to keep me here? Or in all the world, come to that. But my body still would need to be fed and clothed; it would ache and be heavy. I envied the mist its weightless, silent drift, curling through wastes and villages, kissing the faces of the people if it wanted, or mingling with their breath. No one, not even the Queen herself, could lay a hold of it, or ask it to account.

I shook myself. How could I stand still and dream so? He was not here. I descended back into the murk of the village. Still the lane was quiet. I resolved to rouse the houses – surely here people would not turn from me. I would put my foot in the door if need be. The Simons, at least, would aid us. I stumbled. It was one of the stones we had down put to warn of the hole. And there he was, headlong in the trench, his breeches and his jerkin stiff with frost.

17

VERSES, TALES

I must have screamed, for men enough blundered out of sleep to find out what was wrong, and together we shifted him into the house. He was not dead, as I had thought at first, slung out with all the trash, with all that the parish wanted to be rid of into that rent, to be covered over and forgotten like a murderer at the crossways; but he was not far from death.

It seemed my reparation of the day before – how long ago that seemed – had indeed mended relations somewhat with my neighbours for the Widow and Goody Reynolds came by to help me warm him, both of them bloated with piety. They helped get the fire going and chafed his hands and feet. Perhaps I should have been more grateful, but I could not stand their sighs and tuts. It was rare, they said, that even the strongest recovered absolutely from a freezing like this. They wouldn't be surprised if he was an invalid from now on. Do you remember, Judith, Goodwife Reynolds said, old Whittle, who'd lived next to them when they were girls in Woolhope? He'd been caught in the snow one winter, when he'd gone out after the sheep. Never the same again. Ice in his chest from then on, not good for a thing on the land, just sat wheezing by the fire. Ice in his chest and ice in his heart, her sister commented. It was like he was twisted, snapping at anyone who tried to help him, and him such a jolly soul before.

At first I thought we should never get the warmth back into Father, and then he fell into a sleep from which we couldn't wake him, his breath shallow and grating. For two days he lay with his eyelids flickering and I stood over his cot and watched. Then death threw him back.

I thought he would recover, then, but it was

like they said: the ice had found its way into his lungs and he could not cough it out. He sat up, but the strength had gone from his chest and he leaned his hands on his knees for support. I looked at him and felt our future shrink to the narrow rooms of the cottage. Why had I fooled myself? We could no more start afresh than the fire could burn without smoking or the walls be free of the soot. He spat long strings of phlegm into the fire and banged his stick for me to come to bring him broth or a rag or small beer and I came, and I rubbed his back too, and tucked the blanket around his shoulders, but often I could barely speak for rage and sorrow.

Since he was out of danger I went back to my class and the boys were kinder to me than they had been, though I barely focused on the work and they made little progress.

At the end of the second morning there was a knock on the door and Jacob stepped in. I recalled the last time he had entered the schoolroom and felt myself redden. He smiled at my confusion and walked up to me.

'Don't worry,' he said, 'I've learned enough of a

lesson already in here. I know I don't fit,' and he nudged a bench with his foot and grinned at the boys.

'I am sorry for it,' I returned. 'I had a text set aside for you to learn from. It concerns Pride mostly.'

'Then it must be a passage that is very dear to you, Martha.'

'Not at all. I have no need of it, as your mother so often reminds me.'

'Still, you'd better keep it. I am sure it would be too difficult for me to follow.'

The boys were watching us, turning from one to the other as we spoke, unsure if we were in anger or jest. 'What have you come for, then?' I said a little more sharply than I meant to.

'Only this. Miss Elizabeth sends word to go to see her. She has work for you.' Then he turned on his heel and left, and I felt that I had blundered with him once again, although I was not quite sure how.

'Taken pity on you, Miss,' Ned Stolley said, 'on account of your father being so poorly.'

'Is it true,' Robbie put in, 'that he was regular

dead in the hole, and you had to rub the life back in him? Did you charm him back?'

I could see where this was heading. 'It was Widow Spicer and her sister that helped me revive him,' I said quickly. 'They were more skilled than I, but it's true enough that he's poorly.'

'People say,' Ben Ladding put in, 'that deep down in the hole you can hear the screams of hell. May be that he heard them, Martha. It was a bad night with all that fog. There was ghosts abroad, my nan said. They could've pushed him in the hole.'

I thought of the shapes that formed and dissolved before me when I was looking. I could believe there were wraiths in the whiteness, that the mist was thick with their longing and their loss. 'Have you seen a ghost, Ben?' I asked.

'No, I en't, but my nan's seen plenty. She was coming back from Ledbury way once and there was a whole family on the road, walking towards Marcle. She hailed them and they looks right at her and then she fell on her knees for she could see straight through every one of them.'

'All I know,' Robbie, put in, 'is there's summat

going on, and if it isn't a dragon in the hill, then what is it?'

* * *

Mistress Elizabeth herself came to the servants' door to greet me. She took me by the hand and led me to a table in the library. I had not been in there before. What a contrast it was with the cold dusty schoolroom! All of the walls were of dark wood, and the fireplace was of the same dark wood, but carved and gleaming with the warm echoes of the fire in the grate. The air was rich with beeswax and leather.

Miss Elizabeth swept her hand across the room as though to display it. 'My father, alas, is no reader, but I have a modest collection of books, which I add to as much as I am able. I know you have a tolerable fair hand, Martha.'

'I believe I do, ma'am, considering.'

'Yes, considering. Of course, you are no scribe and have not been to school, dear, but I would like you to copy out some verses for me. If you do it well, I shall give you more to do. I have laid out what I want you to copy. There is ample paper. I shall come back and check on you later. And, Martha...'

'Yes, ma'am?'

'Do not wander about the place. If you need anything, ring this bell.'

For the second time that day I blushed to the roots of my hair, though there was no one to see, for she had left already.

It was slow going, for I feared to make a mistake and was distracted by the verses, which were full of love and sighing. As careful as I tried to be, I blotted the paper more than once.

I had not been there above half an hour when the door flew open and Sir William strode in.

'Who the devil are you?' he said, when he saw me sitting at his table.

'I beg your pardon, sir,' I said, bobbing low. 'Miss Elizabeth asked me to copy some work for her.'

He made a show of peering at me more closely. 'Ah, yes, you're Dynely's girl, the one who can read and write. Sorry to hear about your father – bad business altogether – but he's a good man, Dynely, all said and done. He's been through worse than this. He'll pull through. Don't mind me, just looking for something. You get on with Lizzie's dreadful verses.'

An hour passed, and another and no one came. My hand ached; I was not used to writing like this. I stared at the bell on the table, but it felt too much like acting the lady to shake it and I feared how the sound would ring out all through the house. At last a servant appeared and told me brusquely that Miss Elizabeth had bade him give me something to eat. He led me to the big table near the kitchen, where the servants ate, and banged a plate of bread and cheese before me. Before long, half a dozen of the hands loped in, Jacob among them. They started a little to see me, but nodded quickly, sat down at the other end and forgot me entirely in the serious business of filling their plates.

After a little they fell to talking and I kept quiet for I felt sure they would make me the butt of their jokes if I was noticed.

'Did you see the messenger come this morning, from Bishop John?' one said, poking his finger at Jacob.

'Aye, I took his horse, remember.'

'Well, the bishop has heard of all the goings-on around here.'

'What goings-on?'

'The signs, of course: the hole and the hill groaning like an old woman at her stool.'

'Don't you mock,' the oldest one put in. It was Herbert Dinmore, who'd been in charge of the horses and the hounds longer than most could remember. He had a slow way about him, like so many who spend more time with beasts than people. 'It may not be a dragon, though my own grandfather believed in dragons till the day he died – had tales of one too, big as a house and breathing fire, out in the Marches. And which of you does not believe the story of St George? It's easy to mock, but there's something stirring, and there'll be more before it's over.'

'You're right there,' another said, thrusting with his bread to support his words. 'Like Father Paul says, there's something evil unsettling the land and we have to drive it out. These are the signs before the flood.'

Herbert leaned back in his chair. 'I've a cousin who's a woodsman over in Haugh Woods. You've maybe heard the story: he was telling every soul that would listen when he came over to see my mother at Candlemas. No? Well, I'll tell it you then before we go back out. There's a man he works with, Wilf, he's called, crusty old bugger too, but not one to see things. Well, Wilf was out with his son, after catching a hare. Bishop John wouldn't miss it. It was a stark day with the trees all haggard and lifting up their branches as though they were begging mercy of the sky. For hours they trudged and had no luck. Then the son, who was out in front and more nimble, started a hare out in the open, where the land drops down to the Lugg. Off go the dogs and they after, into the woods, the hare ahead but slow. Before a mile one of the dogs has her in the leg and the boy calls them off and picks her up to show his father, for she's a beauty, the biggest he's ever seen. The old man approaches and before his eyes the animal in his son's hands changes into a woman, a young woman, who spits in the boy's eye and curses him for the wound she's taken. No one had seen her before, and no one has seen her since, and the blood that she left on his clothes turned black. For days now the boy's been in his bed, racked with pains in his leg.' Herbert paused and stood up. 'You can say what you like, but I call it devilry.'

No one gainsaid him. They shoved the plates from them and got up to go back out. I had been away from my work too long, but I didn't want to move until they'd gone. They shuffled out, Jacob the last to leave. As he went through the door he turned and looked at me, long and silent, just as he had done all those weeks ago when he had seen me sooted and cut in the stableyard. It was as though Christmas Eve, the wild dance of the Fool, had never been.

I stared back. 'Think what you like,' I said.

18

MISS ELIZABETH'S PROMISE

Miss Elizabeth frowned a little as she ran her delicate hand (for once she had removed her gloves) along the lines I'd copied. I feared I had disappointed her.

'They are very fine verses, ma'am, are they by a poet of the court?'

'No, you silly girl,' she said, but she looked pleased. 'They are just some idle nothings I have written over the years.'

I did my best to look surprised. 'I thought they must be by one who had travelled the world, ma'am, there is so much of it in them.'

Miss Elizabeth sat down. 'I have seen very little, but I was at court once, or rather I brushed against the skirts of the court. A cousin of my mother's was a lady-in-waiting there for a time and we visited her at Windsor. It's a grand palace, grander than you can imagine. It was a fine day and my mother and I were walking in the gardens when a great hustle and bustle filled the air. I declare the leaves on the trees trembled with it. My mother snatched at a servant as he passed to enquire what was the matter and he told her that the King was close behind, that he would be here in a few minutes. My mother was a shy person, not at all like Sir William, and she had no desire to be presented. Above all she feared being in the way, but there was nothing for it, people were arriving. We stood by the roses, turned to stone, as the great ones swept by us. And there was the young King, with the Duke beside him. As he turned he saw us and gestured to us to rise from our curtsying. He had such merry eyes; he looked right at me. I wept such tears when he died.'

'Miss Elizabeth,' I ventured, 'forgive me for asking, but did you dream of staying there, with the jewels and velvet?'

'We are not so very fine. There was never any chance of my stepping in among them. I was very young and foolish then, and my head was full of dancing and the players. I still write my verses, though I confess that I fear Father Paul might not like them. But I believe the Good Lord does not abhor pleasure. And, child, think how much more simple and good we are here in the country, where people are open in their hearts and love their neighbours, without the malice and the plots of the court.'

'You are very kind to us, but I think we are not so good as you say, ma'am,' I said, and when she patted my hand with a complacent smile I burst out, 'There are people who say wicked things about me, ma'am, I am afraid.'

'I myself have heard that you venture off at night alone. You must not, Martha, promise me that. Think how it looks. And there are godless men in the woods at night, child, rogues who'd carry a village girl off and make her their doxy. Imagine! Passed from man to man like a pipe. Here, swear for me now, on this Bible, that you will not do such a thing again.'

I swore for her, but I crossed my fingers behind my back. I told her that I had slipped out once in a moon to watch the badgers play. It was a lie, of course. Mostly I went to steal her father's rabbits and his timber. Once I'd said the words she took my face in her hands.

'Don't think I haven't heard other idle talk. It will come to nothing. You are clever, Martha. People don't like that in a girl: it makes you different. Your father is a good man, but he is not always careful in his speech, or in his actions. He is not unlike my own, you know, in that. You must take care not to give offence where none is needed. And remember, I am your friend. I won't stand by and let you be hurt. You can rely on me, and on my father, too. Come tomorrow after the lesson and I will have more work for you.'

Let them all come on, I thought, as I walked back through the gathering dusk, the greatest lady in the parish has given me her armour.

19

OWEN'S NEWS

I told myself that my father was getting better though I knew in truth that he wasn't. He shuffled around the cottage, almost mute. Very often he had to lean and grip on a chair to haul the air into his chest and each breath scritched like a warped fiddle. I hated to hear it, and although I wouldn't say it even to myself, I hated being at home. After chapel on Sunday I took Owen by the hand and we wandered up into the woods to gather snowdrops and cherry bark.

I asked after his mother and Aggie.

'Oh, she's very much better. Father says he has never seen her so well, only she and Aggie fight because Aggie thinks only of sweethearts and curling her hair.'

'She is very pretty, your sister.'

'Yes, everybody says she is pretty all the time and she believes it, but Mother says golden hair plants no peas.'

'Chase you to the top, Owen.'

He ran, and I after him, up the track and into the trees till we got to the top of the ridge where the wood gives out for the lane to pass. The wind whipped up our hair as it blew west towards the mountains and we leaned on the trees to get our breath back.

'One day,' said Owen, pointing, 'I'm going to walk all the way to the mountains. It's where my mother's people come from.'

'I'll come with you, Owen,' I said. 'We can walk there together.'

Owen sat down and I sat down next to him and we leaned together against the wind.

'I wish you were my brother, Owen,' I said.

'I am, Martha, I often think that. You're much more my sister than Agnes.'

We were silent awhile, staring out over the valleys, towards the mountains.

'Have you ever seen the will-o'-the-wisp?' he asked me.

'No. Why, have you?'

'My mother's seen them. At Craswall – that's her village – she saw them dancing over graves. And sometimes it's like fire and sometimes it's an old woman.'

'The will-o'-the-wisp?'

'Yes, an old woman carrying a wooden can. People see her on the mountains at night, or when the cloud is thick, just ahead. There was a young man in her village, my mother said, he was a shepherd, knew the hills ever so well, but one night he was returning from market and there she was before him. She just turned a little and smiled and carried on up the path and he followed behind – he couldn't do anything else – followed behind her, off the path and on, into the high cloud, and he never came home, not really, after that.'

'What do you mean, "not really"? Was he dead?'

'They found him wandering a few days later

and they brought him back, but his mind stayed lost.'

'How did they know it was her?'

'Why, Martha, who else could it have been? Like I said, he knew the hills. Only, do you think your dad might have seen the will-o'-the-wisp? Not the old woman – she's only over there – but the flame? I've been thinking about it and I wondered if it was that, because if you follow after it, it breaks your heart. Maybe that's why he's so sorrowful.'

I hugged him tighter. 'It could be that, you're right, Owen, but if he did, I think it was a long time ago.'

'Martha?'

'Yes?'

'Miss Elizabeth visited us last week. She looked so tall and bright in the house, like a red swan. She brought a lady and a gentleman with her and the lady said Aggie was so pretty she might take her to be a lady's maid, and then they all sat on the bench and she asked me to read, and while I read Miss Elizabeth kept looking and nodding at the gentleman and gesturing at me as though he mightn't be able to see me, though I was right in front of him and if he stretched his foot out he'd have kicked me. I stumbled on quite a few of the words, but she was pleased with me and brought out tarts for everyone while the gentleman went to talk to my father.'

'What did they talk about?'

'*I* don't know, do I?' and he jumped up and started picking the snowdrops.

I held his hand as we walked back down. Owen might not know what the gentleman was saying, but I thought I did. Miss Elizabeth had not given up on her protégé. Soon, no doubt, when the time came for such things, he would be packed off to the Cathedral School and it would be the making of him, and I would become nothing to him but a village girl who once was kind.

20

THE CHAPEL BELLS

When I was a little girl Sir William still had hunting parties from time to time. Aggie and I would lie in wait near the Hall for their return, to watch the fine gentlemen and catch up a coin or two if they chanced to throw them. She was pretty even then, with a great mop of yellow curls. One time a young gentleman swept her up and placed her on his pommel, declaring her the queen of the hunt, and the ladies who had come out to greet them laughed and ruffled her hair. One took a blue silk ribbon and tied it round Aggie's fore-head for a coronet. I stayed by the hedge, small and brown and silent, and I would not look at the ribbon when we ran back home, or listen to her prattle. Poor wench, she had little enough to treasure; I should not have begrudged her a ribbon. It was right she should work for a lady among perfumes and ribbons and silks. She had the Simons' pale frailty; she could not long have sustained a life like her mother's. All the same, I could not help envying her. It seemed wrong that Aggie, who could barely write her own name, who was frothy as May blossom, should be lifted into the velvet and not I.

It was well past noon. Smells of cooking drifted through the lane. My father would be hungry and cold. I began to hurry, bracing myself for the dreary room. But as I approached I noticed smoke rising. He had lit a fire and was at his bench mending a shutter! I put the snowdrops I had picked in a cup, smiling.

'Why do you pull so many? I'd have thought you'd be wary of bringing bad luck into the house. They won't last, you know.'

'They will last today, Father. I am glad to see you are so much stronger.'

'Well, who's to make the fire if you spend the

day dallying about the fields? Who were you with? Not our neighbour's lout, at least. He came by with some kindling.'

'Very neighbourly of him.'

'No doubt he was on his mother's business, checking whether they could soon take possession.'

'You can be pleased to disappoint her then.'

We grumbled on together through the afternoon. He did not cough so much, and his back seemed straighter, but there was a coldness in him, even to me. I couldn't bear the thought of that. It pained me almost as bad as our dashed plans. Every few moments he leaned his elbows on the desk to gather his breath again, and in one of these pauses I came up behind him and laid my head on the crook of his neck as I used to do when I was a little girl, but he shrugged me off with a curse. Old Whittle, the Widow had said, had grown so after the ice had touched him, a bit of his heart gone black and dead with the frost. I felt very lonely just then, as I went about my work. He had felt bitter towards all the world, but never towards me. It frightened me. This is how I would live now, with this ailing angry man, as months fell into years; Owen would leave, and Aggie too, and sooner or later Jacob would fold a girl into his arms and marry her.

When I came home after evensong the weakness returned and Father had to lie down, but he was softer with it, and held my hand as I sang to him. There are some songs that can make you cry, though you have sung them ever so many times, but the tears are not sad tears, for there's a feeling of fullness with them, like eating well. I was afraid his heart was shrivelling so I sang him the saddest, fullest songs I could think of, till he squeezed my hand and said, 'For the Lord's sake, Martha, sing something a bit more bonny, can't you?' so I sang him the song of the frog and the mouse, I was halfway through it when the shutters rattled and the chapel bell rang out.

'Whyever would it ring, Father, at this hour?'

'It'll be some foolery, no doubt.'

I took up the song again.

Mrs Mouse, will you marry me?
Fa la linkum larum

A loving husband I will be...

But then the bell sounded again, slow and dreadful, as though tolling a death. I could no longer ignore it, but put on my cloak and hurried out into the night. There were others in the lane and together we walked to the chapel. All who could stir from their beds were gathered at the door, but it was locked and there was no one within that we could tell. There were mutterings and glancings, but none could agree whether it was a warning from the Lord or whether the chapel itself were bewitched. I pulled my cloak around my ears and said nothing. All at once there was a hush and Father Paul strode through, carrying a lighted torch so that his face blazed fearfully like one of the carved heads on the chapel eaves. At the door he turned and faced us and the wind whipped up his skirts and hair. He said nothing, just looked sternly from face to face with the fire flickering on his features. We waited for him to speak and it seemed he was about to, but on a sudden he turned, unlocked the door and went inside. Some braver ones looked in after him. He went directly to kneel up by the altar table, his head bowed in prayer. Nobody dared approach him.

We loitered around in the dark, listening to the howl of the wind and the bare trees creaking, and then suddenly there came again the tolling of the bell. A couple of the women screamed; many fell to their knees. I looked about me at the faces that loomed in the lanterns. People were shouting and crying, but no one looked my way. Then Tom strode forward, waving his big arms.

'If the Father will not speak, I will. Listen up. Something is amiss. You'll agree with that.'

People murmured their assent.

'But what it is we don't rightly know. It could be that we have offended, as the Father has told us. I'm not saying no to that, but it could be the offence was not on our part but rather that the Good Lord is not pleased with the Father's new-fangledness. Father Paul likes to tell us all we're in hock to the devil, but mebbe us poor folk are not alone in sinning. Some might say there's sins been done to our Church and a reckoning to be made, and the Almighty pays His debts.'

Folk began to move closer, to attend to him above the wind, but at that moment Goody Reynolds caught my eye and raised her stick.

'It's the devil as is riding on those bells. Look! There she is! Daughter of the devil's harlot. I've seen her, walking the woods at night with the soot of hell upon her. Why does our milk curdle in the pot? And my sister even now abed with a sore heel after she dropped her wax at Candlemas.'

People turned from Tom towards her and there were nods and murmurs. I looked around at the faces. I had known every one of them all my life and yet many looked at me as though they did not know me at all, as though I were a horrible thing.

'Martha,' someone cried out of the dark, 'what did your familiar do to the Simons' baby?'

'Enough of that foolish talk!' Tom shouted at their backs. He walked up to stand beside me and challenged each accusing eye. 'Let the girl be. Can't you see how she is shaking? Jane Reynolds, you've lost your senses to set people on so. We should all go quietly back to our beds and pray.'

He took me by the elbow. 'Best I walk you

home, girl, but don't be afeard, there's not many take heed of the old crone.'

People parted from us, looking shamed, I was glad to see, or maybe it was that Tom was bigger than the lot of them, and liked a good fight. I bent my head; it was more of a run home than a walk. When I recovered my wits I glanced at him. I would not have taken him for a papist. I wondered if he knew about Sir William.

'It was dangerous, what you said about the old religion,' I said.

'Well, yes, I suppose my blood was up. No doubt some good neighbour will report me to Father Paul in the morning. I am near fifty, Martha. I remember King Henry's time when a statue of Our Mother looked down on us with mercy and the walls were bright with pictures. They smashed the faces of the angels and took away our feasts and holidays. Father Paul and his ilk are all about flogging and work. Bishop John rips off the roofs to line his coffers and plants his people in the parishes. All this, the hole, the ringing, it's the earth itself is disgusted. But I've said enough. You be careful, girl, and less of your gadding about.

There's not much done that folks don't see and note.'

'I don't know, Tom,' I said, 'I never knew the pictures, only their shadows through the white-wash. Perhaps there's something in what you say, but it's safer for folk to say I called up the devil.'

At my door I took his hands in both of mine. 'Thank you, Tom' I said. 'I'll take heed.'

21

IN THE STABLES

I made food for Father and set off for the schoolroom well before dawn, for I felt queasy in my
stomach with fear and did not want to meet
anyone before I reached the protection of the
Hall. All night I had lain awake with the vision of
those faces in my head, listening for the bell as
though it sounded my end. At last I had given over
any hope of sleep.

On the road the stars blinked cheerfully. If a
mantle of dread had fallen, the sky was free of it.
It felt good to be alone. The boys I could face, and
after I would sit in the peace of the library where
light fell slow and slantwise and all the books

seemed to promise calm. Miss Elizabeth would ask after my father and then the village would be forgotten and if she came again at all her talk would be of books or history. I wondered if I would have the courage to ask her about Owen. It was none of my business, of course, and she might well scold me for impertinence, but I doubted she would resent my interest in him.

The stables smelled of fresh hay and the only sound was the horses snorting and shuffling in their sleep. I crept up the ladder to the school-room. It was ridiculous to come this early. I had no candle to waste and I could see nothing without one. I made my way to a far corner where I remembered some sacking was piled, kicked it in case of rats and picked up a bundle to cover myself.

I woke to bright light and a scream already in my throat. A lantern was shining in my face and as I began to yelp a hand clapped my mouth. I pulled back my lips to bite it but it pinched my jaws and a familiar voice whispered, 'Good Christ, Martha, you vixen, it is I.'

'Jacob! What are you doing? How did you find

me?' I shrank back from him into the sacking. The lantern threw his shadow huge on the wall behind. If he meant me harm there was very little I could do, and he already thought me a strumpet. I felt in my skirts for my knife. He must have guessed, for he grinned and sat back.

'Don't fret, I've not come for that. You're a puzzle, though. You don't care a bean for your reputation, but you'll pull a knife on me sooner than let me kiss you in a stable. Am I not the one you were expecting, is it that?'

'I will pull my knife on you indeed if you talk so,' I said.

He laughed outright. 'Or curse me – that's more in your line, I think. I'll tell you why I'm here so early, and then you can tell me the same. I was up, watching the heavens. I like to do that on clear nights. Sometimes my mother and aunt make the air in our cottage so thick with all their talk I cannot sleep. You didn't notice me as you passed, but that's not surprising – you were hunched like an old tinker woman. I followed you here. I suppose I was curious and, anyways, I had to saddle a gelding. I did not want to talk to you on the road in case of watchers. There was a rider came to Sir William very late last night and I had to see to his horse, so I missed the goings-on at the chapel. I heard the bell, of course, and when I came home I heard the story. He's an honest man – Tom. That's a debt you won't pay quickly.'

'And that is why you came, to tell me that?'

For a moment he ignored my question. 'It'll not go lightly for Tom with Father Paul, what he said. He'll be fined, I shouldn't wonder, or whipped.' He paused. 'But that's not all I came to say. Martha, I am sorry for my aunt. She is excitable.'

He held the lantern before my face, watching me closely. His own was cast in shadows so that I could not read it and there was that edge of laughter in his voice that irked. For a while it had gone and I had fancied him my friend. I had begun to think about him far too much but still I could not figure where he stood: close or distant, or sidelong. He asked forgiveness for old Goody Reynolds but the laughter was there, as though my existence amused him, so that I did not know whether to take his hand or spit. I could not see

his eyes, but his mouth had not lost its curl. Perhaps I had been awake too long in the night, for
now I found that I was weeping. He reached out
his hand to brush my cheek and when he spoke
his voice was thick and grave. 'My mother limps
since you dropped the wax. I want to know what
brings you to the stables in the dead of night. Tell
me, Martha, are you meeting someone?'

I pulled away and sprang up. 'Only my familiars and Old Nick.' We were standing facing each
other and I could not say why I felt so angry or
why I wanted to poke him to a fury. 'I give them
suck, you see, and sometimes we make love
among the horses.' He stiffened, his mouth thin
and set. I think he would have delighted in
knocking me down, then. I leaned into his face.
'You are not my brother, Jacob,' I said.

As he opened his mouth to reply there was a
noise from below. He pinched out the lantern and
pulled me down next to him in the sacking. It
would not do to be found together like this.

Footsteps – men's footsteps – came into the
stables. They waited till they were well inside be-

fore they struck a light. The unmistakable voice of Sir William rang out.

'If that fellow is right and Bishop John has wind of you, then you'll have to ride like the clappers, Nicholas, like the clappers, mind. Only keep to the back ways. No doubt I'll be searched tomorrow and half the county will peer up my backside to find a rosary. The Berringtons will be expecting you in Little Malvern. John's people will not follow you there.'

'I don't like to leave, Sir William, amid such portents. It is as though the very ground itself is mourning.'

'Something's afoot, certainly. Father Paul won't be happy till he's sent a few souls to hell on a gibbet. I have to tread lightly. Bishop John knows there may be a profit in bringing me down and he'll stop at nothing that might bring a profit.'

'They say half the county is bleeding under his yoke.'

'It is. He's a bejewelled old simoner, and where he can't steal he extorts. No unseating him; bribed the Star Chamber itself when they had a go.'

'I hear he threw off his wife under Queen Mary. He danced to a different tune then.'

'He'd marry his horse if the fiddler demanded it. Now be off with you – it's almost light – I'll not have your blood on my hands.'

A horse clopped out and footsteps shuffled after it. Then all was silent, but for the crowing of a cock. We looked at one another awkwardly enough and then pulled apart and up.

Jacob pressed a finger to his lips. 'Not a word of this,' he said as he turned to go.

I leaned and touched his arm. 'Jacob,' I whispered, 'forgive me. I am not a witch.'

He turned to me. 'What art thou then, Martha Dynely?' and without waiting for an answer he left.

22

THE RIDGE WAKES

All that evening I listened to my father. He was hollowed out with coughing and all his conversation ended with a curse. A frost was creeping through his flesh; it had touched all the tender parts of his spirit so that they had begun to blacken and die. The weight of his hopelessness exhausted me. I knew better than to touch on our leaving, for there could be no thought of that, not this year, at any rate. Our hopes had been blown out easier than a candle at a window. I felt the disappointment like a sharp stone, jagging me – all our sweet future, gone. But I did not have time for self-pity. There was a rattle at the end of each breath, like loose dice in his chest. What he needed was the bright quick flame of a warm fire. No one could heal in this grey cold, but we had run out of wood for burning, or even for heating the pot.

I dared not ask our neighbours for firewood – not after Goody Reynolds had pointed her finger at me before the chapel – and in any case we owed all over the village already. It might be weeks – months, perhaps – before Father earned again. I would have to pilfer; it would not be the first time. There were two ash down north of Hooper's Oak, cut into logs already. All they needed was a bit of splitting and I could carry them home. I could store a small log pile, bring it back little by little, and even if I were caught, and that was unlikely – I was more nimble than the keepers – even if I were, a whipping would be better than this slow freeze. If I went out tonight I could build us a good fire by morning and Father could wake to a broth and oatcakes.

The moon was high: the woods would be well lit. Not a good night for hiding, but there were few abroad these days for fear of witches and thieves and goblins crawling from the unsettled earth. I resolved not to think of all that and broke off a bit of rowan and slipped it into my kirtle for protection. Then I took the axe down from its hook and pulled my cloak about me as quietly as I could, but the latch on the back door was stiff and the click was enough to make my father call out. I turned back towards him and he clutched at me. He can't have been properly awake, for all he said was 'No', holding tight to my cloak. The shadows pooled so dreadfully around his eyes in the candlelight he looked for a moment like a dead man staring. An old man. I gently unclasped his fingers and bent my head down to kiss his forehead.

His eyes closed once more, but just at that moment the hill let out a bellow. A great wrenching, sudden enough to send the crows wheeling up against the moon, louder than anything on the night of the hole or the bells. Then, as sudden as it had come, it subsided. The roar became a sob, then a scraping echo. Yet the night remained clear and still, with the frost hanging in the air, ready like a net. There was no wind. It seemed wrong that the trees, pricked out dark against the sky, should not notice. Or that the stars and moon should not bend to listen.

I turned back to my father. His breath was rasping. When I touched it his forehead was warm. He followed me with his eyes, but said nothing as I piled my blanket on his.

'Don't be alarmed, Father. It was the hill. I am just going out to get some wood. You sleep. I shall not be long.'

He pointed to his chest. 'It has got inside me,' he said. 'Did you hear how it roars inside of me?'

At first I thought he made a joke and offered him a puzzled smile, but I saw he was not joking. It must be the fever, I thought, that had confused him. He needed heat to sweat it out.

'I'll come back soon,' I said. 'Then I'll make us up a fire and I'll sing to you.'

I slipped out the back of the house before he could answer, but then I hesitated, trying to blink back the foreboding that sat like a shadow at the corner of my eye. All was quiet. The ridge rose up as it had always done and the night had resumed its silence, but for the snoring of the pig. I rubbed my fingers and let the stillness and the stars drift through my mind till I felt clear and still, and could push aside the dread.

I set off over the fields to join the way towards Hooper's Oak. It was not easy going, for the mud was churned and not frozen enough to hold me. I kept to the hedges for fear of being seen. Once I reached it, the wet path gleamed like the trail of a snail on cloth, or a ribbon laid down for me to follow. There was nobody about, though I heard voices far down in the village below me. Up here, the land was lonely and free. All my life I had loved to go walking under the moon. People said there were places where the fairies yet danced, though in all my ranging I had never seen them. I had once seen a man, just at dawn. He must have been standing still as a tree for a long, long time. I would have walked straight past him if an owl hadn't caused me to glance up. There he was, scarce five paces away, above me on the ridge, hooded like death itself. I ran and ran. When I glanced back he was still standing there, gaunt as a winter tree.

The moon slid behind clouds and the slopes shrank into shadow. Clusters of sheep glimmered in the hedges below. It was a night for ghosts and strange imaginings. Even a fox startled me, loping long and low across my path. I gripped the axe and told myself I had no reason to feel so flighty, but the roar had left a kind of humming in the air, a kind of unsteadying, as if the trees were loosening their roots.

I found the log pile easily. It was a piece of luck, it being left to be stolen by the likes of me. They would surely move it soon. I steadied a log and began the work of splitting. The blows rang out so loud I was sure they must wake every sleeping soul for a mile or more. I paused and looked around for any sound of a keeper, but there was no one. Only an owl low-hooting after a mate. I placed a fresh log and swung the axe high above my head once more and there, right as I brought it down, the earth rucked beneath me. I was thrown off my feet sidelong into a great mound of ivy. A family of ravens flew up like rags out of the trees.

I should have run. I should have found the axe and run. The roaring was all about my ears; the earth itself staggered. I tried to pray, but my teeth chattered too much in my head. Oh, if this was Judgment Day I was not ready to be judged. Not yet! And what of my father – what state was he in for St Peter? I buried my head in the ivy and counted, one, two, three, four, five... At some point I realised that the earth had stilled; it was my own hands that shook the stems. Slowly I got to my feet. Birds still cawed about the sky and down in the valley the chapel bell was ringing. I should get back to my father and my bed. I took a step, but my legs wobbled beneath me, so I leaned back against a tree and tried to sing to steady myself.

> Come over the burn, Bessie
> My little pretty Bessie
> Come over the burn, Bessie, to me.

> The white dove sat on the castle
>   wall;
> I bend my bow and shoot her I
>   shall;
> I put her in my glove, both feathers
>   and all.

These were lines that my father sang, when he
was well and working. I know he thought of my
mother when he sang it, for he'd often repeat 'my
pretty Bessie' to himself after he'd done, but it always heartened him, and me, too. I sang it over
and over in the dark while the wood quietened
about me, till I could trust my legs not to buckle
and fold. I was so restored I thought to stuff the
logs I'd split into my sack and hide more of them
in the hollow that the tangled ivy covered over.
The moon was sinking low through the bony
branches. It was still early, but nobody would be
asleep, not with the bells ringing out in alarm. I'd
have to go north towards the Cockshoot if I did
not wish to be seen. I could cut cherry bark for
Father's coughing along the way.

The sack banged against my back and it was
hard going, with branches down, and in one place
an old elm fallen into the fork of an ash. I had to
drop to my knees to get past that. On Green Hill I
left the woods to find easier footing at the top of
the pasture where it tumbled down to the village.
The hedges made black lines over the iron-grey
fields, and in the corners pale sheep huddled.

Then a movement caught my eye: a bit of darkness was racing up the grass, as if coming right for me, hopping and darting up the hill. Too small for a man, much too small. My breath caught in my throat. It must be some kind of sprite or goblin, cast out with the roaring. It was coming for me. I ducked back towards the hedge, looking for a way over. The creature began lolloping more slowly, bent down to the earth. It was very close. I could make it out quite clearly now: not a goblin, a boy. Owen!

I stepped forward and near frighted the life out of him. 'Owen, what in our Saviour's name are you doing up here at this hour?'

''S' Truth, Martha,' he said when he had recovered, 'did you not feel it? Agnes fell out of her cot! My father kneels and prays; my mother wails. Goody Reynolds runs from door to door in her nightcap. "It is come!" she shouts, "the great day of His wrath is come. *Blow up a trumpet in Zion, and shout in my holy hill. Let all the inhabitants of the earth tremble: for the day of the Lord is come, for it is nigh at hand. A dark and gloomy day, a cloudy and black day.* Oh, you better pray for mercy now," she shouts, *"for He shall wash His feet in the blood of the wicked."*

Owen grinned, but he was as pale as the shift beneath his thin cloak and he skipped from foot to foot. I put down my sack and pressed my hands on his shoulders to quiet him.

'And you ran up the hill in your shift for fear of an old trot, a mackabroine like Goody Reynolds? For shame, Owen, what will your mother and father think? She's nothing but a loose nail that needs hammering. We are too young for the world to end. Miss Elizabeth says fearful talk is the devil's work.'

He cut me short. 'Listen, it's starting again. Martha, I think it's the dragon. The dragon that sleeps under the ridge.'

At my back I heard it too: a low growl, like the sound a dog makes when he hears a scrit-scratching at the door. I grabbed Owen's hand, heaved my sack over my shoulder and started walking briskly. 'Come, we'll go home by the Cockshoot Lane. It's not coming from that way.'

It was easier to be brave with a child by my side. Every few steps I paused to rest from the sack. The growling did not cease. We could feel it at our shoulders, through our foot soles. Owen's eyes were wide with fright. I tried to set my face to a smile. Perhaps I should have put the sack down and run, but I had settled somehow that we should treat this as a dog that barks and threats; we should not turn our backs and skirr away. And anyhow, my father needed fire. The sky was turning grey in the east and a freezing rain, more sleet than rain, had begun spitting in our faces.

When Owen spoke again it was so quietly beneath the yowling hill I had to bend to hear him. 'Father Paul says a dragon will rise to fight with the angels when the last day comes.'

And like a nod to his words, a great cough came out of the hill. We both looked up. Owen screamed. Perhaps I screamed with him. For above us the slope was rippling like water. A great slab of the ridge began to spill towards us.

23

THE SLIP: THE YEW TREE

I think it was only a second I stared, mouth open, stupid. The wood swept down like a birch brush, a tangle of trees rumpling the field like cloth before it. Then a stone, flung ahead of the mass, struck my temple.

Helter-skelter, we ran down the unfixed slope. There was a gap in the hedge. I pushed Owen ahead, flung myself after, but my skirt snagged on the hawthorn.

'Go, Owen, go on!' I screamed as I tore at the worsted. I was like a ewe held fast by its fleece. For a moment Owen stood transfixed, glancing from me to the tide of earth that rushed down at us. I leaned forward and pushed him as hard as I could. 'Go,' I shrieked above the roar of the slopes. 'I'll catch up.'

He turned to run. It was the last thing I saw before I was hurled headlong into the ditch by a great ash tree, which had been flicked over like a pin.

It saved my life. I was held under its fork with air enough to breathe, while the clay spewed about me. I felt the cold sticky darkness of the grave, moving, jostling, around me. The hill itself had become a monster and I was in its teeth. The rocks themselves were screaming. I thought the sound would burst my bones apart. Soil, sticks, boulders, branches bruised and scraped me. I could not breathe for the panic and the screaming and the press of the clay.

I knew nothing for a long time. When awareness returned to me I was in heavy, suffocating darkness. I lay face down, clay and leaves pasted my tongue and I could scarcely feel my limbs for cold. My fingers by themselves gripped at the ash, which had preserved me. All around and through me there was still the strange terrible sound of the earth being rent. I realised that the ash, the clay, the ruins of the hedge, I myself, all were moving. In jerks and starts the land was sliding. The ash had shaken off most of the dirt that covered it and little by little I turned myself around and pushed at the branches and soil above me until I was able to push my head through to look at the world that was being made.

What I saw goes beyond belief. Yet it is true. If I live till I am old I hope to see nothing so strange. By the light I could tell it was afternoon and a light snow was falling. My field, with its grass and its hedges, with its great fallen ash, was being dragged eastwards. It was as though someone was pulling one of the embroidered tapestries at the Hall across a bed. There were rucks in the fabric, places where a rip had opened, but the picture still was clear. Strangest of all, I saw a clutch of sheep, with terrified stone eyes, snagged with the grass they lay upon. Mistress Reynolds had been right. The Last Day had come. The fiend was hauling the world to hell.

Then at last the rending gave way to a tearing and we ceased to move. I had no idea of hours, but there came a moment when I opened my eyes to the sun in the wrong place. It threw light in strange patterns on the new shapes of the land and I knew with a shock that the earth had come to rest. My head was dizzy with cold and hunger, yet I knew I had to get home. I tried to struggle free so that I could stand, but my ankle hurt very badly.

'Owen,' I called, over and over to the empty fields. There was no answer, only the uncertain bleat of a lamb.

I could not walk, but by pulling myself up on my elbows and using my good leg I succeeded at last to labour over the earth and grass. Ahead of me a great bank of soil was piled up, as though the devil had given up on his load and dumped it. A twisted yew straddled the bank. It looked strangely familiar. Perhaps if I got to it I could see where I had got to. Perhaps I would find Owen. I crawled over the cold mud and the snow, lugging my bad leg behind me. It took so long, so long, I seemed to make no progress. With each pull it felt as if I stuck my ankle with a knife. My mind would not stay fixed to the task. It veered off. I was a child, bounding down the lane to my grand-mother, because she had baked me a honeycake. Oh, the sweet smell of it! 'Let's wait for your moth-er,' my grandam said. But that wasn't right, I re-membered. There was only freezing mud and pain and the yew tree. My mother was dead. Hunger and cold were dispossessing me of my wits. I must reach the yew tree. My mother was dead. But look, there she was, perched on the branches in a white dress. It was a cold day for such a dress! At last I leaned against the rough bark and watched the snow fall. For hours I watched it. *The white dove sat on the castle wall,'* I sang, and laughed, and I felt so light I flew up into the boughs like a bird.

There was a man coming over the field. I looked down at the girl slumped below me. She was trying to shout, but she could not remember how. He came slowly. The light was poor – per-haps he would not see her. After all, her cloak was spotted with snow and she made no sound. She wanted to wave at him, but her arm would not move. Little by little he came nearer; he saw her, he began to call and run. I glanced across at my mother, but she had gone. He was talking to the girl. It was me he was talking to. He bent down and gathered me up and I felt him lift me off the cold clay and hold me close.

24

A VISION

I woke to bright flames. My first thought was that I was in hell, and I was glad for the warmth of it, but I soon came to my senses. The devil does not tuck his sinners in with blankets. I looked around. I was in my own bed. Had I brought the logs home? My head hurt as though the axe had split it. A woman was bent over the fire. She straightened up when she heard me stir.

'Ah, so you have wakened at last. And no fever. You are made of oak, Martha Dynley.' It was the Widow Spicer. I was amazed. Of all people to see at our hearth, busying around our house, making broth, smiling at me.

She nodded at me now as though she understood my thoughts.

'It was my Jacob as found you. He was out with the others looking for the Simons boy. Nobody really believed you were lost, you know, what with your father... well, not being his right self. No, Jacob had been out for hours, calling and calling for the boy, but getting no answer. Then he thinks he hears a moaning from the great yew tree. Goodness, there's a story there, my dear. I'll tell you later. Anyway he wasn't affrighted, not my Jacob, although nineteen out of twenty would have hightailed it at such a sound, with night falling. He went straight up and there you were, strewn on the ground like wreckage from a boat. Thought you were dead, he did, but he picked you up, gentle, as if you was one of his birds. Like carrying one of the pheasants, he said it was, and your heart began to flutter like a bird's, just like a bird's. He knew by that you were alive.'

'My father,' I said, but I couldn't go on, for I saw that his cot was empty.

'Is up at the Hall,' she answered. 'Sir William directed it himself, and very good of him it was, too.

There's many who wouldn't extend the hand of charity to those who work their own ruin. You have a debt to pay there, Martha, though you live to be a hundred. And that's not all. Mistress Elizabeth directed wood be brought, and food and a blanket. Stopped by herself, she did; charged me to leave the linen and tend to you. All the gentry have been out to see what's left of Marcle Ridge. Of course we saw it all, down here. Heard it too. The hill woke up and walked. The land itself. It's a judgment, that's sure and certain. Why, we all thought the end of the world had come. You've never heard such wailing and beseeching. There's some say Tom should never have been put to the whipping post,' she dropped her voice to a loud whisper, 'after his words about the old religion. But if it were so, if it is turning from the old ways has done it, why should it be the Simons boy taken? Everyone knows the statue of St Ann that was found again under Queen Mary had been tucked away under Ann Simons' bed. It's not a turning back that's needed now. You mark my words, girl, this is punishment for superstition and idolatry. The Good Lord has sent a warning.'

'Owen,' I interrupted her, 'have they found him?'

'They have not.' And she fell quiet, but only for a moment. 'His mother is distracted, running hither and thither without much sense. There's a party gone out now to look for him. Ranged as far as the Fosbury yesternight, sweeping back southerly tonight, Jacob says. Even some of the gentry have joined in. But there's not much hope now. Little mite like that in this cold. He was never strong. It's horrible to think of it. The earth pressing down and crushing the life out of him. I said to his mother: "You had best pray for his soul, Ann. He is with the angels now, my dear." Well, she turned on me with a look as should never be used on a neighbour. There's some as won't be helped. That's the truth of it.'

'Tell them,' I said. 'Tell them to look for him in Stockings Field, near the Aylton road.'

'Oh, don't you worry, dear, they'll have looked there. I said to my Jacob: "Make sure you go through Grover's meadow, through Stockings Field and the Readings." "Mother," he said, "I'll go there first." And the Lord be praised he found you. Oh, you'd be dead if it wasn't for that boy.'

'Please,' I said, 'tell them to look there again.'

'I'm sure they have it under control,' she said, a little more tartly. 'Sir William himself is out there. I know you've always been fond of the boy, Martha, but it was a hard night last night, ice as thick as my finger in the troughs. Snow coming, too, by the look of it. The hill itself rose up and made a grave for him. Best to pray for him. He's in the Lord's hands now. The potage should be ready.'

I regarded her from my bed. Silly prattler, all pleased and comfortable with herself in front of the fire. I pulled my legs to the ground and stood, gathering the blanket around me like a cloak. My head swam, I thought my legs would buckle, but I grasped at the wall to steady myself and dragged at my wet boots. My right ankle had swollen but somehow I forced it in. Mistress Spicer stirred the pot and noticed nothing. Each step felt like a knife in my ankle bone, but I reached the door. My hand was on the latch when she turned and saw me.

'And wherever do you think you are going, child?' she said, waving the ladle in my face.

My head began to swim again and I clung to the latch for support. I didn't think I had the strength to argue with her.

'Stockings Field,' I said.

'Get back into your bed at once. Wilful girl! Who do you think will be blamed when they find you dead in the dirt? You may walk yourself to hell when your sot of a father returns, but till then I am charged to look after you and look after you I will. You'll not lose me my favour with Mistress Elizabeth. Oh, no.' And with every word she lunged at me with the ladle as though we were jousting with spoons.

I pulled the door open; a rush of cold air and darkness slapped me back. There was a man turning towards the house. At the sight of me he ran forward. I had not known I was falling.

'Oh, thank the Lord, Jacob.' Mistress Spicer bustled behind us as he laid me back on the cot. 'Perhaps she'll listen to you. If she was anything of mine she'd know the rod, that she would. Tell her. She has to bide here and drink her broth. Good-

ness! What I have to put up with. She had no business surviving up there all that time. Who knows
but she might be dangerous, never mind that she's
half dead.'

'Martha,' Jacob said, ignoring his mother, 'you
must rest. It's not safe for you to be out yet. What
is it?'

He laid his hand on mine and it felt strong
and warm, and tears began to prick behind my
eyes. I pulled my own hand away.

'I beg your pardon, Miss Dynely,' he chuckled.

I'm not a child, I thought, to be laughed at like
that. I waited for the room to stop whirling. Then
I made myself look straight at him, trying to push
from my mind our last meeting in the stables and
how he despised me.

'Thank you, for bringing me home,' I said
stiffly. 'It seems I owe you my life. But you need to
go out again, go directly to Stockings Field. I think
Owen will be there, or near there.'

'He will do no such thing,' his mother put in.
'He will sit down here and drink some broth
with us.'

'Please go. Now,' I said.

'Why, why do you think he is there?' he asked, not smiling now, brushing his mother back as she tried to interrupt.

'He was with me. We saw the hill falling and I pushed him into the field to run. He may not have got far. I feel in my heart he is hiding, in the crook of the hedge where the spring rises.' And suddenly I could see him in my mind, crouched still, covered over by a grey-white mass. It must be the snow, the snow that was coming. I felt a great weight of hopelessness.

'What is it?' Jacob said, seeing me look blank.

'I don't know,' I answered, my voice sliding into a wail. 'I saw Owen in my mind, all under the white snow. I think it's too late; it must be too late already. You'll not find him.'

'That's an evil vision, Martha. Put it aside.' he said. 'The fields are all twisted about, but I'll trace the lines of Stockings Field. No, Mother, don't try to stop me. I'll come back soon.'

He put out his fingers as though to squeeze my hand but thought better of it, nodded, stooped under the low door and stepped out into the night.

'Well, I hope you're satisfied. Sending him out on a wild-goose chase and him not eaten for hours. And bad weather coming in. I won't sleep a wink tonight, not one wink.'

She held the ladle up as though she had a mind to step over and strike me. I had no stomach for a fight.

'I'm sorry, Mistress Spicer. I know the debt I owe to your family. If Jacob had not found me it would be me freezing to death out there. If anyone is like to find the boy it is Jacob. Oh, yes,' I added as if to myself, 'what a hero he'll be, and all the gentry coming from round about to hear about the happenings here. Sir William will be sure to honour him. I wouldn't be surprised if the bishop himself came to hear of it.'

I watched her anger turn to pride and preening as I spoke. 'Well,' she said, 'you're a wild unbridled thing but you've got a head on your shoulders. There's those who make trouble and those who make good the trouble others cause.'

'I shouldn't wonder if a ballad were not written of it,' I added, grimacing at myself that I had gone too far. But she nodded as she ladled out the broth at last and hummed an air, as if trying out the tune already.

25

JACOB'S SEARCH

When I woke all was quiet. Every part of me ached – even lifting my arm to my face exhausted me. I could feel that I was cut about, too. My eye felt swollen and in places my skin stuck to the rough cloth of the blanket. I listened for my father's cough and then remembered he was not there. The smell in the cottage was all wrong. Tears leaked out of my eyes. Through the gap in the curtains that shut off my cot I could see Goody Reynolds asleep in my father's chair before the fire. Her scrawny hands twitched in her lap and she mumbled, but I could not make out the words. Then came the sound of the latch and voices and stamping feet. She jumped up in a flurry and one after another men stumbled in, till the place could hold no more. Jacob was with them, and the Widow. Groggy with sleep though I was, I recognised Sir William himself take a cup from her. I lay very still behind the curtain.

He spread his large hands wide. 'Well, madam,' he bellowed, as though to Parliament itself, 'there's no better feeling in the world than to be proud of a fine son and, madam, you can be proud today. Why, the boy has rescued not one, but two strays from the flock. Not one, but two, mark you.' And he grabbed Jacob by the shoulder and clapped him on the back.

I leaned up on my arm. So Owen was found! I wanted to shout out for particulars, but fear prevented me. The presence of so many men in our cottage quite confounded me. Even if I had been able to speak, I should have been ashamed to appear like this before gentlemen – for there were at least two others with Sir William whom I recognised from the Hall.

I did not have to wait long for the news. With a great bustle the party departed, leaving Goody

Reynolds, Jacob, and his mother, who was rubbing away with her apron at the coin Sir William had pressed into her hand. Jacob sat quiet on a stool, warming his hands on a great bowl of broth. After a moment he addressed me.

'It is all right, Martha, they are gone. You were right, you know. But it was not an evil vision.' He laughed. 'Not snow, Martha, sheep.'

'Whatever are you talking about?' his mother put in. 'Why, the boy is losing his wits. Did you hear Sir William, sister? I am so glad I insisted on Jacob's going out again. Drink your soup, boy, and tell us what happened.'

I hooked the curtain back and carefully sat up on my bed to listen.

'Remember, Mother,' Jacob went on, 'Martha insisted I looked in Stockings Field. Said she had a vision of Owen smothered by whiteness? Well, listen. I went out, meaning to find the other men and tell them what Martha had said. I thought they might laugh, but I found old George Tanner first, and he heard me out and nodded.

'"Aye," he said, "there might be something in it. She's a queer one and no mistake. It's not the first time she has seen things. There's good in some of her visions, whatever people say. Found my pig for me, she did, that time it had wandered over to Millpound Coppice."

'We hailed the others and made our way to the remains of Stockings Field, or what we could make of it, what with the dark and the snow blowing in our faces. It was hard going, too, for the ground is now all soil and rubble, with trees and hedges thrown out of place. We feared what we might find, with the chapel itself thrown down and the dead that lie there scattered.'

'The chapel gone?' I blurted.

'Aye, Martha, you didn't know? Well, it's no surprise, seeing as you were being carried along with it. The slide of earth took the chapel with it. There are blocks of stone strewn about, but much is buried. The biggest wonder of all is the great yew. The tree you came to rest in, Martha, it is that same tree from the graveyard. Carried over a hundred paces and planted again by the grace of God. I can only think you were guided to it. But to get back to Owen's story. Some of the men were afraid, and truth be told, I was afraid myself of what might lie beneath us. We dared not look down. Our feet slid on the frozen mud and every lurch sickened us, in case we pressed down on the face of one of the dead, ripped out of its resting place and writhing in the earth. The screech of an owl sent us all cowering; it seemed to us like the howl of a damned soul. Every one of us knows someone in that burial ground. We tried to put it out of our minds.

'I won't lie to you; I was beginning to despair of little Owen. It was in all our thoughts that, what with the freeze and the snow, there was little hope. We searched every knot and scrap of hedge, but the fields are thrown about, Martha. One of us would swear he recognised a thorn, but in the lamplight all shapes are estranged from themselves. Rob Tanner muttered that it was no use and the others agreed with him. I must be soft, they said, listening to the chatter of a witless girl. The snow was getting thicker. Rob said it was the dead: they were calling out for a shroud. Unless Owen made shrift somehow to come to us by himself he was lost. I couldn't argue with them, for it was plain they were right. But then Master Simons himself appeared with a lantern. Grey as the snow, he was, and his face set grim. He'd heard, somehow, about your vision. I hadn't the heart to leave, though the others nodded to him and shrugged their way off. We didn't speak, but set off eastwards, side by side.

'I'd not gone far when I stumbled over a branch and was flung headlong. My fingers closed on wool – wool, and an animal struggling against my grasp. A ewe. I let out a cry. Richard Simons rushed over, thinking me to have cried out in pain. But it was not pain. I was thinking of your vision, Martha, and what you had taken for snow. Of a sudden I had a great hope the boy was still living.

'There were three of them, bundled together up against a fallen tree. They were all breathing, although the smallest one had its legs broke and was dying, with a great branch across its back. I pulled the big ones aside as Master Simons held up the lantern, praying over and over. And there was Owen, curled up like a rabbit, his big eyes staring up at his father.'

'Well, praise the Lord,' put in his mother, 'and of course it's like his lordship said, it's down to you, Jacob. There's two souls in this parish as would be facing judgment if it hadn't been for you, my son.'

I couldn't help interrupting. 'Will he live, Jacob?'

'Aye, Martha, he will. He was caught up between the sheep, wrapped in wool all around. His head was cut – not a bad wound, not deep – but he was distracted. He didn't seem to recognise his father, not even when the old man yelled and caught him up in his arms.'

'Well, what do you expect,' said his mother, 'holed up like that for two whole days, all alone with the earth roaring above him and around him? Nothing to eat and drink. It's a wonder if he's not touched for life. He was never a big strapping child like you were. It may be it would have been a mercy for him to have been taken, rather than to linger on a stranger to his own senses.'

'Mother,' Jacob said sharply, rising from his stool, 'don't speak like that. I won't hear that. The boy will mend, God willing. His mother's tears will cure him. You should have seen her, when we brought him home. I've never seen such joy.'

'Well, it wouldn't be the first child Ann Simons has lost. We will leave you now, Martha. I'll
call by again in the morning. I think you can spare
us one or two of these logs Mistress Elizabeth left.
Look, Jacob, Sir William gave me an Angel; very
handsome of him.' And the silver coin flashed in
the firelight as she held it up.

26

AGGIE VISITS

People began to call it the Wonder, for they had no words for it or what it meant. The hill was rent and the chapel gone – that we could say easily enough – but that was barely to begin to talk of it. In those days after the Wonder we kept repeating what we knew – the rent hill, the chapel gone – as a man in the flood clings to the wreckage of the bridge; it kept us afloat, but it was wreckage nonetheless. Where we had used to watch the sun set was now an ugly wound. Our old horizon was piled in drifts beneath the dirty snow and even the house of God was buried. For the rest, we were waiting to learn how to talk of it, how to find the words to understand.

The particular truth I clung to was Owen – that he had been brought home – though the Widow told me he was a broken thing now, that he had not said a word since they had scooped him out the snow. In honesty, I thought of the arms that had lifted me out too, but I tried to push that by. Of my father, no one would speak in that first week, except to repeat he was being nursed by Ruth Tranter, in her cottage up at the Hall. When I pressed the Widow or old Goody Reynolds, they exchanged glances and pursed their lips and said he was as well as could be expected, and that surely soon I should have him home to nurse. Just as soon as my ankle healed a little more. 'It's the Lord Jesus as can help him as much as any doctor,' Mistress Reynolds liked to say, and they would piously lower their heads, though not before the Widow had darted a glance at my consternation.

That first Sunday Father Paul led a service in the open, near where the great yew had come to rest. Two hours in the wind and sleet, till barely a soul could bear it.

'Oh, he was all fire,' the Widow told me later. 'Couldn't feel the weather, not he. You can imagine how my poor swollen hands and feet suffered with the bone-ache that I have to put up with, rain or shine, and rain in particular. We felt sure that he'd talk of Jacob, of the Lord rejoicing over the bringing back of the lost sheep, but not a word. Two hours and not a single word, mark you. How can he expect us to follow the stony path if good deeds get buried deep as the chapel bell? There we were, with the red earth piled like washing, and for all we knew the bodies of our dead scattered in the soil beneath us and not a word of comfort. If he had dropped his eyes from the heavens for one minute he'd have seen that people weren't happy about it. Not happy at all. Idolatry, he said it was, that we cared more for the stones than the risen Christ. The Lord needed no roof, he said Our Saviour preached in the desert, under the burning sun of the Holy Land. Mary Tucker nudged me. "Wouldn't mind a bit of burning sun," she says. "Any sun whatever would be welcome." You have no idea, Martha, cosy in your bed, just how desolate it felt, stuck out on that hillside, with the ruin of the ridge above us and Father Paul competing with the sleet to freeze our blood with fear of His vengeance. I'm not one to set my face against the Church, and when all's said and done Father Paul's a university man and God's word is laid open before him, but if he keeps this up there'll be more than Tom of the mill spending time at the whipping post.'

Miss Elizabeth had charged Widow Spicer to care for me, and she had hopes of another silver coin if she did her duty well. Very often I woke to hear her moving about; my latch was not my own to say who came and went. But I gathered, too, from bits and pieces that she dropped as she chattered, that there was a shift in the air towards me that encouraged her to play the nursemaid. The Lord Himself had a hand in my deliverance, people said, or why else would I survive, and why be found in the holy yew of the graveyard? Besides, I had pointed the way to the boy. People called with gifts of cheese or oats – even, once, a wrapped piece of bacon – at the door. My neighbours pitied me, but to my surprise I did not mind. I sat in my father's chair and sniffed at the bacon and, amazed at my weakness, found myself weeping with fondness.

'Come, girl,' the Widow said, taking it from me to 'store it safe', though I knew she'd be cutting off a part for herself as she never failed to do, 'stop that weeping. You're not the frost brought in beside the fire to melt. Whatever next! You should be giving thanks – all this kindness, to a waif like you, and one that's caused her share of trouble.'

Jacob did not come, or rather, he came once. I drifted out of sleep to the sharp rich smell of the warrens and for a moment I lay with my eyes still closed, breathing it in and smiling – because it was the smell of the fields and I was sick of being cooped up. He must have been resting his hand next to my face. I could feel the warmth of it.

'Fie, boy,' came the Widow's voice. 'Leave off gawping. There's girls far more worth looking at than she, as you well know. You might have saved her from the hillside, but that doesn't make you her brother. Come over here and eat your stew.'

He moved away, taking the smell of the woods

and fields with him. I slid back into sleep. When I woke the cottage was dark but for a pile of embers smoking on the hearth. I vainly reached my hand out to where the scent had been and closed it on darkness.

A few days later Aggie came. There was a knock and the latch lifted gently, and there she was, wan and hesitant and hovering on the threshold. I felt so pleased to see her I tried to jump out of my chair and near fell headlong. She leaped forward to grab me and any awkwardness sloughed off in an instant like a spent adder skin.

"S' Truth, Aggie,' I said as soon as I was settled again, 'but you are more pretty than the morning. I wish I were a gentleman so I could buy you a silk gown. But how is Owen faring? The Widow tells me nothing, or only shreds I can do nothing with.'

'Well, he is doing well, or not well yet, but we have hopes. He is getting stronger, but he will not speak. Father Paul says he saw the devil and is struck dumb with fear.'

'Why the devil? Why not an angel, calling the sheep to shield him?'

'No, Father Paul says it is a devil, or one of the

walking dead, ripped from the earth by the hill as it fell, but Sir William – he's come himself, you know; stayed ever so long – he said it was more likely the boy was exhausted and needed time to mend and that he had more faith in ham than exorcists.'

'What do you think, Aggie?'

She glanced at me and all her mask gave way. After a bit she took my hands in hers and leaned in towards me so that our heads touched. I could not see her face, but I could feel that she was crying. 'Oh, Martha, I don't know. It is all so horrible, and just as our lives were about to change! Poor Owen, Jacob says that without you he may never have been found. That you had a vision. Is that true, Martha? The whole parish is talking of it.'

'I don't know, Aggie, it is all a whirl. There was a kind of picture, but Jacob and your father would have been led to him without me. Has Jacob been visiting, then?'

'Oh, yes, he's been on his own account to check on Owen and, then, the Widow is always sending him – for gossip, I suppose.'

Not just for gossip, I thought, looking at

Agnes' lovely face, and you know it, or you wouldn't smile so. I closed my eyes and leaned my forehead against hers. I had no right to mind him visiting her.

'Will you tell Owen I love him,' I said, 'and that I will come as soon as my leg will bear me?'

'Oh, Martha, I will. Of course I will. But you won't believe the change in him. He lies curled silent on his cot and barely seems to know a soul, except Mother, although that is her say-so. I am not sure he knows even her. His eyes are open and he looks at you, but it's like he has shutters drawn. His soul is all closed off. People say he's not likely to ever speak again. It's so cruel. You know there was plans for him to be sent to school? People say he's like to be an idiot for the rest of his life.'

'Nonsense, idle prattling, there's people who always love to see the worst. He's had a fright, that's all. Think, Aggie, what it must have been like for him in the cold, with those dying, bleating animals about him and the earth giving way as if hell itself were opening. His head is more full of fancy than anyone's at the best of times. It's no wonder at all he's retreated a while. There's herbs can help call him back. I can make a remedy that might help him, Aggie. Monkshood.'

'Wolfsbane, you mean? I don't know, Martha. It can kill a grown man. I know you helped Mother so, but I'm sorry, after the baby, Father would not like it, and Father Paul said very strongly we must trust in prayer alone and any other meddling was sinful.'

'What does he know of herbs? Remember when old Father Geoffrey was vicar here? He used to call my grandmother in himself. He had no thought that it was wicked to be cunning with plants. Wolfsbane is a poison, it's true, but used right it could purge the stoppage that holds Owen from himself. I would not want anyone else to give it to him, but I could bring it myself, when I come.'

'Well, you might ask Mother, if Father is not by.' She got up, but I could not let her go without asking about my father. His absence hung around the cottage, around every object, every corner and yet no one would speak of it.

She looked a little nervous and then sat down again. 'Miss Elizabeth said it would distress you,' she said, hesitating. 'Said we weren't to say a thing about him till you had recovered.' She sat down again. 'But if it was me I should want to know. He is very ill, Martha.

'This is all from what I've heard, mind,' she went on. 'We were out in all the roaring, searching for Owen. The fever must have grown on your father after you went up the ridge, and in the early morning he was raving. You could hear him from the lane, they say, hollering fit to burst, but everyone was too busy being afraid to pay him any notice, what with the hill collapsing, and the earth buckling and sliding. Folks was running back and forth, one minute believing the houses were about to fall and the next hiding under their beds. And no one knew you weren't there within. Then just before noon he appeared at Robert Tanner's door in his nightshift, screaming that he could see the devils dancing and that they had carried you away. He was going to dance with the devils all the way to hell and get you back. And he started tearing at his shirt.

'His eyes were terrible, blazed like branding irons, I'm told. They tried to wrap him up, but he wouldn't have a stitch of blanket on him, just cast it aside, though it was near freezing. He was running with sweat. There was a great scream, then, from the hill. He grinned wide and started pointing. "That is Moloch," he said. "He is waking up. Go lock up your children. He has taken mine." And some of the old people made the sign of the cross and drew back from him. Mistress Reynolds began howling that he must be possessed, that they should call for the priest, that he should be bound and held for the Justice.' Agnes glanced at me. 'Shall I go on, Martha? Do you want me to?'

I nodded.

'Very well, then. There was a gaggle round him then, and he pointed at Goody Reynolds. "You have Bessie's blood on you!" he cried, and he started rubbing at her with his shirt. "It will not come off! Moloch and Lucifer, Moloch and Lucifer!" Then he grabbed her by the scarf shouting, "*They came to thee and said surely thou know her for thy speech bewrayeth thee, but thou curst and swore thou knew her not.* Listen, Mistress, the cock crows." And it was true – there were roosters crowing all over the village. Oh, Martha, I'm sorry, my mother said you shouldn't hear of all this. Bessie was your mother, wasn't she?'

'Yes, she was. Oh, I think he must have been raving. I can't think what he meant. Goody Reynolds grew up in Woolhope, which is not so far from Moccas. Perhaps their paths crossed when they were girls. Oh, he's mad.'

But I remembered the look he gave her after Plough Monday and knew in my heart there was more to it. And subtly, like a pulled thread, I began to see how the unravelling had begun when the Widow's sister had come. She had been picking at our past, and especially my mother's past, peddling stories I could only guess at. It must be that.

'There, Martha, don't weep. Please, stop weeping. I think you should be told, but I'll stop if you wish it. Very well, then. He was wild, Martha, and it seemed he might do something violent so men laid hands on him and bound him. And he spat in their faces. Mistress Reynolds gave him a sharp kick and others might have turned on him too, but that a violent fit of coughing made him collapse in their arms. "For the Lord's sake," Tom cried, "he's sick. There's been whipping enough; the man needs physic, not the constable." That brought them to their senses. By good fortune a number of the gentry happened by, out to see the Wonder. Sir William was among them. He commanded that your father be taken up to the Hall to be looked after. He is lodged with the gardener, Ben Tranter, and his wife, and he's quiet now, but he's very poorly, Martha.'

After she'd gone I lay in the dark and listened to the night thickening around me. Pictures of Owen and my father drifted through my head, the one locked in silence, the other broken into speech that made no sense. I could not bear to think. Tears ran down towards my ears and I let them, for they comforted me, like the sound of rain pouring from the eaves.

27

BESSIE DYNELY

Aggie had promised me a cart to take me to my father, but it took her days to wheedle it. Widow Spicer insisted on joining me, for she was taking mending up to the Hall.

It was near two weeks since I had been outside. I opened the cottage door to the morning and the bright grey sky was endless. Worried as I was, I could not help smiling at the light and the cold air that had the sting of newness in it. The ridges in the tilled fields glinted. He would recover – I could not believe otherwise on such a morning. I stretched out my bad leg before me on the cart and braced the ankle in sacking. At every lunge of the wheels it rolled a little and pained me. Beneath the hedge by the Yapps' place I saw primroses. He would get strong again. It would just take a little time. Like my leg.

The Widow was watching me and now she cut in on my thinking. 'Well, Martha, you know I've always been your friend, and it's as your friend I tell you that any fool can see that that ankle is not going to mend straight. It's twisted good and proper. You'll be lame, my dear, like old rolling Mary out at Aylton. It was God's will and you must bide with it and be content.'

'Content to be lame?'

'Content with your lot, and your fortune. Even before this it was never likely that you'd marry. You're a little brown thing and your family is not fortunate. But there's no question of it now. Best to put it right out of your head.'

I stared at the red scar on the ridge, but it made my eyes hurt to look at it. The horizon was ripped and beneath it all was ragged and raw, with scraps of snow lying in the wreckage. I had to blink hard. I had no wish to marry, I assured her.

The Widow eyed me closely. 'The world's not

a kind place for a plain girl with no family and no prospect of gaining one.'

'I have my father,' I said. I would have said more, but I couldn't trust my voice.

'Your father,' she said, smiling. 'You need to find yourself a place, girl. Don't think they'll let you keep your cottage when he's gone. There's others as could make use of a roof. You need to think about the future lest you end up one of those wantons sleeping in ditches, good for nothing but rogues and thieving. Come now, don't take on. I'm saying this for your own good, girl, because you haven't anyone to guide you.'

'People have been kind. There's been no end of gifts left at our door. You've said so yourself.'

'There was gratitude the boy was found, I'll not deny that, but the hand you had in it was heaped and pooked, if you ask me, out of all measure. That is one way of telling the story and it'll do for the present. What if it goes ill with the boy? Folks might remember then that you've done things and said things that've put fear in the hearts of good people, people who've ever tried to defend you and stand by you. Folks might call you by another name then. Then there'd be an end to any freeness towards you, right enough. You'd be turned out before you could say cock robin.'

She was right, though she herself was the worm in the apple. I could have cursed my own eyes for welling up. I seemed to have taken in weakness with the cold. Fie on her and her counsel, time was I should not have given two peas, but since I had been carried back from dying I seemed to be made of water. I pulled my cloak about me, to wrap myself tight in myself, as I used to do. Then I stared at old Bert. His head was sunk into his shoulders and he creased his eyes against the road and us. A large papery wart grew by his nose. If he turns to me and speaks, or if he helps me down and wishes my father well, I thought, I will make him up some tormentil and dandelion milk, birch-bark and skullcap, and charm it gone. I would I could pick it off and stick it on the Widow. Her face was long and thin and had all the comfort of wet-wrung linen. For all that, she was tall and had once been fair enough. The lines of her bones were strong still; she was like her son in that. Little nut my father used to call me when he still sat me on his knee, little cob. In my dreams my mother wears white, but she was small and dark like me and yet my father loved her.

I turned away from the Widow, rude as I could, but the cart was small and at every turn of the wheel I was slung against her and the jag of pain made me gasp once or twice. It was all she could have wished.

Then I saw Jacob a field away up at the warrens. I forgot myself and called to him. Turn, I thought, turn and look at me and let your mother see it. He looked up sure enough, took us in: the cart with old Bert driving, his mother, the mending, me. But he didn't smile. He just nodded quickly, then studied the grass as he walked towards us, fondling the muzzle of the dog that bounced at his heels. I remembered his visits to Aggie, then. Perhaps they were paddling palms already. I looked at the way he cupped his fingers and tickled the dog beneath its chin. My face burned. His mother saw, of course; she savoured it like honey on her tongue.

'Oh, that's a fine boy,' the Widow said when he had finally done his 'good days' and we were on our way again. 'Our Lord sent him to me, and no mistake. He'd never take a step without my blessing. Mother, he'll say, you brought me up. All alone you did it, and I'm not about to repay you with ingratitude.'

I gazed out where the plough had ripped and scored the earth. One of these days soon I would have to hobble up to the Hall for work. No good cart to lollop in for ever. The Widow wanted rid of me – well and good, I had no love for her – but I had depended on her these last weeks for food and fire. She was right: with father gone the village would brush me off its skirts and turn away. My grandmother's bones were strewn from the churchyard and who else would stir themselves an inch for me? There was only Miss Elizabeth. I looked out across to the east where the road to Gloucester must lie, and tried to summon all my old dreams of flight, but all I could see was a coming cloudbank and a band of thick slant rain.

Bert dropped me off with barely a glance and no word for my father. Let your wart grow all over your face, I thought, thanking him.

When Goody Tranter opened her door, all

smiles, and beckoned me in, I hung back a moment in a dizzy kind of fear. The cottage was dark. There was a fire, but it was pitiful. The flame staggered worse than a weary pedlar. But it wasn't the dark that made my eyes smart, it was the sour smell of sickness.

Ruth Tranter took both of my hands. 'Oh, Martha, you've come,' she said, pulling me gently in. 'I said to your father only yesterday, it'll be today or tomorrow, mark my words. And here you are. He's sleeping now. Come sit down with me – you can help me with the yarn. Can you hear how easy he's breathing? If only the bile would let up. A few hours like this and he'd have his strength coming back.'

She drew up old Ben's chair for me and I sat down beside the thread of a fire while she built it up. Then I held my hands out so that she could wind her wool. She was about the age of the Widow, but as unlike her as honey is sour cider, for her body was soft as cushions and her face was creased with kindness. They had a daughter living – she'd married the miller out at Sollers Hope – but she'd had three other children, two babies and a boy of nine, who'd been lying by the chapel when it was torn and scattered. Nobody knew where they might be now. Perhaps they were among those some said that they'd seen walking in the hours before dawn. If their boy had not drowned he'd have been about my age, or a little older. I remembered him. He was always after water. We'd built dams together on Pentaloe Brook, where it falls along from Canwood Knoll, and we'd swung from a willow bough all across the stream with the water skiffing at our feet. When he died, I remember old Ben had come to my father for a coffin, because Robert was away and there was no one else to make it. His face worked without speaking as they measured at the wood and every now and then he cuffed at his leaking eyes.

With the fire built up the room was not so desolate. Light from the flames played over a basket hung on the wall and the leeks and ham tied to the beam, and threw a glow on us both as we sat drawing on the warmth of it. It seemed natural not to say a word; Ruth smiled at me from time to time, lifting her eyes from the yarn. Her son, my friend, had been called William. It had been easy to like him. There'd been none of the pain my liking for Jacob brought me. If he'd lived perhaps he would have loved me and then she would in time have been my mother, too. I would spend my evenings in the firelight and we'd tell one another stories as we baked good food to eat, and during the day I would walk in Miss Elizabeth's garden, through the rows of box and the roses to the Hall and Miss Elizabeth would say, 'I cannot do without you, Martha, now my eyes are weak.'

A long spasm of a cough jolted me out of silly fancies. Goody Tranter leaned in to me. 'That's him; he must have woken. He's his right self again, has been these last few days. As gentle as a lamb. Seeing you will do him better than any physic.'

She led me to the back of the cottage and drew back the curtain around a bed, pushing me forwards. 'Walter, it's your daughter, it's Martha. Don't mind me,' she added. 'You sit as long as you like. I'll be making oatcakes. I'll bring you some when they're done.'

The pale figure in the bed opened his eyes and roused himself up onto his elbows. I busied myself with the bolster to help him sit up, so I wouldn't have to look. This was not my father. My father was a big-boned man, who could lift a length of oak as if it were a petticoat. Time was, I would place my hand on his just to feel the size and strength of it. The man on the bed seemed made of paper; he patted at my hand as if unsure that it was there. His breath was like the whining of a saw. It came to me that he had crumpled like the hill. Or perhaps I had forgotten how the drink had shrunk him.

I sat down on the bed with his hand between both my own. I had done this to him. It came to me like a blow to the chest. He had wanted me to stay and I had gone. The Widow was right, I was wilful. Whatever I did, wherever I went, my father's ruin would be like a shadow at my shoulder. I cast my gaze down and tried to stop from crying.

He pulled his hand away and waved it in my face. 'Martha, stop that. What good does that do? Why, child, I am not dead yet.' And though he gasped it out, his voice was strong enough and had the old impatience to it. 'Look at me!'

I got down on my knees, wincing at the stretch

it gave my ankle, and looked at him properly. Even in the darkness of the cottage his eyes were my father's eyes, fierce with love and bitterness. 'Forgive me, Father. Bless me,' I said, but my voice came out a wail.

'Away with all that, Martha. Let's not waste time. You're not to blame, you hear me? You're sad now, ready to weep yourself into any kind of guilt, but by and by you'll be angry too. I did this to myself; over years I did it. I know that and you do too. You left to get some wood. You did not know what was coming. I had an idea it was time. For weeks I'd had a sense of it, though it could have been then, or next week, or never, but the skies have fallen down on me before. We are cracked, me and the world both. You survived, girl. You should be glad. I'm glad. I thought they had buried you.'

He paused then and sat staring into a dark corner of the hut. Minutes passed. I turned to look at Ruth Tranter, shaping each oatcake with a swift swivel before tossing it into the pan. Soon the baking smell filled the room and pushed aside the tang of sickness. Still he stayed quiet. A bit of talk had made him weary, but it wasn't only that. This was an old game for me: the silences when he'd be thinking of his other life, the life before we came here. I used to think that if I sat quiet enough and thought hard enough I would be able to see the visions that passed before his eyes, but I never did. Sometimes he would shake himself and smile and return, and sometimes a cold look would gather in his eyes and he would take his coat and leave for the alehouse.

It was a surprise when he finally spoke. 'Do you remember her?' he asked. 'Your mother? You were two years old when... when she was taken from us. Do you recollect her at all? Do you remember how she died?' I glanced sharply at him. He never talked of her death, never. My grandmother had warned me not to ask about it. Some wounds stay raw, she'd said.

'I have a memory of before,' I said. 'I don't know if it's true or if it is a picture I made up. I remember being held and her hair falling around my face and listening to her sing to me. And I remember walking, with my arm stretched up and my hand held firm, near to an unmeasurable stone building. I think it was the Cathedral.

And we turned a corner and the sun splashed golden, and she swooped me up and round and round, and above me all the goblin faces whirled.' And, I thought, I dream about a white bird in a tree and I know I must not speak of that.

He nodded. 'You were born in Gloucester, as you know, in the shadow of the dockyard and the tall-masted ships. It may be we should have stayed there, but after she died I was headlong in the gutter more than I was upright. There was a kind of peace in that. In the gutter you have a choice of prospects: stinking filth or the reachless sky; both offer a satisfying torment. I loved you, child, but I could not see how I could bear to live. Too much of my pity was for myself, of course.

'I have often thought it strange that we came here, to your mother's country, after all that happened. For a long time I thought it must be fate, or the will of God. Your grandmother was here. That was a part of it. But to go back to your mother's story. She was in service and when her mistress married a Gloucester merchant she was taken along too. They were fine people – oh, very fine –

and the mistress wanted Bessie for a pretty lady's maid, for all that she was just a country girl.'

He paused again and I waited, but differently now, because I knew he was telling me a story he had not told before, though I had patched much of it together from the tales my grandmother told. I waited for more.

'The mistress liked Bessie, but the master liked her too. She was never safe from him, not in the kitchen, not in the parlour, not even in his lady's chamber. The mistress saw what was going on and because she could not hate her husband she hated your mother. Bessie was turned out without a penny, the mistress howling her a strumpet in the street. It was not easy for her, friendless like that. I had done work at the house and noticed her then, but scarcely dared to speak. When I found her she was waiting tables at a tavern. I did not drink overmuch then, but I'd had a thirsty morning and stooped in at The Mermaid. There she was, shrugging off a sailor who was grabbing at her like she was so much cloth. She looked at me and knew me and did not look away.

Oh, she was proud, Martha. She could not bear contempt or pity.

'After she was taken, after no hope was left, I think I went mad for a while. Like I said, my soul was blasted with pity for itself. I put you out to a nurse. I worked and then when I had money I haunted the alehouses near the wood yards, till I was dirty and sodden as the sawdust on the floor. Soon there was no work and I had to get money however I could. Sometimes at dawn I came to in the street, ringing out curses to the stars. Even the beggars kicked me as they hobbled by. There came a day, though – it was early, I had barely started drinking – when I... well, I was able to do someone a good turn and that led me here.'

He nodded and glanced up over my head. A figure had come into the cottage and approached the bed. It was Miss Elizabeth.

28

MISS ELIZABETH INTERRUPTS

'Martha, don't curtsy. I doubt your leg will stand it and I came to visit your father. It is good that I did, for he has left out the most important part of the story. I will let him gather his strength while I tell you myself. It is true that he had listened too much to the devil at his left ear, but there was an angel at his right. I believe it was the angel that woke him that morning and led him to that inn so that our paths would cross. No man is so lost but that our Shepherd cannot find him and lead him back to the flock. Many times I have praised God for His mercy in leading your father to the yard that morning, so that he could prove our salvation and we could do what was in our power to raise him.'

I glanced at my father. The suggestion of a smile played at the corners of his mouth. Miss Elizabeth liked the pulpit. Father used to come back from the Hall laughing that she'd have made a fine Doctor of Divinity, if she could only swap her skirts for hose. I did not like to hear him mock her, for it led me to look at her askance, and that interfered with my delight at her favour. But to-day, for the first time in her presence, I found myself nettled. I wished she would get on with the story, now she had seized it.

'We were changing horses in Gloucester,' she went on at last, 'and my mother and I were waiting at the inn while my father saw to some business. I was only a girl then and the parlour where we waited was stifling. The nurse who should have been attending me had business in the jakes; I slipped away to go to see the horses. There was a young Spanish jennet in the yard. Oh, she was a delicate, fine creature, red-brown as our Herefordshire earth, with a white star on her forehead. I came forward to greet her, and she let me place my hand on her neck. It was so warm and alive, thrilling with spirit. I could see the fool of a stable-hand was handling her roughly and I was about to chide him, when she kicked out. The dolt struck her and she went wild. One moment later and the yard was in uproar, carriage horses rearing in their traces, the stable lad knocked into the straw. Heavenly providence was with me that I was not struck. I could see my mother by the gates, screaming for the hands to help me, but no one dared approach. No one except your father. He walked over, bent down among the shying, kicking beasts, picked me up and took me to my mother. Then he went back and took hold of the frightened filly and talked to her gently till he could lead her to a stall. By chance we had lost a carpenter, and my father, seeing he was in dire need, offered him a position on the estate. Two weeks later he appeared at the Hall, with a little girl beside him.'

Miss Elizabeth looked down at me, pleased with her story. My father's eyes were closing. We should be going now, she told Goody Tranter, or we would tire him too much. As I pulled my hand away he pressed my fingers lightly. I did not want to go. I did not want to leave him there in the dark, gathering each breath in so slowly. But Miss Elizabeth guided me away. I felt aggrieved. Why did she have to interrupt us? I glanced back at his face and knew this was not the story he had wanted to tell me. He had wanted to talk to me about my mother and how she died. About the white bird.

Miss Elizabeth smilingly brushed aside the dish of oatcakes Ruth Tranter entreated us to share with her. They smelled so good, I felt giddish at the sight of them. I was about to sit down despite her but she was firm.

'Come, Martha. I think we have intruded on Mother Tranter's goodwill quite enough.' Oh, the pang in my belly at that! At the cottage door Ruth Tranter's voice brought me back to the present.

'Very well, thank you, your ladyship. And young Martha here was saying when she got here how very grateful she was for all your kindness. Weren't you, Martha my dear?'

'Yes, ma'am,' I said.

Miss Elizabeth turned to me graciously. 'There is good in you, Martha. You are like your father –

and your mother, too, I dare say – in that, but in all of you there is something of that wild horse, child, and you will need to be careful. I will do what I can for you, not just more copying, though there is some of that. The schoolroom is the darling of my heart, but there are those who might make it difficult for us to continue. And now Owen. Poor, poor Owen, I had such plans for him. But God is merciful.' She sighed. 'Come to me at the Hall when your ankle is well and we will talk about your future.'

'Miss Elizabeth,' I said, 'I thank you for honouring me with your story today. I did not think it possible to be even further in your debt, but I find I am. I would like to bring my father home, ma'am, if I may, so that I may look after him.'

'Martha, my dear, of course you do, but how will you fare, child? How will you provide for him and for yourself?'

'Miss Elizabeth, ma'am,' Ruth Tranter put in, 'I am very happy to keep him here, but it is natural for the girl to want to tend her father. Perhaps if young Jacob could help with heavy work until her leg is mended...? He has been here near every day to look in on Walter.'

'Jacob?' I was amazed, but I dared not show it.

Miss Elizabeth looked closely at me. 'Of course, his mother, I am sure, asked it of him. She has been most attentive to you, has she not, Martha? I will send over the cart for Walter, if he is well enough tomorrow. Come, child, don't let the cold air blow in. I will give you a ride back.'

Miss Elizabeth stepped lightly into the carriage and waited serenely while I laboured up at the back. I was glad there was only old Bert at the reins to see me hauling my awkward body. No sooner had we rumbled off when Ruth Tranter came out of the cottage, waving at us to stop. My heart went to my mouth at the sight of her flurry, but there was no crisis, only a batch of oatcakes, warm from the griddle, which she thrust into my lap.

29

VIOLETS

My father did not come home the next day, nor the next, and I had word by the Widow that he had been so weak they feared to move him. On the third day, Bert brought me to him, but he did not wake the three hours of my visit. He had grown feverish again and at times he'd fling his head about from side to side, muttering constantly. All I caught of it was mad and wild, and I feared Miss Elizabeth would call again and hear him.

'Go fling your prayers to hell. I say, I'll none of them. What! Is the devil on the bench again? Curse the lot of you. Our true villains wear purple and velvet. Come close, pray you, I've a secret to tell you. It was an angel whispered it in my ear. The priests know it already, those that know Greek, but they are all of them at the trough, and besides, they must have us obedient. Jesus was a liar, the angel said, the meek shall inherit nothing and the rich man belches through grace, for his mutton means more to him than mercy.'

It was good the Tranters had poor ears. When he started on this talk I got down on my knees right away and prayed faster than he could mumble for the Good Lord to forgive him. For a while he'd subside and be quiet, and I'd feel the fever fall again. All the time his fingers trembled between my own, like the wings of a sparrow when you hold it in your hand.

There were a couple of rabbits hanging up at the door. Ruth Tranter saw me glance at them. 'I expect you can guess where they came from. He was here not an hour since and stayed a good while, staring down at your father while he slept, just as though,' she smiled, 'he were looking for a resemblance to someone.'

I felt myself blush, and it was not just the pain

her mistake caused me. Jacob was not deaf; he'd have heard every bit of my father's blasphemies. Please, I thought uselessly, I do not think like my father. I pictured him standing just where I stood, only an hour back. I could almost sense the echo of his spirit in the air, but I had more chance of grasping the light that fell across my hand than sensing what he felt.

'Master Jacob is very kind,' I said at last, and with some effort, 'but you are mistaken if you think it anything but courtesy or his mother's bidding. He is attached to Aggie Simons.'

'Is he so?' Ruth Tranter replied. 'Then I'll say no more on that subject.'

I turned back to my father. He was deep in his dreams and all this surface world was lost to him. What did Jacob want here? Why did he come? All I could think was that the Widow had sent him, to be at the ready for any change, so as to not lose ground in claiming our cottage. He had no wish to see me. That had been clear when I hailed him from the cart on my last visit.

Two days later I came again. My father was no better. Goody Tranter made me up a bed on the floor and plied me with food and pity, so that I could hardly keep from weeping and that grieved me for I knew that half my tears were wicked and for myself. She wanted to call for Father Paul, but I would not believe it was time. I asked her to brew him tea from cherry bark. I gave him feverfew and spoke the charms over him that my grandmother taught me. Perhaps it worked, for in the morning he opened his eyes and smiled and chided me for sitting around by his bedside when I could be working.

'Take me home, Martha,' he said. 'These are good people, but when all's said and done they are not kin, and I don't want to die among strangers.'

'I'll not move you if you talk of dying,' I answered, but I bent myself to persuading Goody Tranter he should go home and by the third strike of the Hall bell we were in the cart.

Bert carried Father to his cot while I lit a lamp, and then he abruptly left. I thought he had gone without our thanking him, but after a minute he returned with a load of wood, which he dumped down by the fire.

'Come by soon,' I said to him, 'if you want to be rid of that wart. I'll charm it off for you.'

'Happen I will,' he said. 'Good night, young Martha. Keep him sat up and make him up some broth. That's better nor all your potions.'

It felt good to be at home, making potage for my father; I could pretend, at least for a little while, that all was as it used to be, or as it should have been. Light from the lamp and the flames flicked and danced around the walls, and I saw something I had not noticed: a pot of violets on the table. But who had placed them there? Was Owen perhaps recovered? They must be near the first of the year. I picked one up and held it against the firelight. Veins threaded the petals, the colour was a cloudless day sliding towards night, a promise of the summer in the spring. But who had brought them? I could not help smiling and smiling, for it had to be Jacob. He had brought me violets: violets, my own flower. Violets that clutch and mat themselves into the earth, even on the rocks and banks that would seem to offer them no purchase. They grow little and dark and then they throw up flowers more delicate than silk, finer than the bluest glass.

I was afraid my father would worsen in the night, but the fever stayed down and in the morning he was still himself. We talked of the Wonder. He knew of what had happened from the Tranters – the horror of the chapel – but he had heard nothing about Owen, that he had been lost and found, or found at least in body.

'But you must go, Martha, if you can walk as far as their cottage. Will you go? It may be you can treat him. You owe him that.'

I was loath to leave my father, but eager to see Owen, and for once I was grateful when the Widow lifted the latch with barely a knock and marched in. I think she had not expected to see my father alert, for she checked her advance when he saluted her.

'Walter,' she said, 'I heard that you were brought back. I have brought some butter, not much, and indeed we can scarcely spare it.'

I thanked her, from my heart, I think, and begged her to drop by again as I was going to visit Owen with the remedy I'd promised Agnes.

'Is that wise,' she said, in a low voice so that my father did not hear, 'after all that's happened between you and them? I mean, I know his mother never gave any credence to the evil talk about the babe, but there's those who say you have not brought that family luck, Martha Dynely, that's all I'm saying.'

I did not want to quarrel. 'I promised Agnes,' I said.

'We're talking of Agnes Simons,' she exclaimed in a loud voice as though my father were an idiot as well as weak. 'Such a sweet, pliant way she has. Not headstrong at all. My Jacob is that taken with her – I don't mind admitting, neighbours, I've got hopes in that quarter. Of course, they're both so young, but no use waiting for grey hairs, say I. It may be Agnes will want you for a bridesmaid, Martha – you were always such friends.' She turned to me again. 'Well, doubtless you'll take no regard of my counsel. I'll send Jacob with the long barrow to fetch you back – he'll be willing enough – any excuse to visit that *particular* house.'

I tried to argue that there was no need, no

need at all, but she insisted. 'There's a change in the weather, girl, lately. Maybe it's the warden meeting that's done it, maybe something else, but you'll be safer coming along with Jacob. You do as I say, now. I made a promise to Miss Elizabeth for you and I'll thank you not to cause trouble.'

I barely heard a word of what she said. I was thinking of the violets. They made me so bold and sentimental, and I reached out and grabbed both her hands. She flinched a little and looked at me in alarm. Perhaps she thought I'd caught some of my father's madness.

'I need to thank you, good neighbour, for sending Jacob round to my father. Ruth Tranter said he'd been near every day and Miss Elizabeth, for she was by, said she was sure you must have sent him, that it was all of a piece with your concern for me.' And to cap it, I leaned forward and pecked her on her chapped cheek, as though I thought it true, and she smiled, endeavouring to make it seem so.

30

AT THE SIMONS' HOUSE

It was barely any distance to the Simons' house. I could have hopped it before the slip, but now I was slow, so slow, lurching from step to step with my twisted foot pushing me always to the left. More crooked than the crooked moon, I thought bitterly, but not so alone. The violets, fragments of the evening sky, filled my thoughts. Warmth tickled me from my belly to my toes. I was beloved. The further I walked, the more the pain in my ankle tugged me down to earth. What had she meant, 'safer'? What new mischief was being put about? It struck me I'd not passed a soul, though it was near dinnertime. Were people lurking behind their windows? A silly, foolish thought. There was Mary Tucker, out in her front garden across the lane, tending to her herbs.

'Good morning to you,' I called as soon as she looked up. 'I am going to visit Owen Simons. I have to thank you for the fine batch of cakes you gave me when I was ill.'

Mary smiled warmly enough, though I fancied her eyes darted up and down the lane. 'You are welcome, Martha. Your father does well, I hope? I am surprised to see you out alone so soon. Your leg still ails you, I see.'

'I am much better, and I have faith he too will mend in time. I must accustom myself to a roll.' I tried to sound light, but my voice betrayed me a little.

Mary darted to her gate and leaned forward. 'Have a care, child. Best not stir about too much at present, unless it is to Mass,' she whispered, glancing around and patting my hand. 'It will pass. Ezekiel and I, we are praying for you and your father.'

With that she scuttled back into her cottage. There was some evil stirred once more about me –

that was evident enough – but I told myself I would not mind it. Jacob had given me violets. My father lived and Owen would get well.

Aggie opened the door almost before I had knocked and plucked me inside faster than my lame leg could manage. But then she hugged me hard.

'So, you have brought your father back? And he is recovering? We heard that you had almost called for the priest. See, Mother, see, Father, here is Martha. She can tell you how miracles happen every day. Her father has pulled through.'

'He is not out of danger yet, Aggie, but please God he grows stronger.' I would have said more, but Ann Simons came running down from the sleeping loft and grabbed me.

'Oh, Martha,' she said, 'how good it is to see you. And have you struggled here on your bad leg? I have prayed for you every day. I have not had chance to thank you, for Owen. Without you we should have lost him. Richard, it is Martha come. We are both so grateful to you, are we not, Richard?'

Richard Simons was standing grave in the

shadows behind the door, watching me without smiling. He came forward and bent towards me. 'My wife tells me that without you and your visions we should have lost our son. Perhaps she is right, although I rather think it is the Lord's mercy we have to thank, is that not so, Martha?'

'It is, Master Simons, and what I saw was sent me in answer to a prayer.'

'And your prayers carry more weight in Heaven than a desperate mother's, an anxious father's, could?'

'No, no,' I began, feeling my leg grow unsteady beneath me.

'Richard, dear husband,' Ann put a hand on his arm, 'Martha has always been a good friend to Owen...'

But Richard put a hand out to bid her be quiet and she closed her lips and looked down with the air of someone used to doing so, though unseen she took my hand and squeezed it.

He did not take his eyes off mine. 'I walked the fields back and forth for hours for my son, for a sign of him, with the snow blowing in my eyes and the wind mocking me with its whining. And

God's house torn up and the dead mangled where they slept. So, no more talk of visions, girl.' He seemed to smile and tapped me on the shoulder as if he was done and he half turned away, but then he whipped back and said with a slow deliberateness that frightened me, 'But what I should like to know is, why was my son out in the fields at that hour with you? What did you want with him at that hour of the night?'

'I was not out with him, Master Richard, I was gathering cherry bark for my father and – and stealing wood, too, truth be told, and I came across Owen. He had been tumbled from his bed by the earth's shivering and he'd run out afraid. I swear it by all the saints.'

'And we believe you, Martha,' Ann put in, though not without an anxious glance at her husband. 'Richard, dearest husband, the poor girl speaks the truth. Come and sit down, Martha. It will do Owen good to see you. He always has loved you like a sister.'

'Better,' put in Agnes.

All at once Richard Simons seemed to soften a little. 'I am sorry if I have been harsh, Martha. I scarcely know what to think, the whole world is so out of joint. I found my boy but I have lost him all the same. I'll say good day to you all. I have business to attend to.'

'Don't mind him, don't mind him,' his wife said as soon as the door closed. 'He has aged twenty years this last month. He cannot bear to look at Owen any more, or when he does it seems more in anger than in love.' She turned to the loft stairs but did not at first go up, just stood there, and patted her hands, rubbing the skin of her knuckles back and forth, back and forth. Presently she turned and gave me a quick sad smile. 'Owen has much changed, Martha. He barely eats. It's like his whole body is shrinking into his eyes.'

Owen was huddled in a long cot with his head near the window. At first, in the dusty light, I thought he must be sleeping, but as we drew nearer I saw that his eyes were open. I couldn't help but gasp at the sight of him. He barely looked like a child any more, for his skin was papery and flaking on his face and his lips so pale his mouth looked like a wound. He did not seem to notice us at all and I wondered if he was blind as well as dumb. His mother bent down to him and stroked his thin pale hair, then found his hand and pressed it.

'Owen, here's Martha come to see you.' She smiled at me and gestured me forward, but for a moment I was locked in sorrow at the sight of him, and couldn't move. Oh, Owen, I thought, oh, my beautiful boy. I don't know what I had imagined, but not this staring shadow.

He'd not responded, either to his mother's touch or to my name. From behind, Agnes nudged me forward.

'Go on,' she said. 'He's better when people go up close. At least that's what Mother says; he's made no sign for me.'

'Ssh, Agnes. It is true,' Ann Simons put in, 'you have good hours, don't you, Owen love, when the world comes into focus. He's just gone in so deep, Martha, he can't seem to find a way out, is all. But he can hear and he can see, I know it. He's still there, aren't you, my boy? You will help us find him, Martha, I know it.' For the first time her voice was not steady. 'Agnes, come down and help me. You'll sit with him a while, won't you, dear? He can't be doing with too many people at once.'

I nodded, and ducked forward to the bed. Behind me Agnes was muttering to her mother. 'I know that, but what if Father should come back... he made me promise... not alone with him.' Then Ann Simons was gone and only Agnes remained.

I threw Agnes a look and she giggled awkwardly. 'I'm sorry, I can't go against my father. You can understand that, Martha, can't you? I know you wouldn't do anything to hurt him. Poor Owen,' she looked across me to where he was still staring straight ahead. 'I don't believe there's anything anyone could do to make things worse, in any case. Mother declares he looks right at her sometimes as though he is about to speak. Or at least he did. The last couple of days, though... Look at him, he seems barely alive at all.' Her voice slid into a wail and she slumped down on the floor beside the bed. 'I've not got any tears left, Martha. It's worse than a death.'

I sat myself on the cot and reached for the hand his mother had held. It was thin and small in mine and lay limp as though he were sleeping.

'You must not talk so, Agnes, not with him by and listening.'

Did I feel his fingers stirring when I spoke, just a little, just a little? I pressed his hand against my chest where my heart was beating.

'Owen, it's Martha,' I said, with my head bent down to his face so that my mouth was at his ear. 'It's Martha. Owen, come back to us. Owen, I'm calling you. The hill fell on you, all the earth fell down on you and it carried you with it and you thought you were in the grave and it was so cold and so lonely, and the clay is so bitter and sticky in your mouth, and the ewes pressing into you so you could hardly breathe, and each time you woke the screaming earth was in your ears and the hot quick heartbeat of the ewe so heavy you thought it would crush the breath from your body, and all you could see was the striped slit eye of the sheep that panicked and clouded and was dead staring back at you, and then there was just the greasy wool and the weight against you, and the cold and death coming, but it didn't come, Owen, it was your father and Jacob that came – I sent him, Owen – and he lifted you out and lifted you up. Come up, Owen, the dead are in the earth and you are here. Come back, Owen, listen to my heart, yours is beating too, it's beating.'

It seemed for hours that I spoke like this, without pausing, with my head down by his ear, and I could feel him listening. I could feel the words begin to flow around his body as though they were looking for the place he kept his name. And over and over I said a finding charm and called on God to aid him.

When at last I lifted my head there was Agnes, drop-jawed, staring at me. 'Go,' I said, before she could speak. 'I think he should have light and flame, if you have candles enough. It will help him find his way.'

She nodded and came back with a lit stub and her mother. I took the flame and gestured to them to be soft, for any knock would send his soul reeling back towards all its horrors. In the candle-light we sat and stroked his hair and his shoulders and called him and we felt him slowly coming back.

He looked right at me and then at his mother and back again and we felt he was gathering his breath, as though trying to remember how to speak.

But then the door downstairs opened and the house was all loud boots and men's voices. Ann rose and put her finger to her lips. She'd not got down the ladder before her husband was calling for her.

'Ale, wife, and bread for my friends. Has the cripple gone? I'm glad of it. She's nothing to us, and we owe her nothing. Do you hear me, Ann? Nothing. I don't want her in my house, d'you hear me? What? Less of that, Ann.'

'I said nothing, Richard, please.'

'Your silence is as bad. It defies me as loud as shouting. Get that look from your eyes, judging me all the time, judging. I will not have it. God damn you, woman, you will do as I say,' and something was shoved back hard against wood.

Agnes squeezed my arm and flew down the ladder. 'Father, you forget your friends. Come, Father, shall I bring the ale? Owen is looking so much better – will you see him?'

'Not now, not now,' Richard Simons replied,

his voice no longer dangerous. 'At least there's one female knows how to be useful in this house.'

I looked back at Owen. He had slipped back. There was some focus in his eyes still, but it was going like a dream that's not held onto quick. 'Please,' I said, bending my head down low to his, 'don't go, Owen. Stay, come back. I'll save you yet, I promise, out of this house too. We'll live by the Cathedral and eat pies every day for our dinner.' But he was gone again.

I did not know what to do. I needed to get back to my father, but knew I could not be seen. In my pocket was the monkshood mixture. I mixed it to a paste with water from Owen's cup and dabbed it on his lips. Perhaps I would get a chance to give Ann the rest and explain it, too. The bitterness made him cough a little.

'What are you doing?' I had not seen Agnes come up behind me.

'I have given him the preparation I talked of. I have more. Agnes, I can tell you what to do.'

'You should not have, not without us by and without asking. Father does not want you here in the house. He'll go wild if he thinks you've been doctoring.'

'Your father!' I burst out, then hung my head, for she'd started back at my tone. 'Please, Agnes, you saw how Owen was coming back; you saw I was doing him good.'

'You were whispering so strangely, Martha, it was like someone was speaking through you. You frightened me a little. Sometimes you feel as familiar as kin, and sometimes I am not sure I know you at all.'

'Your mother trusts me.'

'And my father doesn't.'

I was about to reply, when I caught my own name among the men downstairs.

'She's Bessie Gould's daughter, right enough. There's something more than natural in her, with her reading and her potions, but I still say she en't no witch. Didn't she help you find the boy?'

I looked back to Agnes; my face must have been a picture of fright, for she let go of her stiffness and sat down beside me and took my hand. Next to us Owen had assumed his glassy-eyed stare, but his tongue softly ran over his lips. I felt

sure he heard every word spoken. The talk
went on.

'I'll give you that she had no business being
out. Her being out at that hour is against her, and
with your boy, too. But the Lord alone knows what
goes on in that cottage of their'n with her crazy
father...'

'He was two sheets to the wind before all this.'

'Could 'a' done with a sheet – or a shirt, come
to that – last I saw on him.'

'You know what some folks have been saying,'
put in another voice. 'That it's not to do with the
girl at all, but on account of the stripping of the
altars. Why else would the chapel be tore down?'

'Tom the mill better be careful who he farts
his thoughts at. It's as like to be the other way
around, with the smells and bells we got round
here. Father Paul said it's our idolatry that we
cared more for carvings than the Word of the
Lord.'

'Father Paul's the bishop's man. The bishop's
got his eye on Sir William. He'd happily bring
him down. Being a gentleman won't protect him if
he's been hiding priests.'

'It'll be the worse for us all if aught happens to Sir William. God forgive me but the bishop's a bastard. He'd happily see us all starve if he gets Sir William's lands.'

'You be careful where you talk like that.'

'We're friends here, aren't we? The whole county knows it to be true.'

'True ain't got nothing to do with it.'

'It was a year ago almost to the very day of the Wonder that the Pope in Rome excommunicated the Queen. Damned her he did. A year ago nearly to the very day he did it.'

'God save the Queen and the Jenny Wren. Why would our hill take a tumble at the hest of the Bishop of Rome? And why take a whole year about it?'

'It's the dead that frightens me. Every night my mother has come into my dreams. She was ripped out of where she lay and now she can't settle. How many were in that graveyard? A hundred? More? Strewn all about the place now. The Lord would never tear His own house down. It's the devil's work. That's the only certain sure thing.'

'You're right, Sam,' Richard Simons' voice

broke in again, 'the chapel is gone and the graves are gone and my boy is bewitched. Our own earth is infected with devilry – there's nowhere safe to tread. The hill broke open like a foul sore. Some nights I think I hear the chapel bell ring.'

'My Mary's heard it, too.'

'What did your boy see that's struck him dumb? What did that girl do to him? I tell you, Richard, the Good Lord is talking through that bell. He's saying we've got to rip out the source of the demons.'

'We must all pray on our knees for Christ's mercy.'

'I've prayed till my knees are stiff, I tell you. The dead need more than prayers to help them sleep.'

I sat there listening while the candle danced around the roof beams and played over Owen's still face. His eyes were open and black. They seemed sightless, but had they turned, just a little, towards me? I felt a pain in my chest that seemed part fear and part weeping, though I did not cry. Agnes put her arm around me.

'I'm sorry, Martha,' she whispered, 'for what I

said. I do believe in you, truly. You can have faith in me. Didn't I put violets in your cottage to welcome you home?'

'It was you?' I said. 'You placed the violets, Agnes?'

'Yes, silly, who else? Don't cry, I liked to do it. Now you must go. If I help you, you can wriggle out of Owen's window and slide down. I'll run down and whistle. When I do, you let go and I'll catch you.'

How we managed it I don't know, with me half in, half out of the window, afraid any minute Richard Simons would take it upon himself to climb upstairs as I waited for her to come below. A fine sight I must have been for any coming across the fields. I couldn't help smiling despite it all.

Then the whistle came and I let go, not daring to look, for I knew she would not catch me well. But the arms I fell into were strong and held me safe, and didn't hardly stagger. Not Agnes, but Jacob, come with the barrow.

Agnes was grinning. 'Look who I found loitering in the lane, all ready to rescue you again.' She pushed him playfully and the puzzle on his face broke into a smile. Oh, I felt so wretched and stupid at that moment. That I'd thought he'd gather me flowers! They two were hale and beautiful. The violets were for kindness and pity, not for love.

31

THE WATER CALLS

I would not ride in any barrow. I limped beside Jacob as we walked back, struggling to keep pace, for I knew he would be needed back at the warrens. Once or twice I nearly stumbled, and my bent foot ached in the bone, but I did not let it show. For his part he grew silent after we left Agnes. We walked on through the mud, with the spring sun leaking through the cloud.

At length, he stopped abruptly and regarded me, head thrown back. 'You think I can't see? Every step and your mouth is tight with pain, but you won't ride. You are the proudest creature alive.

No stooping, never, not to the likes of us. The Queen herself couldn't hold her nose higher.'

'What do you mean? It does me good to walk, is all. I'm grateful to you and to Aggie, both of you together,' my voice began to wobble so I made it harder. 'What do you want me to do, grovel? I will if you wish it. I'll down in the dirt on my knees. Is that it?' As soon as the words were out I regretted them. 'No, no, I didn't mean that, that's not what I meant at all. I'm sorry, Jacob. I'm thankful for all you have done for me, and for Father, truly. As soon as I am able I shall tell Miss Elizabeth how good you have been to us.'

I was never good at mollifying; he turned away with an oath as I spoke. For a moment he stood with his back to me, his fists all balled up. I did not know, I could not fathom what I had done. Always this seemed to happen. Yet people said he was steady. Steady Jacob, no surprises, true as oak, but to me he was as flighty as a fairy clock seed, when they lift on the breeze for the children to snatch and wish on. I could not catch hold of him at all. And I was so tired. My eyes welled up.

'Please,' I said to his back, 'please, Jacob, I don't mean to provoke. I'll get in the barrow. What would you have me do?'

'It's not safe, Martha,' he said, turning back, all brisk and steady once again, 'the way the talk is turning. Is there someone you could stay with awhile? Your mother's family at Moccas?'

'No. There's no one. And I cannot move my father. It would kill him. But you are wrong, Jacob. Things cannot have turned so quickly. Only a week ago folks were leaving presents at my door. And anyhow, Miss Elizabeth loves me; no one would dare move against me or my father. This will pass. In a week or so, when Father is recovered, I will open the school again. I'll just be the lame girl who is good with herbs.'

It was not a comforting picture. I would become a hobbling spinster, pounding village boys with letters, crooked as the tinker woman I glimpsed the day I threw Jacob from the class. I gazed at my future, full of pity, till Jacob yanked me back by the arm.

'Stop it, Martha. Can't you see? You won't open

the school again, not ever. Not ever, do you hear me? The hillside fell on top of you and you crawled out, but the earth hasn't settled. There are those who'll pull it down around your ears and bury you again.'

'Miss Elizabeth promised to protect me, Jacob. She and her father. No one would dare lift a finger against us.'

'Miss Elizabeth!' The mockery in his voice surprised me. 'Miss Elizabeth, who puts on her gloves before she talks to you! You don't know much, Martha, for all your reading.'

'She values me,' I said, stung, 'and she has an obligation to my father. You wouldn't understand.'

'Oh, wouldn't I? Well, so be it. Damn you and your pride both.' He looked at me a long while and said nothing, so that I became awkward. When he spoke his voice was different. 'I want to help you, Martha – you cannot guess how much – but even I, sometimes...'

'Sometimes? What do you mean, sometimes what?'

'I'm not lettered like you, Martha, but I'm not a

fool. It's dangerous to dabble in things you can't rightly control. No, don't turn up your nose and snort. It's gone past time for that. There is something stirring, you can't deny it. Breathe it, go on, the air is full of it.'

'It's just the spring is all.'

'The spring, is it? If it is, the spring is cankered. There's a worm in it. Listen,' he leaned forward and lowered his voice, though there was not a soul by, 'I don't believe you're a witch, or not on purpose. But any fool can see that you have gifts. I fear you may have awoken something; that you won't be able to rein it in, that perhaps you didn't even know you had a hand in it.'

He stretched out his palms as though he were handing me the matter; as though it were a bundle of clouts. As though I were a washer-woman, like his mother, who could scrub them clean. I frowned down at the rough strong hands that had caught me and held me so that for a moment the world seemed safe and simple. There was a white scar on his right thumb just above the knuckle, shiny and smooth and white like a dove's wing. Like silk, it would feel, next to that rough skin. And suddenly the pale golden light was gone and there was only cloud and a fine rain. It struck me he was right, there was a devil whispering through my flesh. Didn't the light itself flee from my thinking? I *had* awoken something. 'What art thou, Martha Dynely?' he had asked me once. I had no idea who or what I was, not any more.

I remembered how I had stood in the chapel and picked out words from the Holy Book. *Cover us, and to the hills, Fall upon us.* And the hills had fallen and Owen had been hurt. If it was a prayer it had been answered. Who had answered it? And now, even now, when Jacob spoke to me of danger I could not listen, for the thought of his calloused fingers on my lips and the small white scar.

'Jacob,' I said, 'don't doubt me, I would not do anything that's forbidden.' I stretched out my hands and pressed his lightly, and I tried to smile away the puzzle in his face, but I had to drop my head for fear my eyes would talk too plainly. We started on again in silence.

'Well, God be with you, Martha,' he said as we

neared the cottage, and his voice was sad. 'My good wishes to your father.' He waited while I raised my head, then gave a short nod and left. I limped off to my door. Somebody had left a message – a bundle of rowan. Witchbane. I kicked it aside and looked up and down the lane. Jacob was striding towards the Hall, his hands stuffed in the pockets of his breeches. There was no one else around. Cowards. No doubt it was the same folk who only days ago had left me gifts.

The Widow, God be thanked, had gone back home, and my father was sleeping, his breathing steady, if shallow. He had eaten (or the Widow had eaten) the porridge I had left for him. A swimming in my head recalled to me that I had not had a bite since yesterday, but I was too much in a whirl for eating. I sat down on the cot next to him and waited for my thoughts to stop their eddies. There was talk against me, but it was just talk, surely. It would die down once people felt the fields quickening and the darkness and the fear shrinking back into the earth. Owen was worse than I had feared or imagined. It would not be easy to see him. But all the better part of me was

with him... with him and my father. I would bring
Owen back and we would be as we were before,
and no school would ever part us. Then I remem-
bered the men at the Simons' house, and Richard
Simons' anger. And Jacob. He was in love with
Aggie and she with him – it couldn't be otherwise.
Both had looked at me bewildered. If even they
could not trust me...?

Perhaps they had reason. I did not know any
longer. I looked into the last weeks and months
and they drifted from me like the mist. What had
I done? What might be working through me? I
considered how my blood rebelled against me; it
burned. It whispered of deeds a maid should not
think of. I had come out from the earth twisted. I
had called up havoc and set it loose.

I rocked to and fro on the bed and the panic in
me clutched and tightened, but I could not weep.
When I tried to stand, the walls of the cottage
reeled. Even my father's face I could not see
clearly. I bent my head to the blanket and stuffed
my mouth with wool to keep from shaking. Please,
God, I prayed, please, God, bring me back to
righteousness. And the prayer steadied me till I

could raise my head and look about me once again.

My father's breaths began to sigh and knock. I remembered how, when I was a little girl, we would sit and listen to the storm wind straining through the door and he would smile and hold my hand and I felt safe. And now his chest heaved and he sighed with the weight of the gale pushing at him.

Was I damned? Was it my wishing that had wrenched the earth apart and brought down the horizons? But then there was my vision of Owen – that had done good, at least. Maybe that was a last flicker of God's grace before the spirits blew it from my soul for ever. My deformity affirmed it. A terrible blackness opened up before me and I forced myself to look. You ripped the hole, the blackness said. You let out demons; your father lay down in it and it made him mad. He is dying. Why is he dying, why is Owen dying and not you?

It all became clear. My eyes were opened. When I swallowed the flung dirt that day before the chapel, I had bargained away my soul. It was thick with filth. I had not died on the hill because filth cannot kill itself. With each breath now I smelled it, dank and rotten on my skin. I patted my hair, expecting a slick of clay on my fingers. How could I limp through life with hell already in my soul, bringing dirt and ruin and pollution? I was a stain on the earth and in God's eye. My death would be a cleansing, that my father and Owen might live.

The river was in flood. It was not so very far away if I found a cart to carry me. The current would take my skirts and whirl me under and then pound and pummel all the dirt away. Nothing left but a bubble rising to the surface of the water, breaking into air. I hauled myself up. My head was light; I saw everything with a terrible clarity. I think I would have gone then, but my moving had woken my father.

His voice broke into my reverie. 'So, Martha, how was he – how was Owen? How did old Richard Simons thank you for the finding of his son?' His voice was gentle.

It was with difficulty that I returned to the moment, and I looked down with pity at this father I had ruined. He would grieve for me but he would get well. It surprised me how easy and smooth the lies came. 'Owen is poorly, but he's mending, Father. He almost spoke, I think. And the whole family greeted me warmly.'

'And so they should, girl. They're an ignorant lot, every last one of them, but they won't forget what you've done. Even if they talk of your father as broken and mad.'

'No, Father, there's goodwill towards you. Folks know the fit has gone now, that you were wild with worry. I've had no end of gifts left at our door.'

He smiled with real contentment and patted my hand. 'Bessie will be proud,' he said.

'Father,' I said, leaning close, 'when Miss Elizabeth visited you last week and told me how you saved her, you had begun to tell me another story.'

But he had drifted off back to sleep. If he woke and told me, I thought, it would show me how to take my mother's hand to join her. I did my work around the cottage. My ankle did not pain me for I glided above the earth.

Death stood at my shoulder. He was a fine

gentleman; Jacob was a rustic beside him. His breath smelled of water. Don't be afraid, he said, she sent me. When evening fell he sank into the gurgle in my father's chest and he was the river that called to me and sang that my mother was waiting in the moon, that she would set me free.

32

PENTALOE WELL

It seemed to me that I should lie down and sleep. In the thick of the night a song wove itself into my dreams. 'Maiden in the moor lay,' it sang, and sometimes the voice was mine and sometimes it was hers, my mother's. 'In the moor lay, seven nights full, seven nights full and a day.' It was so very peaceful lying on the moor, where the soft grass brushed my face like a fall of hair and the moon looked down and sang to me.

Good was her meat
What was her meat?
The primrose and the

The primrose and the
Good was her meat
What was her meat?
The primrose and the violet.

When I woke the vision remained with me, more real than the wood of my cot or my father's jagged gasping. I knew the place, too. It was the slope by Pentaloe Well, where the open land fell down to deep pools that never dried, even in years when the clay was baked to dust and the brooks sank into the earth. We used to find pretty pebbles and throw them in, presents for the fairy of the well. They would flick and spin through the air, but once in the water it was as though they had fallen into a dream and they drifted slowly down.

I did not pause to reason, for I had none. My father's forehead felt clammy to my lips, but I closed the door without a glance, because the water would make him well. I set off across the Goosefoot, and sometimes I rose above the grass and every step was a sloughing off of pain until my ankle tugged me down again. There was the moon, cold and shining. I heard my own voice singing high and quiet,

> Good was her meat
> What was her meat?
> The primrose and the violet.

If my ankle did not pin me to the wet clay I knew I should rise and spin with the moon. They thought they could fasten me to the earth, but she knew another way. She was waiting for me in the water.

'I am coming, Mother,' I said, and even as I reached the track there was a cart. I stood before it and its old nag near reared in alarm. A man was sitting in front, idly whistling, all gathered up in a shawl.

At the sight of me he yelped, 'By the Lord Jesus, what are you, starting up out of the hedge like that? If there's more of you, come forth. I'll face the lot of you, devil or rogue. I've no money anyhow, I tell you.'

The moonlight fell on his bony old face and picked out his eyes. He shrank back into his seat as though he could wish himself wood. Try as I might I could not speak. My mouth fell open in a grin, and I spread my arms wide. I drank the moonlight in. He suspected me of friendship with the moon, but he did not know my feet hovered above the earth. The thought made me giggle. I was more empty than the air. I threw my head back and laughed at emptiness and the moon, and the cart that would take me, and the foolish man who clutched at the reins and tried to urge the horse on. I had hold of the bridle and I put it in my teeth to bite back my wide, wide smile at the silly man. He kept repeating the Lord's Prayer, over and over. I pushed my head into the horse's flank to steady myself, then I clambered up beside him. He didn't try to stop me.

'I know what you are,' he said. 'I heard the talk, over at Little Marcle. You're the girl who bought your life back with a boy's soul. You leave me alone. I'll have none of you, you hear?'

What use had I with words? I pointed over the hill where the stars were dancing. Staring, terrified, he nodded.

He didn't let off his mumbling, nor take his

eyes off me neither, unless it was to glance nervously behind us. More than once I thought I heard a pebble roll or the suck of a boot in mud, but the track was empty. As if any would trouble to follow us, or keep it a secret if they did. As if any could hinder the moon!

It took so long through the Nighbrooks I panicked I had lost her. The woods covered over us completely. The track was barely a glimmer in the dark. I floated above the cart, watching this old man who flinched each time the girl at his side moved. He had a knife in his belt. His fingers crept to it now and again, and I wondered if he might suddenly stab her. It would not matter, only she had to find the moon in Pentaloe Well and it would not wait for ever. When the light silvered the trees and fell on the old man's face, it was wet with tears. Again, he darted a quick glance back. Something was following. A dog, or a fox; a demon?

There where the road curved round before it dropped, a crack of darkness opened in the trees. The moment I got down he whipped the old nag up into a trot. It would be dawn soon. The moon held on for me, but she was growing pale and sinking. As I toiled up the path I could not quite remember what I was doing here. All my giddy lightness was gone, but where had it gone? I remembered I was going to find my mother. The song came back to me.

> Well was her drink
> What was her drink?
> The cold water of the
> The cold water of the
> Well was her drink
> What was her drink?
> The cold water of the well spring.

There was the well with its two pools, and there on the dark water, the moon. I sobbed to see her. After all, after so long, she was true to me; she was waiting! There was the willow we had used to swing from, jutting out to where the water was so deep it did not end. I leaned along the trunk and let myself fall into the moon.

33

THE RED ROSE AND THE LILY FLOWER

The moon scattered and slid off, leaving black water. I lay and floated in darkness, till my gown grew heavy and pulled me down into the weeds, and they parted gently for me and softly noosed my arms and feet and drew me under. The water closed over my face, the chill, chill water in my eyes and mouth. It woke me.

What was I doing here? How could I have left my father? If I died I would be damned. The cold licked me, told my skin it was alive. I did not want to die; I could hold my breath no longer; my chest was full, tight; I must breathe. I thrashed and kicked, but the weeds knotted me in. All the world was blackness and ropes. And shouting. I began to swallow, kicking into the bank. I reached my arms up. Something, someone, grasped my wrist.

He had followed me from my door, he said, staying a little way behind. Each time the tinker had glanced back he'd thought himself seen, but the shadows had held him. Then when I turned to the pools he'd missed the path I'd taken and had come aslant, looking down from the slope to see a figure on the willow tree drop like a leaf into the water.

'What were you doing, Martha? Are you gone mad like your father?'

I wanted to answer him, but when the coughing stopped the world tilted strangely, and though I was lying still on the grass where he'd lain me down I was afraid I might slide off. I didn't want to, so I fixed my eyes on the fading stars and on his face as he crouched above me, rubbing at my hands and feet.

'You are too cold,' he said. 'Were you trialling if it's true, what people are saying about you? A witch can't drown, can she – was it that?'

For a while his face kept dissolving and

coming together again. I worked very hard to keep it there before me. 'Jacob,' I said, and lifted my hand to touch his beautiful face to see if it was real.

'You are too cold,' he said again. 'Can you take your gown off? You can have my cloak.' His words did not feel real. Only his face was real, his face and his hands. When I made no move, he began to unbutton me, but he turned away his eyes and I could not see them.

A voice began singing, soft and clear.

Well was her bower
What was her bower
The red rose and the
The red rose and the
Well her bower
What was her bower
The red rose and the lily flower.

It was a fairy voice, I thought, and then I realised it was my own. As long as I sing, I thought, he will not go away. The moon had gone and I was on the earth and my skin glimmered.

'You are too cold,' he kept saying, and he took off his own shirt and lay down with his chest against mine and wrapped us both under the cloak while the light grew around him. All the time his hands stroked my bare arms and then my belly and then my breasts; it was as though he were pressing my soul back into my flesh. And I took his face between my hands and turned it to look at mine, and before he could speak I drew him to me and I kissed him, and he was warm, so warm. He hesitated for a second, only a second. I drew my hands across his back, his buttocks, the warm place between his thighs and then I drew him into me and it was like a knife, but oh, how sharp and good and real.

* * *

The birds woke me. For a moment I lay conscious only of the pale sun, of lying safe between the earth and Jacob's sleeping body. Then I heard voices somewhere down below us. He must have heard them too, for he sprang up and began dragging on his clothes. When he looked at me his face was full of shock and confusion. I sat up, but I could not think what to say. I knew what we had done. A soreness as I moved reminded me. There would be blood on his cloak. I had been pulled from one mortal sin into another, but I could not find it in me to be sorry. I had let go of the lonely moon for the rich soil beneath my fingernails. I had felt him and the stars within me and I knew that I belonged.

'Jacob,' I said, 'it was not your fault. I made you do it, when I sang. You had no choice.' I don't know why I said this. Perhaps it was the shame in his face – I could not bear it – or perhaps it was true.

In any case, his expression hardened. 'You will have to put your wet things back on. We must not go back together. I'll walk round by Woolhope. There should be a cart on the track. Your father will be needing you.' He turned his back as I dressed and when I was done I stood there staring at his back, awkward.

'Thank you,' I said. 'For pulling me out of the water,' I added, and I felt my cheeks turn red. The horizon reeled a little, but I knew it to be hunger, not lunacy. 'Jacob, have you a little bread you could give me?'

He turned then and rummaged through his bag for a piece of bread. Our fingers touched as he handed it to me; it was like the sting of a wasp. 'Promise me that you will not try to harm yourself again, Martha. Whatever your trials may be, it is against all holy law,' he said, not meeting my eyes, not taking his hand away either.

'Do you trust me, Jacob?' I asked. The bread and the touch made me bold.

He looked at me then. 'No. I don't know – I cannot believe you have given yourself over to evil; you unsettle me. That's the truth of it, Martha, you make me – I don't know what it is – but when you are by I feel a wildness... Were you in earnest, that you made me make love to you? It was very like a dream. I don't know. I cannot trust you. I barely trust myself any more.'

I stepped up to him and kissed his lips until I felt his rough tongue on my own.

'I made you,' I said, and walked back down the path to the track.

34

TWO DEATHS

I sat on the side of the lane and threaded flowers in my hair, wood anemones and stitchwort, until I saw a cart come rumbling up.

'Decked out for the May already, are you, wench?' the man said. 'Off to see your sweetheart? Come on up then.'

He didn't notice my clothes, and happily for me soon fell to talking of himself. He was a barrel maker come to bring barrels to the Court at Little Marcle. Lived over at Sufton, he did, twenty years now and no better place on earth, got two fine sons coming up and the eldest could taper a stave better nor any man in the county, though he said it himself. No end of coopering work these last years, though the price of oak was shameful and Bishop John to blame. He was sorry to talk so of one of the cloth to a maid, but it had to be said. John Scory was a scoundrel and would sell the last oak in the diocese to increase his son's portion. Hadn't he sold off Bear's Wood, which had always been for Sufton folk...?

We were nearly at my door when a fine black horse came up with Father Paul upon it. He reined in at the sight of us and I bobbed him a curtsy as well as I could. The cooper hailed him, 'How be, Father? Fine morning, thank the Lord.'

Father Paul looked past him as though he were not there. I could feel his eyes locked on the flowers in my hair. One by one, I thought, they will wilt and die under that gaze.

'I do not wonder you are too ashamed to face me, wanton, decked out like a strumpet, with your father dying in his own filth and the poor boy a dumb idiot. You can't fool heaven with flowers, Martha. Sin smells rank as any midden.'

I felt my eyes drawn up to his face.

'That's right,' he said, 'you cannot hide from your God. Confess. It may not be too late. God is merciful.'

A great trembling took hold of me and the cooper glanced in puzzlement from one to the other and back again.

'Why,' he said, 'she's soaked through. Whatever have you been up to, child?'

But I could no more have answered him than flown away. Was it written on my face what I had done last night? Was that what the Father's eyes were searching out? What would happen if I laid it all before him? That against God's law I had sought to destroy myself and then seduced my rescuer? It might have been a demon usurped my mother's spirit to tempt me to self-slaughter, I could believe it. But after? Had the devil had a hand in that? I'd almost said as much to Jacob. But I did not believe it; it had not felt like devilry. When I kissed him, it had felt like coming home. Despair was the greater sin and I had vanquished it. It was a good thing to be alive. Tears of relief welled up.

Father Paul was nodding, leaning from the saddle towards me. 'Yes, weep. That is the Lord working. Open yourself to Him.'

Yes, I thought, looking back at Father Paul, I have opened my soul. I have been restored. If my heart was truly black as he said, how was it that I felt so light? As if I were made of petals. I breathed in the scent of earth and flowers and it did not feel like shame. Last night I had been mad, but I was not mad now. I felt a vacancy where all my repentance ought to be. But then the cooper got down and came over to where I sat. Before I knew it he was bundling me off the wagon.

'I'm sorry, Father,' he said, 'but confessing will have to wait. This child is not well. To think I've been pattering on for goodness knows how long and her not said a word, and I'd not noticed she was dripping. What would my Lucy say? This your cottage, is it? In you go, then. That's right. No, don't thank me. I've a soul needs saving as much as you.'

'You're an impudent fellow,' I heard Father Paul saying behind me as I leaned against the door in the darkness of our cottage. 'How dare you interfere? Still, it is of little matter, she can wait. Good day to you.'

The room smelled of shit and of fever. I put on dry things, then cleaned my father up as best I could. I moistened his mouth, but he slept on, every now and then muttering or shaking his clammy head. Then I took the dirty things and hobbled out to try if the stream could scour them. If anyone meant me ill they could find me at home easy enough. I would not stay a prisoner.

I scrubbed at the cloth in the water and thought how I had believed myself polluted and had longed to plunge into water and be drowned clean. I still felt strange, but the demon that had whispered of the moon was gone. Father Paul wished me to confess. But to confess what? I looked down at my hands through the clear water, I pounded the cloth and mud billowed around it, and I took a handful of grit and rubbed the foulness off. I let the shift spool out on the current then, like a shroud or a fresh kirtle; it was all one. And I thought about the way the clear water cleaved a way through the mud and grit, and the grit rubbed off the dirt it was a part of, and all things rolled into and away from earth and were never pure, but could be clear and fresh.

The slap of a cloak on the water beside me yanked me out of my musings. It was the Widow, and close enough to spray my side with her laundering, as well she knew.

'There's not many would sit down next to you, girl, as things stand, but I've never been one to follow the crowd or to see evil till it pokes me in the eye. How is your father?' She eyed me closely. I blushed, for I remembered the flowers in my hair and why I had threaded them there.

'You might be brown as a beechnut, but there's something colouring you up. What is it? You've no business garlanding yourself up with trash from the verges. At a time like this, with your father near to drawing his last breath on God's earth. Oh, the shame of it, Martha. Some gypsy from the camp by the Noggin, is it?'

I said nothing. For half a minute I said nothing, but I could not bear the pursing of her lips. 'I have not been with any gypsy, Widow Spicer, but I thank you kindly, for I would rather be thought a wanton than a witch.'

'You won't be laughing in the stocks, my girl. And you'll be lucky if it's only the stocks that pin you. That poor lad is nothing but a warm corpse in his father's house – there's many would like to know how you had a hand in that. Coming so soon after the baby's death, too. If you had any idea how often I've had to stop folks going to the law. Richard Simons would have had you in irons ere now if he wasn't persuaded he could make you unwitch the poor boy. Your kind aren't good for a place. As a friend I'm telling you, it's time you left.'

'As a friend?'

'Yes, girl, as a friend,' she said. 'You're a plain little thing, but you've a fine neck and I doubt you fancy swinging. I said to my Jacob this morning – though he barely listened, he was that tired with lambing all night, and his cloak all muddied – I said to my Jacob, that girl... why do you smile?'

'I was not smiling, Widow, please,' I said, frightened by the colour I could feel rising in my cheeks.

'Well. I said to my Jacob, we are not...' and she

trailed off, looking at me intently, her gaze returning to the flowers in my hair. A slow recognition rippled through her and she stood up, swung out her arm and whacked me with the dripping cloak. The droplets sprayed off in the sun and I was knocked sideways to the bank.

'Hussy,' she hissed, standing over me, 'so you thought to witch my Jacob, who saved you from the snow, with your lewdness?' She bent down and grabbed a handful of my hair; taking the knife from her girdle she sawed it off. 'You'll hang first.' For a moment she looked at the knife in her hand and at me and I think she might have used it, but there came the sound of voices behind her and she stepped back.

* * *

There was no rowan at the door, only a small parcel wrapped in cloth. I opened it carefully in case it held some horror meant to fright me off, but it was kindly meant, for it held bacon and beans. Agnes, perhaps, or even Jacob? We were not altogether hated. It struck me that Miss Elizabeth could not have known of the strength of the talk against me, or surely she would have come before now. The Widow would not let things wait. Tomorrow, early, I would go to the Hall.

My father was awake when I came in, but more pale than the walls. His eyes followed me around the room as I worked. Truth be told, I could not bear to see how weak he was. The thought went through me that I had bought my life for his, but I did not entertain it. I had done with that foolishness. When the food was ready I brought him a bowl of it.

'You have it, Martha,' he said. 'I am dying, I don't need food. Sit here beside me; take my hand, there. The dark crowds round so.'

I sat down and took his hand. It was light, lighter than a sparrow. The fever had gone. 'Perhaps if you could sleep, you'll be stronger when you wake.'

'No, Martha, I must talk. It's coming; it's not far off now. Reach under my bed for the wooden box. You know where the key is. Open it. What do you see?'

'There's a ring.'

'Her wedding ring. Take it. Give it to your true love. What else?'

'There's a small bird: a dove, a white dove. I think you made it, Father.'

'Yes, I made it. She was a dove, Martha. Though she came from this country sewer, she flew above it like the singing birds do. She was more air than earth.' He began coughing and could not say any more.

I held his hand and sang,

> Come over the burn, Bessie
> My little pretty Bessie
> Come over the burn, Bessie, to me.
>
> The white dove sat on the castle
> wall;
> I bend my bow and shoot her I
> shall;
> I put her in my glove, both feathers
> and all.

Tears ran down his face, as the coughing

stilled and he gathered his breath. 'It's not all, it's not all. Look again. Your knife...'

I looked. It was a plain wood box. There seemed to be nothing in it, till I took my knife and slid the blade around the base. Sure enough the wood sprang back a little and I was able to lift it out. Beneath lay a few papers. Not many. One was a set of drawings. I held it up.

'The drawings I made for him, Sir William, the safe places... Best burn those, Martha.'

The other was a single folded sheet, with a few lines on it. The hand was clumsy, with round letters such as one of my pupils might attempt, but my name was written on it. I looked up at my father, my heart beating in my chest so strong the paper shook in my hand.

'Aye, that one. She wrote it for you. Wouldn't let me scribe it. Should have handed it to you long ago, but well... No, don't read it now. Please, keep it folded. I'll stay strong that way. She was hanged, Martha. Did you guess at it?'

'You told me she died of a fever when I was two years old.'

'It was a lie!' His voice rang out loud. The

weakness seemed to have fled him and he stared at me with a bright intensity. 'You know that by now. I killed my Bessie. After we were wed she begged me to move – somewhere, anywhere else – so long as it was away from him. But I was a freeman of the city, I knew my rights and I would not listen. My father had been an alderman; everybody said I should have been a university man. Everybody said so. All was lost: my mother, my father in a single night. Did I ever tell you, Martha, of the fire?'

'Yes, Father, you told me. Go on. Why do you say you killed my mother?'

'There was no going to sea. I learned how to mend wheels. There's beauty in a wheel, every part true to the centre, and that centre a god, and not an absent god, but a block grasped and held by its circumference. I found Bessie. We were happy, three years, more. You were a fine, strong baby. I had work and money.'

He paused and stared ahead with a faint smile. I did not like to hurry him, for his breathing had grown easier and there was more colour and joy in his face than I had seen since before he froze. We sat like that awhile, with the past playing out for him. I should have liked to pay a penny and see the sights he saw.

But then he frowned and shrank back to me. 'I was a fool. I could not let go of the grievance. The thought of that scall-headed lecher who used my Bessie like a whore tormented me. More and more I dwelled on it, till one day I found myself in his yard offering work as a wheelwright. He happened to walk down his fancy steps... They locked me up, of course, for breaking his nose and the Lord knows I could have had worse than a whipping. Bessie pleaded for me to him, and to the mistress too; showed them the bonny infant I'd leave an orphan. My fault. His lady wife had flicked Bessie away to sit on sailors' knees at the tavern. She wasn't about to grow merciful. She extended her ringed finger and crushed my Bessie like a flea.'

I could see how it was taxing him to talk. I rubbed his shoulders and said he should wait, there would be time enough to tell the story, but he batted me away.

'It was early when they came for her. I was

standing in the doorway watching the light fall on her hands as she plaited your hair. You fidgeted and she sang to quiet you. Then they came and took her away. There was a dolly she had made for you. It had a tear in its bodice and they said she'd done it a purpose to harm the mistress. They said she was the reason the mistress' babies died.

'Her mother, your grandmother, came from Moccas to plead for her, begged others to, but they were afraid of contagion. Accuse one, accuse all. There was a young serving girl from the house, though; one Bessie had been friendly with. They'd shared a room, giggled through the winter. Jane'd known all about the master, what he'd done. They hauled her up and swore her on the Bible. Bessie thought herself saved. Jane mumbled so low the court couldn't hear her. Speak up, they shouted. Then she spoke up right enough. She testified Bessie had witched the master, turned the milk and made the doll to harm the mistress. That's it, she screamed when they showed it, that very doll. Look at the rip that the nail made in the belly. Jane Wade her name was, till she married a ploughman named Reynolds out at Maisemore.'

'Goody Reynolds!'

'Aye, Martha. I didn't know her straight off, but she knew me. She spat her filth about Bessie up and down the village. It was after she moved here, after the summer, that things began to go ill for us, that the air around us fouled.'

He fell to coughing then. It did not stop. He was racked with it, each breath catching into another bout as he tried to speak. All the colour, all the strength that had come to him, was gone.

'Please, please, Father, no more talking. You must pray. You must try to be reconciled with God. Let me call for Father Paul. He cannot refuse you, not now.'

'No,' he said at last. 'No priest. No prayers.'

At last the coughing petered out. He lay back, oily and ashen. I took his hand and kneeled down beside him. 'If you will not pray at least you must bless me. Grant me that.'

He laid his hand on my head, hacking gently as he did so. There was blood on his lips and though I dabbed it away with a cloth there was always more. His eyes were still blue, but they were clouded. I thought how they had held the promise of the sea for me, how they'd been the colour of the Virgin's gown in the chapel before it fell. All his features were clenched with anger. Did Our Lady's face turn angry, too, when they killed her son? In the window glass she was always smooth cheeked and gentle, her pain was soft and sorrowful like a lamenting tune, not like my father's rages. His pain scored and twisted him like a storm-struck oak. The grain of his mind had been marred.

'What good are prayers? They didn't stop her swinging. Leave this muck. I have raised you to be better. To have better.'

I thought of Jacob and my cheeks burned. I do not want better, I thought, what I want is here. I swallowed and tried to find him in his eyes. 'Father,' I said, 'I love Jacob, Jacob Spicer.'

He seemed to look back at me and smiled and nodded. When he spoke his voice was steadier, stronger. 'I know you love me, child. You're a good girl. These last months have been hard. But you are safe. Gifts at our door, it's only right – you saved the boy. People know your worth. They'll stand by you. The Mortimers, they are great folk and Miss Elizabeth has promised she will protect you. Hark, do you hear the knocking. Go to the door and let her in. Go, child.'

I looked towards the door, there was no sound, no knock, but his arm fluttered and pointed so I went and opened it as he bid me. He broke into a big smile and nodded, gesturing to a stool.

'Why, Sir William – and Miss Elizabeth too – thank you.' He turned to me. 'You know they have come every day, Martha. Look at this embroidered quilt. Take the ham from them, take it now.'

I took the air that he handed me and as I turned to set it down I heard a little cough, like one that a man might use to clear his throat before speaking. It had loosened the catch. His lifeblood streamed out from him. So much blood. Still he struggled to speak. I bent down to make out his words.

'Damn them all,' he whispered, 'plague and damnation on them, great and small.'

His head fell back and he was dead. I stayed all night by his side, hoping that if I held his hand it might stay warm in mine. Now that it could not hurt him, now he could not shout I told him everything – all that had happened and all my fears. Slowly his hand grew colder and the candle burned down, till I was speaking into the darkness.

35

THE LETTER AND THE WHITE DOVE

It was morning before I could bring myself to open my mother's letter. I held the paper in my hand and unfolded it, but my eyes filled and I could not read the lines. For a while I brushed my fingers over the words, for the impressions left in the paper by the push of her hand as it had gripped the quill. In one place there was a large rimmed stain and the letters had run. I brought it to my lips and fancied I could taste the salt.

My dear child,
When you read this I will be watching you

with not one jot less of love than I feel now. Until this last sorrow, my daughter, we had never been parted, thou and I. You are grown too big to sit on my hip hour on hour, and yet I cannot refuse you for it brings your cheek so close to mine. We walk and gabble together and when you are afraid – you must not be afraid, my darling – you bury your head in my shoulder. I think you have made a hollow for it there.

I will die tomorrow. The words are strange. I feel such strength and life in me. I could dance five hours together. How can it be that I will be dead ere sundown?

A tangle of windflowers bloom outside my cell. They might have blown here from the woods at home. How I wish I was breathing the wet oak after rain. The petals of the windflower are so delicate, they cannot abide picking. Tissue of the moon, though they grow in dark places. I will wear white when they take me tomorrow, like the windflower. Know it in your heart, Martha, I am not tainted. I am no witch. They can tie my body to the gibbet, but my heart and mind fly free, like the innocent dove.

Walter says I must hurry. There is no time in heaven. In the blink of an angel's eye you will be with me, though you die an old woman and we will hold hands and laugh together at your children's children's children.

I will not say goodbye, daughter.

Your loving mother,

Elizabeth Dynely

I read the letter over and over. Why had he not given it to me before, years before? There was so much unsaid. In the morning light his face was grey, but a peace had come to it, which, God forgive me, at that moment I did not think that he deserved. He had protected himself, not me, in keeping the letter. I folded it up and placed it carefully in my bosom, just as a loud knocking called me to the day.

* * *

Most of the parish turned out for the funeral, but

they were not mourners. Tom stood with me, and Aggie and Jacob stood together, behind. Next to them the Tranters. I was grateful for them. I stood by the grave and felt nothing; relief, perhaps, that it was the Putley vicar, not Father Paul. I held the small dove my father had carved and I smoothed my fingers along its feathered wings. I had gathered flowers and we threw them in the grave, but when I tried to throw my father's adze the Widow stepped forward and grabbed my arm.

'That's not yours to throw, girl. There's debts your father owes must be settled.'

I pictured the blade in her scrawny neck and said nothing. Jacob turned to her. 'Mother,' he said.

'Don't you mother me. She is practising upon you, boy, even now, with that good innocent girl beside you.' Aggie pretended to hear nothing, but I could see her colour rising. 'She's a charm in her hand even now she's a rubbing on. She suckles her familiars in her sleep.' And I saw Jacob glance at my hand and I, without thinking, hid the dove in my pocket.

Father David gave her a curt look to quiet her,

though unlike half the village, he had not heard her words. I looked down at the grave, where my father's coffin lay. I could not grieve. It was wicked, but I could not do it. Soon, I promised him, when all of this was done with.

Father Paul was in Hereford with Bishop John, Tom told me as he drove me back from Putley church. I glanced back. The crowd was gone, even the Widow and Goody Reynolds, but Aggie and Jacob were standing talking to each other. She was leaning in, waving her arms. As we turned from the grave I had clasped her hand and asked her to come to see me, but though she quickly nodded I could see the Widow's words working in her eyes and her embrace was stiff and awkward.

'I thought Sir William and Miss Elizabeth would come,' I said. 'Perhaps they had not heard.'

Tom snorted softly. 'Happen they are caught up in the bishop's business. Matters over Hoar Wood have come to a head. Bishop John and Sir William are at loggerheads and the bishop talks of plots and papists. Word is, the bishop needs a scandal. Folks in the Court have him on the rack. Sir William's head might save his own.'

'How is Father Paul part of it?'

'Him? Chance of advancement, see; get his long weaselling fingers into a bit more pie. He don't want to be stuck out here with the likes of us, not if there's a chance of rising. He'll be thinking how he can be useful, what the bishop might like to hear. And he's too low for Sir William, as you know yourself. He wanted the glass out of the chapel windows long before the Wonder came.'

He was silent awhile, then shot me a sharp glance. 'Martha,' he said, 'I don't hold no truck with all this talk of your witching poor young Owen, but you've not done yourself any favours, carrying on with your herbs and potions like a cunning woman, cursing the folks out at the Underhill the night your father fell in the hole. And now there's gossip you drew Jacob Spicer under the crooked moon when he's all but promised to young Aggie.'

I glanced across at him. 'Has he said this?'

'No, you fool, it's his aunt and his mother. I'm telling you this as a friend, and you've precious few of those just now. Tomorrow's Sunday, they'll leave you alone on the Lord's day, with your father fresh in the ground, but Monday you need to be gone. As it happens, I think I might be better somewhere else when the bishop comes calling on Sir William. I've said a few things myself that might be remembered if they are looking round for necks. I'm going to my sister for a week or two in Worcester. You should come with me. It might not be for ever, girl. You could come back when things were safe.'

We had pulled up outside my door and I still had not replied. I had not cried for my father, but I was quick enough to weep for myself.

'Look,' Tom said, as he handed me down, 'perhaps you love the lad, but you are a cripple and his mother hates you. There's no future in it. You know by now what was done to your mother?'

I nodded.

'Well then, think. Do you want to follow her to the scaffold, Martha? Do you want to follow her, when you could leave?'

We agreed to meet by Aylhill before dawn. It wasn't far. I could hide my things tomorrow near the cottage for him to pick up on his way back from the Hall.

I stepped out the back of the house and looked up at the wounded hill. The spring sun was warm, but the grass and branches were still beaded from the rain that had fallen hours before. The drops shone like brilliants. I could hear the burrburr of a turtle dove. The trees were beginning to come into leaf. Jacob would be heading up to the ewes by now, or down to the Hall to the horses. Somehow after my night at the well, and with my father gone, I felt free to love the land. Had my mother loved it too?

More than anything I wanted to see Owen, but I could not do that without his sister. I was afraid of seeing Aggie, but my heart would not be at peace till I had. Yet what was there to say? I was sorry, yet I was not sorry. I did not know even if I had practised on Jacob as they said. Until the water slapped me and he pulled me to the bank I had thought myself drawn by the moon and the song. I had thought the song would bring me to the cold water and my mother, but it brought me him, the red rose and the lily flower. I was no witch, but there was magic worked through me and I didn't know if it were for good or ill.

I sat in the empty house on the cot where my father used to lie and conjured Aggie to come. And just as the sun began to droop she came. She did not smile at me or embrace me, but sat primly in the chair. Her lips were pressed tight together.

'You must miss him. He was a good man,' she said, without conviction. We sat stiffly, either side of the table. She was holding a bunch of early columbines, and she thrust them at me as though she wanted none of them.

'Aggie,' I said, taking them, 'would you wish I gathered rue to mix with them?' I tried to take her hand, then, but she flinched and snatched it away. For a while she sat with her shoulder tilted towards me, saying nothing, but throwing me fierce looks. Then she got up and turned to the door.

'Aggie, talk. I know what's on your mind.'

I got up and stood in front of her. To my surprise she slapped me, full in the face. I stepped back, my conscience stinging more than my cheek. She glanced defiantly at her hand, then looked me up and down. 'I only came because

Mother made me.' She crumpled her face in disgust. 'When your father lay dying. How could you, Martha?'

'How could I what?'

'The Widow herself has said it. You were wet through with half a meadow in your hair. You lay with him. Jacob doesn't deny it, not outright, just fell to cursing and walked off back to the Hall. You used your herbs and your enchantments and drew him after you like a tame dog.'

I had meant to be meek with her, not angry, but my spirit rebelled. I talked calm enough, but I knew the words could spin off at any moment.

'Had he promised himself to you, Aggie?'

'You knew it was what we wanted.'

'Had he promised himself? Had any word been spoken?'

'That is of no consequence. We did not need to speak of it. Both our families were happy, the Widow and my father especially. There could be no engagement while Owen lay so ill.'

I sat back down; my heart was pounding in my chest, and yes, with relief. I was half smiling, I could not help it.

Aggie stepped back, full of shock and indignation. 'Martha, I have always been your friend, I have helped you and pitied you, but how could you think it? It's almost disgusting. No respectable family could have you. Perhaps if you were fair... but even then... And now, suspected as you are, limping with the mark of the Lord's disfavour...'

The truth she spoke sucked the air from my chest and all the silly fancies lurking in my brain. She had said it. The idea of his choosing me was almost disgusting. That was what I had seen in his eyes in the morning. I clutched the table and waited for my heart to calm enough for me to turn to her and lie.

'Aggie, listen. I lay down that night and listened to my father dying and I could not bear it. I fell into a great sin, but it was despair, not lust. I left the house, meaning to throw myself in the river, to be washed away. To prove with my death I was no witch. Unbeknownst to me he followed, fearing what I might do – I had hinted as much when he helped me home with the barrow. I did not get to the river. I threw myself in Pentaloe Well and he dragged me out and made me pray forgiveness for the deed I had attempted. That is all, Aggie. He had no interest in my flesh – you said yourself I am not fair like you. I do not have magic enough to make him choose a little dark cripple over you. It was my soul he sought to bring back to the light.'

She crouched down and stared at me a long while to divine if it were true, biting her lip all the while. I returned her gaze, filling my eyes with a look of honest confession, until she nodded and smiled and pulled me to her.

'Oh, Martha,' she said, 'I should not have doubted you. You are so small and dark and spiky; you are like blackthorn and you scratch and tear whether you will or no.'

I was glad of her embrace and her warm soft shoulders, and pleased with myself to have won her back so easy. I felt a little wretched too, for she was right; I was full of thorns and deceit and yearning.

36

OWEN RETURNS

I was surprised how quickly Aggie put by her fears. Within minutes she was happily telling me that a messenger from the Hall had come by, asking after Owen and saying she must attend Miss Elizabeth on Monday, early, to discuss a position.

'But, Agnes, if you are to be betrothed soon?'

'Oh, don't be silly, Martha. I may not marry for years. I have nothing against long engagements. There is no hurry. And the joy of it is, the position is not with Miss Elizabeth, but an acquaintance of hers, the lady who found me pretty all those weeks ago. And just think, Martha, she dwells in

Hereford and her husband is a rich man, a cap merchant. He is said to have a house in London. There will be dances, the players, I will have my hands in ribbons all day long.'

Her face fell and she remembered where she was. 'I should not be talking like this now. It is my turn to be sorry. But after all these months of suffering, I can't help it if my mind keeps lighting on silks and satin slippers. How I would love to be away from all this.'

'How is Owen?' I asked. 'I should love to see him.'

'That's just the thing: Mother wants you to come. Father left this morning, said he wouldn't be back till after nightfall. There is a group he meets with over by Cockyard Farm. As you know, he is grown very strict in his religion. They are for rooting out idolatry where it lingers and...' She blushed.

'... and witchcraft. You can say it, Aggie. Your father wants me at the end of a rope.'

We toiled over the back way, keeping to the field edges in the hope of passing without notice. I could not enter by the front door any more. It would be safe for no one. Ann Simons was waiting for me by the window with a box to help me in.

'Oh, you poor, poor girl,' she said. 'I would have come, only Richard would not allow it. And you all alone now. Come in, come in. Have you the monkshood? We used up what you left us and I dare not attempt to mix it myself.'

'You must not,' I said. 'It is powerful. How is he?'

'You will see,' she said, smiling broadly. 'I believe he is coming back to us, Martha, only Aggie and Richard will not take heed.'

I glanced across at Aggie, who shook her head slightly at me. She had told me as we walked that she feared her mother's long watching and seclusion had affected her mind.

Owen was where I had last seen him, his face turned to the window. He was sleeping peacefully enough, though there was a lassitude in the placing of his limbs that spoke of weakness. He was so pitifully small. I sat down and stroked his hair.

'He knows me,' Ann said, 'I am sure of it, and

there are times I think he wishes to speak, only he can't seem to find where his voice has gone. After I have given him your tincture, in particular, he seems more alert, more understanding. He has squeezed my hand no end of times. Aggie, don't look like that. I know you have given up hope, but I have not. My husband and Father Paul believe you have possessed him, Martha. If Richard knew you were here, I don't know what he would do. It is selfish of me to put us all in danger like this. I don't know what I was thinking. Owen is sleeping. He might not wake for hours. Maybe you should go before any harm comes of it.'

'I asked to come,' I said quietly. 'Please let me stay awhile. Might I lie down with him? I am very tired.'

She went away to make me food and Aggie, too, let us be. I lay down on the bed, suddenly filled with a weariness that seemed ancient. As I stroked Owen's shoulder I noticed they had put a tiny book around his neck: St John's Gospel, no doubt, proof against the witch. I talked to him softly as I fell asleep, for though he was little he saw the world through eyes like mine, and understood what others never would. I hugged him in my arms and wept for both of us.

A slight movement woke me. For an instant I could not remember where I was and I started and sat up, staring at the unfamiliar beams and the clanging of pots below. This must be the gaol; I had been taken. Then I remembered and looked across at Owen. His eyes were open, but more than that, he was looking at me. I smiled at him and slowly, silently, he smiled back.

He had smiled back! He had returned! I opened my mouth to shout it out. But at once a picture came into my mind of myself as a tiny child, coaxing a blackbird that hung about our door. For days it had avoided me and then at last it came, in short bounds, cocking its head as it paused and considered the grain I held. 'Go easy,' my grandmother said, 'stay quiet, do not fright it or it will fly off for ever.'

I sat on the bed next to him and took his hand. 'Do you know me?' I said.

He nodded.

'Oh, Owen,' I said, forgetting the blackbird, 'I am so sorry, I am so sorry I couldn't bring you home. You must have had such nightmares out there. But you are home now, you are safe. The Good Lord has preserved you. Oh, Owen, you have come back.'

I stood up to call his mother, but he pressed my hand. 'Martha,' he said, 'you won't go? Please don't go.'

I sat down again. 'Oh, Owen, love, I have to, but I'll come back. I'll come back just as soon as I can and we'll live together and you can go to school and I'll keep house. And at night we'll look out over all the roofs in the city to the great Cathedral.'

'Stay, Martha,' he said again.

I heard a cry behind me and a small crash. It was Ann coming up with a bowl of stew for me. 'Oh my darling,' she said, rushing forward to bury his head in her bosom. 'Oh, Martha, I will not forget this.'

'Don't hurry him, please, Ann. Maybe best not to tell Master Richard right away, not till Owen is more settled into himself. We must let him back gently into the world; they'd ply him with talk.'

'Yes, yes, you're right. Oh, Owen, how I've

missed you, my boy. Oh, my darling child...' and she rocked back and forth with tears streaming down her face. Then she shook herself and turned to me.

'I'm sorry, Martha, I was coming to say you had best shift yourself soon. You've been asleep hours, you know. It's quite dark outside. Aggie'll walk back with you. Best say nothing to her of this, not yet. She is her father's girl before all.'

We both promised Owen I'd be back very soon – the next day, even. To say goodbye, I thought, for a while at least. Aggie and I stole back by the fields. I told her there was no need to come, but she seemed ill at ease for me. She said I was safer with her by. Every second step she pestered me to rest until it irked me, though I was glad to have her goodwill. Truth was, I barely felt my ankle. I was floating. Owen had come back, his eyes were quick and full as they had ever been. Perhaps the evil set loose in the hill had at last sunk back into the dark places I had helped to wake it from.

Aggie was all of a jitter and kept flying ahead of me along the path till I could scarce make her out in the gloom. Then a second later she would run back and exhort me to rest. I was relieved to reach my door; the night would be long and lonely, but I had a yen to sit quiet among my father's tools and to think of him.

'Good night, Aggie, and thank you. I could not bear for us to be at odds. Oh, Aggie, it means the world to me that we are reconciled.' We embraced one another and her innocent curls fell across my face as I laid my head on her shoulder and thought how easy, after all, it had been to betray her and how quick I would be to betray her again.

I did not want a light. I sat in the darkness, on my father's ash chair. He had turned the wood in the green and the back fitted to his own. I pressed my spine against it, aware of a pain in my chest that rose and sank, and blocked my breathing. His hasp knife lay on the table where I had placed it, wondering if I should throw it in his grave. I patted my hand around till I found it. It was solid and smooth in my fist and I gripped it till my heart calmed and I could picture him alive. It was in the workshop I could see him most distinctly, seated at his lathe with the draw knife steady in his hands. The tools held the memory of his hands when they were strong. I got up. I would sort through them tonight, pack up such as I might carry and sell. I was searching out a candle stub when the door banged sharply.

'Martha, it's me, Aggie. You must come, there's been an accident. There's hopes you can help.'

'What was it? On the road, on your way back?'

Aggie looked confused, then she nodded hurriedly, 'Yes, yes, Robert Tanner, on the road, that's it. They've taken him to the Widow's.'

So, I thought, they are ready to hang me, but are not above asking my help.

'Let them look to their own,' I said. 'Why should I stir? The Tanners have been no friends to me.'

Aggie looked nonplussed. Her face darted this way and that like a bird's. There was something strange about her. Then she brightened into speech. 'You should come, Martha. Who knows but what if you help, it'll lay some of the ill will that threatens you? Think, it can only do you good.'

She was right, I had to admit it. I let her lead

me out. No sooner were we in the road however, than her manner changed again.

'But you may be no use at all, Martha, and after all, perhaps it would be better if you did not come.'

'Oh, do not dither so, Aggie. First you call me, then you hold me back. I cannot make you out at all. Come, it is hardly even a step. We are at the door already.' I banged and waited. Light seeped below the door and through the shutters. In the noise before I knocked I'd heard many voices. Richard Simons' voice loud among them. Suddenly all had gone quiet. Something was wrong. I turned to Aggie, and her face was contorted with fear and something else: shame, perhaps.

'I'm sorry, Martha, I'm sorry. Father said I was to bring you. It is to help Owen and stop you... They will not harm you, they promised, they...' But her words were cut off by the door flinging open and Richard Simons himself was there before me with blood on his hands.

37

PROTECTION

The room blazed with candles. There must have been a dozen of them, pooling the faces that turned and stared: Robert Tanner, nothing amiss with him, then; Dick Loader; the Laddings; Goody Reynolds and the Widow either side of a yellow fire. Every one of them was turned towards me with hands sticky with gore. I glanced around for Jacob but he was not there. That was good. But did he know what they did here? Had he simply chosen to be absent?

'Aggie,' I said, but she had gone. It was only as the door slammed behind me that I took in the reek of blood. The air was so hot and thick with it my knees buckled beneath me and I found myself clutching the arm of Richard Simons.

'Look!' cried the widow, 'her strength is leaving her. It is working, it is working.'

Richard Simons grabbed the back of my head and thrust me forward. 'What do you say, witch, what do you say?'

The room was swimming. I felt my stomach heave, but somewhere my mind was quite at liberty, watching, as though this were a scene acted out by the players in an inn yard. I looked into the fire and saw what caused the stench: it was the blackened heart of a pig, stuck with pins. My part now was to say a blessing. It was a healing charm to do away witching. I had heard of it working when the Cleggs' boy had been made ill out at Sapness. He'd been sick a fortnight when they called in a cunning woman to unwitch him. No sooner had the heart blackened and burned than an old neighbour had knocked on the door and blessed the house. The boy got better directly. A month or so later the witch was found; she'd been dead a week. A fall, it was said. What would they do with me if I said the blessing? Let me home to bed? I did not think so. I would not name myself a witch.

I backed away from the fire, but it was a small room and the assembly pressed around me.

'Listen,' I said, 'I do not bless you, I curse you. All of you. The curse of an orphan with her father fresh in his grave. You've broken his rest.' They shifted uneasily and glanced at one another. Dick Loader stepped back into the shadows, as if my curse were water and he thought not to get splashed. Even Richard Simons shrank back away from me. Only the Widow seemed unperturbed.

'Your father's safe in hell, Martha Dynely. Why, if he tried to, he'd never find his way home, with all the drink that's in him. The only spirit he ever had came from a barrel. You say what you ought to say and promise to let my boy be and we'll let you alone.'

There were nods and murmurs, but no one spoke. All clutched their candles and stared at me, faces I had known all my life, but just then more horrid and contorted than the gargoyles that had sneered at us from the chapel roof. They'd smashed the faces of the angels and the saints, but the monsters survived, too high to reach.

I heard my voice rise high and shrill: 'The seed will rot in the earth and your milk will turn.' I took out the hasp knife, pulled it open and the blade flashed in the candlelight. Then I snicked my thumb. 'Lay hands on me and you'll be dead within a twelvemonth, I swear it.'

There was a pause, and I felt if someone moved I might be ripped to pieces, but the pause held and just then the fire coughed. A great belch of smoke tumbled into the room. Goody Reynolds screamed. God or the devil had saved me. I shuffled to the door and everyone drew back to let me pass.

I dared not go back home. It may be that was wrong, I don't know. It may be they would have thought better of it all if I had emerged from my father's house to go to church in the morning, but once out of the Widow's house all the fear in my heart seized me and I crumpled to my knees and fell to vomiting. Then I drew my cloak about me and crept into the fields. As soon as folk set off for the service, I thought, I would venture to the Hall and seek shelter there. That would be safer than trusting to Tom.

I was lucky, it was a warm night and a dry one. I found a hollow between two beech trees in the coppice above the warrens. I would try to send word to Tom to gather my things for me. Miss Elizabeth would be white with rage to hear how I'd been treated. She might well go directly to the village and call out all those who threatened me. I fell asleep picturing Goody Reynolds, the Widow, Richard Simons, all of them, on their knees, wringing their hands with shame.

The birds were loud and lightsome with the morning when I woke. I hung about in the trees for a while, for I could not venture out till folks had set off for church. I told myself I was only waiting, but I kept an eye, too, on the warrens in case Jacob should appear. I had no idea how things stood between us. I had given him leave to hate me – hadn't I as good as told him I had worked on him to lie with me? It was not true, or I did not think it could be true. Yet I had asked the hills to fall and they had fallen, I had yearned for Jacob and he had come. Enough of that, I would not think that. I cast no spells. I suckled no familiar in my sleep. Still my heart misgave me.

All at the Hall seemed quiet. I passed the stables without a single soul spying me. And there seemed indeed no one to notice. Perhaps the hands were gone to Putley to worship and only the family was left. After the Wonder they had fitted out a chapel within the house and had scarcely been seen in church. I had not thought of that: how they would be sequestered within the house. It would not do for the likes of me to knock at the main door as though I were a person of quality come calling, but if I should be shown off from the servants' door, Miss Elizabeth would not know of it, nor even hear me if I shouted.

I hovered around the kitchen, willing the door to the scullery to open and the kitchen boy, Roger, or some other I knew to come issuing forth, but the door was barred and I feared knocking. The morning was wearing on, but I knew I could not go back – with each breath I seemed to smell last night's reeking fire. I took courage and banged at the servants' door. I glanced at myself as I waited, and did what I could to smooth my gown and pluck leaves and grasses from my cloak.

The door opened barely a crack. I recognised the man who opened it: Peter, a weaselly manservant of Sir William.

'Yes, what can you want here?' he said. 'Is it begging you're after? I tell you, his lordship is not in a giving mood. You'd best be gone.'

'Please,' I said, 'I must speak with Miss Elizabeth. She will not refuse me. Tell her Martha, Martha Dynely is come.'

'I know well enough who you are. I tell you, and this is for your own good because you were ever civil to me: you better make yourself scarce. Every house this side of Ledbury is talking of the cripple witch who sucked the soul out of the Simons boy and threw over God's own house.'

His words made me gasp. I knew the talk in the village, but somehow I had not thought the Hall contaminated, let alone the world beyond. To be published a monster through the lanes and roads!

'Look at your eyes,' he said, 'round as beakers! What, is it news to you? Look, I don't say everyone believes it – you know how people love a tale, and the dolt that stole a peck of grain is Springheeled Jack, who leaps over barns, by the time the teller's done, though he's a poor dolt still and you may be nothing more than a cuckoo – but trouble sticks to you like burrs.'

I did not know what to say. I was like the hare, standing fixed in the grass because it has heard the dogs.

'Between you and me,' he said, leaning a little towards me, 'all is not well at the Hall today. Nicholas Craddock the Jesuit has been taken at Little Malvern Court. There's a great many papish plots to be unearthed. Bishop John scents blood and is on the hunt. We expect his men at any moment. Sir William has suddenly a great many things he does not wish to be on view and he's not quite sure which of us are the bishop's men. Miss Elizabeth follows him like a shadow, rubbing her pearls.' He smiled. 'Let them at it, I say. There's always money to be made when great men quarrel.'

'But Miss Elizabeth, she will not refuse me. Please let her know I am here. As a friend, please tell her,' I said, as soon as he paused. He started as though he'd forgotten I was there, that he was talking to another person. He put his airs back on.

'As a friend,' he said frowning, 'I tell you, get you gone.' He closed the door. I banged on it with both my fists and the noise rang out across the courtyard and set the dogs barking. At last it opened narrowly. 'Wait,' he said. 'I will ask, and then you must leave. It will not do for you to be here when the bishop's men come.'

I sank down on the step, and looked up at the empty sky. High, high above me two crows mobbed a kite. Not long now and I would be safe. The bell in the tower rang the hour. It was a thin sound, nothing like the deep clamour of the chapel bell that lay buried somewhere in the fields, with the dead tumbled around it. Maybe it would not be found for years. Maybe a hundred years hence some plough would snag it and they'd dig it up and place it in the new chapel that would be built. And even after that, for years after, the earth would turn over a hipbone or a skull, the jaw hanging open as if it would speak, but for the soil that stopped its mouth.

When the door opened I sprang up, as quick as my leg would let me, and a rush of joy set me grinning, till Peter's grim face knocked me back. 'She is not at home,' he said.

'But she is. You said yourself she was.'

He sighed. 'She is not at home to you,' he said, emphasising each word. 'For what it's worth, I'm sorry.' He smiled, showing his brown teeth. 'Go to the city or follow the mustered men. You've a kind of dark prettiness, you'll earn on your back well enough for a few years yet. Here,' he fumbled in his purse, and tossed me a coin, 'you can owe me a tumble.' And he shut the door.

It was not true. It could not be true. She would not abandon me like that. She would hold out her arms as she sat on her velvet chair and I would lay my head on her lap and weep as she stroked my hair. He had lied, it was surely that.

I went around to the front of the house and hovered at the far end of the bridge that led directly to the great oak doors. It would not have seemed marvellous if the bridge itself had crumbled at the liberty of my crossing it. As I dithered, a horse came clattering up, panting and spittle flecked. The rider flung himself down and knocked sharply. He was evidently expected, for he had barely finished knocking before he was ushered in and a man issued out to take the gelding. A messenger. Some trouble for Sir William afoot. It was not a good time to intrude with my troubles, but what choice had I?

The door was answered directly and a maid I well recognised stood there. 'Mary,' I said, 'may I come in? I must speak with Miss Elizabeth. They would not take my message from the servants' door.'

'You,' she said. 'My, you're a brazen hussy. How dare you come to this door? She got your message all right. She'll have none of you, you hear? Be gone. An' if I were you,' she added, 'I wouldn't hang about, neither,' and she pointed down the approach to a rabble at the other end of it. They looked odd next to the little hedges, a flurry of rags and tags and washed-out browns against the clipped yews and the grass, as though they had no right to be among such colour. But they were advancing steadily enough.

38

TORN: TIED

They paused the other side of the moat, their boldness not quite up to crossing the bridge, though there was no gate. Mary smiled. She did not close the door, but placed herself to bar me from the house. A couple of other servants gathered behind her. This was worth a watch.

They had come for me. It was almost a relief to face them. Almost. As long as I could keep the knot of panic in my guts from rising. Last night's faces and more, with the Widow and Richard Simons at their head, Goody Reynolds jittering behind them, chewing on her tongue.

'You'd best hand her over,' Richard Simons

called. 'We're Sir William's men, but there's my boy lying in his bed an idiot, aye, and others too,' he glanced at the Widow, 'taken from their right minds because of her. Good God, the dead with their bones scattered underneath the sheep are crying out! We won't stand for it. Hand her to us and we'll pass her over to the constables.'

'What's left of her!' someone shouted.

'Take her and good riddance,' Mary said, poking my back with a finger. 'Only don't start anything here. You let her get the other side of the gatehouse and conduct your business there. John here will walk her out and you can keep your distance.'

'Very well,' Master Simons said.

'I mean it, mind,' Mary went on. 'Any funny business in sight of the Hall and you'll be out of your houses come Lady Day.' She poked me again, but I would not move to please her. I clutched ahold of the doorway and screamed for Miss Elizabeth with all my might. Then I felt myself shoved forwards. They had got a broom and were prodding me out like a pig in the corn. A great shout went up as I was pushed out over the bridge to where they stood. I stared at the gravel, and did not bother to wipe off the spittle that hit my cheek as I was goaded out in front.

'What'll you do to her?' John said, over his shoulder as he poked me forward.

'Don't you worry,' the Widow said, 'we're God-fearing folk. We want to see her hang, not swing for her ourselves. But we've not time to wait for the gallows tree to help our loved ones find the sense she's scattered to the winds. We've given her one chance already to undo what's done, and now we're going to scratch her. We'll let a bit of bleeding put an end to her mischief. Then the law can put a stop to her for good.'

As if to underscore her words a small stone stung my ear. I felt blood trickle down my neck. 'Not so quick with your curses in the morning, are you?' someone shouted.

I glanced back to the house. There on the first floor, through the mullion, I glimpsed a figure, a lady, peering through the casement. A red-gloved hand rested on the glass. I looked at her as long as I could, till the handle poked me forwards again.

The journey to the gatehouse seemed a mile

long. I bent my head down and let tears fall in
the dust. Insults buzzed around my ears like flies,
like stones. I had been at the cockfight once,
looking for my father, and seen how the men jos-
tled and shouted, rousing themselves to a need
for blood.

'Bessie Dynely was a witch,' one half-sang,
half-shouted.

'And they hanged the filthy bitch,' another answered, laughing. They kicked the lines, one to
the other like a football.

> Now her daughter is the devil's
>   little slut.
> The Good Lord marked her as a
>   cripple
> For a pulling down His chapel
> But we'll see how she can charm
>   when she is cut.

'That's enough!' John said, rounding on them.
'I don't like this. I'll have no part in it. You, there,
Robert Tanner, you put that blade away. You wait
till I'm back through. I know your names, mind,

every one of you. If there's murder, you'll answer for it.'

I had hardly noticed passing under the gatehouse. He prodded me now onto the track that ran around the outside of the gardens. 'I'm sorry, child,' he said, leaning me against a tree, 'I would help you if I could.' I clung to him and wailed. He had to pull my fingers from his arm and push me to my knees before he could get himself free of me.

A bright spring sun smiled on the snarling faces. There was a soft breeze. I buried my head into my knees and pressed my hands over my ears and rocked. Somewhere a bell rang. Was I going to die? My breath snagged in my chest. It was horrible, this waiting. Then I felt my hair grabbed and my head was snatched back so that I had to face them all. The twisted faces wobbled and ran. There were not so many, I saw. Maybe only eight or nine.

'Here's for your curses,' Goody Reynolds said. Her sister wrenched my head back and the old woman pushed a handful of foul dirt into my open mouth.

I doubled over, retching, choking.

'What, did the devil's arse taste sweeter?' someone shouted. 'You were ready enough to swallow then.'

And then there were hands about me, ripping off my cloak, tearing my gown while I puked and gasped, and then a thousand nails clawed at my skin, all across my open back.

'Her blood must flow,' Goody Reynolds was screaming. 'Let out the witch's blood. Do it for your boy, Richard.'

'Set yourself up like a grammar school boy. We can write, too.'

'Pute.'

'Daggle-tailed slut.'

'Drassock.'

'Piss-breathing harlot.'

Nails scratched me, scraped and tore at me. I heaved and my gorge rose into my mouth. Then all at once another voice: Ruth Tranter's.

'Shame on you all, and her poor father not yet cold in his grave. Judith Spicer, how can you act so? And you, Jane Reynolds, are you after the devil's work? Who are you to take on God's justice?

This is a child.' I dared not raise my head, but I saw her familiar skirts beside me and she was bending down over my back, tutting and cooing.

'Leave her to us, old woman,' Robert Tanner cried, hoarse with excitement. 'We've no grudge with you, but I swear we'll take a hand to you if you get in our way.'

'Hark at you,' she said. 'Lift a hand against a grandmother? Fine Christian man you are. There's Ben, my husband, on his way, and Bert I doubt you'll be so fiery before them.'

I raised my head; they were clustered before her. Goody and the Widow pursed their thin lips, but others laughed outright. 'Go to, Mistress. Do you think we're afeard of two old hands who've never swung more than a rake since they were two foot tall?'

Behind them a horse appeared; unnoticed, quietly, it advanced. It was the messenger I had seen admitted as I stood waiting by the moat. A gentleman by the looks of him, on a fine black with a sword by his side. He coughed and they turned, astonished.

'So, you're spending the Lord's day attacking a

girl and a grandmother? Honourable work, fellows. I think you better go home now, or better still, get back to chapel, or I might have you all whipped.'

Richard Simons squared up to him. 'Begging your pardon, sir, but this is parish business. The girl is arrested for a witch and we're holding her till the constables come.'

'Meaning I should let well alone?'

'Begging your pardon, sir, yes.'

The rider laughed and leaned down from his saddle. 'Why, you ignorant superstitious curs. I will not have you whipped. I will whip you myself.' And he took his crop and began to lay about with it willy-nilly, man and woman, till they had all scurried off.

Ruth Tranter fell to her knees before him but he pulled her up.

'Go,' he said. 'Don't linger here. The bishop is on his way and he'd like nothing better than a little witch to hang.' And with that he cantered off, whistling.

Ruth found what was left of my cloak and laid it around my naked shoulders, for decency's sake, though the rough wool scoured my wounds. Now the retching had stopped, I found I was juddering with sobs. I think if the moat had been by, I would have sought out the cool oblivion of the mud.

'Why you're all laid open,' she said. 'You poor, poor thing, can you walk? It was a lie about my Ben, I'm afraid. He's in bed with the toothache. I was taking this way home so that I could beg clove oil from the kitchens.'

I felt stronger with her arms about me, though the pain in my back was a constant screaming. 'I think they would have killed me. Oh, Ruth, they hate me. If it wasn't for you, I would be dead.'

'Nonsense, dear, I couldn't let another of my children die. I think of you as my child, you know, after tending to your poor father. They don't hate you so much, you know, or only the idea of you. They are afraid... all these goings-on. Who's to know what's behind it all? It's easier for them to decide it must be you. You have a bit of elsewhere about you.'

'Miss Elizabeth...' I said. 'Ruth, I saw her watching. She gave me to them.'

'Did she so? You set store by her, didn't you?

Well, she's not bad as they go. It's not a good idea, all told, to depend on the likes of them. They only care for their own kind, in the end, and there's a deal of trouble her father is in. He has been named, you know. They say Nicholas Craddock has given a list of names. The last thing they want is to be found harbouring a witch. She'll be thinking of her own skin. She had you writing all kinds of things. Wouldn't take much to draw her under suspicion.'

'But she's a lady, Ruth.'

'There's folks as grand as her have found themselves swinging. No, there's nothing steady these days.'

Some time later I was lying on my stomach in the cot my father had lain in. I pressed my nose into the tick and tried to catch the scent of him, but Ruth was a good housewife and had aired it well; all I smelled was straw and lavender. My back stung, but this was a tight kind of pain, more bearable than the raw agony I had felt at first. Ruth stood above me, finishing her pasting.

'I don't say I've your gifts, Martha, but there's no end of injuries I've healed over the years.

You're young and hale, and the wounds aren't deep: you'll do. Not but they've made a fine mess of your back. Written all over, it is; looks like the scribes have been at it. If I hadn't witnessed it myself, I'd have sworn they'd used knives, not nails. May they never scrub the guilt from their fingers.'

The door banged and Ben Tranter came in heavily and stood beside his wife. 'He'll come as soon as he can harness her,' he said to his wife, throwing a hand up now and then to his sore mouth. 'No, don't worry,' he said, as I made some feeble attempt to cover myself. 'I've seen a girl before. We nursed your father and we'll stand by you. You should have come to us, child. Right, well, you're in no fit state to be moved, but moved you'll have to be. Bert will be over here within the hour. He'll take you where Tom can pick you up in the morning.'

I began to thank him, but he cut me off. 'I don't want thanking. Or not yet, any road. Thank me when you're safe.'

Ruth helped me to dress and then made up a parcel of food for me. Outside a cuckoo sang. 'Always a cuckoo we have out the back door in April.

Wouldn't be spring without it,' she said, smiling, and taking my hand. I felt such love – had I ever known such love for people? Not knotted up like my love for Father, or full of thorns as my feelings for Jacob were, but simple, nourishing as porridge laced with honey. Ruth stroked my face and smiled, and Ben came up and patted my hand and called me 'child', and they neither of them had a doubt or a shred of fear of me. The dread that clutched at my heart and my belly finally gave up its hold. I am no witch, I suddenly thought, and I believed it to be true. I must have said it aloud, for Ruth nodded.

'Of course you're not, dearie,' she said. 'I would know one a mile off.'

Ben stood with his pitchfork by the door, keeping lookout up and down the lane. Now and again he turned to me and smiled too broadly, his old hands kneading anxiously.

'Not long now, child,' he said, again. 'Bert will see you right.'

I perched on the cot and did my best to smile back.

Then all at once the door burst open. Ben was

thrown forward. Ruth and I seized hold of one another in alarm. A man near fell in, but sprang up in an instant and grabbed old Ben by the smock.

'What has happened? Is she dead? Has my mother killed her? Where have you taken her?' Jacob. It was Jacob.

Ruth had stepped forward to hide me, but I rose. Everyone knew I was here. It could only be a short while before the constables came, and if it was Jacob at their head I wanted to know it.

'I am here,' I said.

He turned as I spoke the words. All the fences had gone from his gaze. He was before me, reaching to take my hands. He turned them over and kissed my palms and cupped them about his face and leaned his head against my own and I would have stepped into fire for him then.

'Come, come,' Ben said, 'a bit more temperate, lad. If you're so fond of the girl where were you when they came at her and half tore the skin off her back?'

Jacob coloured a little, and stepped away, but he kept hold of my hands. After the funeral, he told us, he had had to take a load of rabbit skins to be sold in town. There were things he'd needed to consider, and here I could not meet his eyes. He'd not thought me in danger, with the earth fresh on my father's grave, and though he had little faith in Sir William or Miss Elizabeth he had reckoned their protection would stay folk from any direct show of violence. Saturday night had been so fair he had slept out by Sleaves Oak and counted stars. He paused, embarrassed. It was not only that, he said, meeting my eyes, his mother had wrought him so he half believed I had ensnared his soul somehow, and indeed my own words had seemed to say so.

'Why, Martha?' he said now. 'Why did you say that?'

I flushed. What could I say? I didn't hardly know myself. Except, I was afraid of his disgust and had thought somehow I could ambush it. 'You looked so shamed,' I said. 'I thought my willing it must have worked upon you, or it could not be true. I was afraid there must be magic in it. And you, why have you returned to me?'

'I could not be freed, whether I wished it or no. And I realised I did not. I do not wish to be free, Martha. It was strange. I lay on the warm earth and dreamed you were there too, sleeping, and there was nothing in the world but the breast of the hill and the stars and we two. And I woke and knew you were dearer to me than the pulse of my own blood. I cursed myself for leaving you alone. The second I entered the stables the hands told me how you had been turned away. And, oh, Martha, I thought you might be dead!'

'It could have come to that,' said Ruth, 'and your own mother and aunt set it on,' and she turned me round and uncovered my back a little.

'Oh,' he said, his voice long and drawn and low so that I was afraid at what he saw. 'Oh God, oh God, I was the cause of this.'

'No cause,' I said, turning back to him, 'no cause.' And I took his face and kissed his eyes and his forehead and his mouth.

'Well,' Ben interrupted us, 'enough billing and cooing. If you mean what you say and are not here to work a foul trick on the girl you had best say your goodbyes. She has to be off. Bert should have been here already. It'll be too late if we leave it an hour more.'

Ruth bound me again and helped me with my cloak.

Jacob straightened himself. 'I'll not leave her,' he said. 'I'll not leave you, Martha, not any more. I shall marry you.' He turned to the Tranters. 'We must marry, now. You must be our witnesses, in the sight of God.'

'Oh dear Christ,' Ruth said, 'save the young from themselves. Steady on, this is too fast.'

'No,' Jacob said, 'it is much too slow. I have known it must be so since the hole appeared, only I doubted my own heart.'

Ruth raised her brows at her husband, who was shaking his head. 'If anything were to take the sting out of Judith Spicer it is their being wed. And I do not wish to pry, but it is clear things have gone so far that you had better be knit.'

Ben frowned and shrugged at her. 'A handfast. I suppose it is legal,' he said. 'They are old enough.'

Jacob sank to his knees and I kneeled too, and he took both my hands in his. 'Martha Dynely, in the sight of our Redeemer and these good people, I marry you.' He smiled and poked me, for I kneeled stupid and silent beside him. 'You have to say it too.'

'Jacob,' I said, hardly believing my own voice. 'Jacob Spicer, I marry you, here, now, for my whole life long in the sight of God.' And I reached into my gown and found where I had sewn the ring my father gave me and I pulled it out and put it on his finger.

'Goodness,' Ruth said, 'who'd have thought you'd have a ring ready. Well, that was quickly done, but better so, perhaps. Listen, that's the cart now. Bert has sacks to hide you. Tend to her back, Jacob, that the wounds stay clean. Send us word when you are safe.'

39

THE BLACKBIRD

Bert's face was as hard to read as a sheep's is as it chews over the grass. He stowed us between sacks and hogsheads, saying nothing, but taking care my back was clear of aught that might jolt on it.

'I don't say as it's decent, you two laid up together, married or not. In my book a priest should have a hand in that, though the law's the law,' he said to Jacob. 'I'll take you up Pixley way and you can wait for Tom by the Roman road. And I'll tend your poor father's grave, girl, till such time as you can come back and fetch flowers for yourself. Lay still, the pair of you, and don't say a word.'

The hours that followed were the softest and the harshest I had ever known. He took us right through the village. We knew just where we were by the greetings people threw at him. Even the ruts were familiar. As we went past our own cottages we put our hands over one another's mouth.

'Good day to you, Bert.' It was the Widow. I felt Jacob's jaw tense beneath my palm. She sounded nervous. 'What news at the Hall? Have the constables taken her yet? You might have passed them. It was an hour ago, at least, they set off and Father Paul with them.'

'Aye, missus, I passed them. Father Paul looked very well pleased. Heard you had a bit of justice of your own. Wet your whistles a little, before the law and the vicar could take a good long drink.'

'We only did what was right, Bert, to protect our own. There's a boy lying near death yonder, remember that. Have you seen my Jacob, by any chance? You tell him to come home, if you see him.'

'Oh, I doubt he'll stray now you've seen to her, Judith Spicer. He'll know where his heart lies.

Wait a moment... Take this toothpick to clean out your nails.'

We lay pressed together between the hogsheads, under the burlap sacking, and the joy of lying so was greater than the pain in my back. He smelled of wet grass and the stables. Softly, quietly, so that a mouse would scarce have seen a movement, I took my hand from his mouth and we kissed, long and slow, as though we were drinking one another's souls.

We were past the village and long past the house before I thought of Owen. Had he been waiting for me all day in that dark room, with the sour smell of his cot and his bitter family about him? Or perhaps he had heard I was to be taken. Perhaps his father was crouching over him, waiting to see if the scratching had released him. Agnes I did not want to think about. She had betrayed me. Worse, I had betrayed her too.

Bert set us down in the woods south of Pixley, at a long-abandoned cottage. A rowan tree grew out of a broken wall and a blackbird alighted as we approached and did not take fright. I took that as a good sign. We dared not make a fire, but Bert left us sacking that we placed over a drift of last year's fallen leaves.

As evening came the pain grew worse, each slight shift of my limbs ached and I began to fear the wounds grew infected, but Ruth had bound them up tight and I thought it better to leave the dressing in place. Jacob peeled back my gown to check for swelling and whistled low as if he were seeing it for the first time. Then he stood and swore.

'What do I do?' he said at last. 'Do I hate my own mother, my silly old aunt? They did this.'

'Not only them.'

'Chiefly them.'

'It was for love of you.'

'Love of me be damned. It was for love of position.'

You have forgot, I thought, that you, too, lately questioned what I was; that I myself sought out the green well in despair, to try if I was guilty. But I said nothing and presently he came and kneeled before me where I sat, and kissed my shoulders and my bare arms and my sides, and he went on kissing till I felt no pain, only swooning, and then he laid himself down on his back and drew me to him. We did not speak, but softly, gently, we moved together and the blackbird trilled in me and through me and for me, and all was singing.

40

TAKEN

In the dawn the road and trees were dewed and mantled by the mist. I do not think we spoke at all; our voices would have broken something of the stillness and the peace. Jacob went down to the road and waited. It did not seem a good sign that the horizon was veiled from us. At length I heard his whistle. There was Tom, with his laden cart and my father's beautiful chair atop of it all. How had he managed that?

He grinned when he saw me. 'Thought I might not find you standing after what you've been through, but you're a tough one, Martha.

Can't keep yourself from saving her, can you, Jacob? First the earth and now the noose, is that it? I hope you've not done ought you shouldn't.'

'We are married, Tom. The Tranters witnessed it.'

'The Tranters, eh?' and I could not but help noticing a cloud cross his brow, though he blinked it off. 'Well, that's as may be; I don't doubt you love one another and you'll make a fine couple, but if you don't want to find yourself a widower before you've brought your bride under a lintel you'd best get back, Jacob.'

'I've made my choice, Tom. I'm coming with her to Worcester.'

'And what'll you do there, pray?'

'I'll find work. I know horses, and every inn has a stables.'

'Every short-breeched boy knows horses, or says he does. All the work you know is here. Wait here, save your money and when the land is settled fetch her home, or near home. Or if you must, join her when you've got a place set up and money in your purse. Come now and afore long you'll find yourselves in a stinking room with a puking baby in your arms and you'll have no comfort for it, or each other. My sister will see Martha right, find her a place and send word by me.'

It was all good sense. I glanced at Jacob and the set of his jaw. There was a whisper of the Widow in the line of it, though I scuttled the thought away.

'Thank you, Tom,' he said, 'but I'll take my chances.'

Tom opened his mouth to reply, but just then a horseman emerged from the mist and trotted by. Jacob and Tom touched their caps and I dropped my head. As they set to again I ventured a glance back and to my consternation saw the horse had stalled and the man was craning back to look right at me. The others had not noticed and when I looked again he had gone.

'Tom,' I said, butting in, 'I am anxious to get going.' We agreed that Jacob should walk alongside at least as far as Stony Brook, where Tom had a friend with whom we could break our fast.

'I think you should go back,' I said to Jacob as he helped me up.

'No,' he said.

'Ha,' I said, 'I wondered how long before we fell back into argument.'

He threw his head back in the way that used to puzzle me so, and then he grinned. 'It was falling into difference that felled me. I am fallen, I am at your feet.'

'Nothing like a bit of chafing to warm a body up,' said Tom.

The sun came up and the mist began curling up into the branches. I was leaving all the world I had ever known, but the sun was shining and as we neared Pixley church the pear blossom was beginning in the orchards. The road did not wind and meander like the lanes I knew, it sliced through the country with a purpose. Far in the west the ripples of the land rose into waves. I thought of the Roman soldiers in the ancient days when it was built; who knew how many miles they had walked? Had they dreamed of settling here, or of returning to their own country?

I felt the tilt of possibilities in the rise of the road as we drew towards the horizon. And after all, what was I leaving, but a ruined name and the bitterness of neighbours I had never loved? Although that too was not true, or not all of that was true. I remembered sitting up on the ridge with Owen, before the Wonder finally ripped the world apart, with the redwings in the rowans and our talk of Hereford, and I thought of my grandmother's and my father's graves and I knew the lines of the land were written into me as deeply as my veins. No scratch could score them out.

A fair number of folk passed us, on their way to the orchards and the fields. At first I cowered, but after the first one or two I saw we were nothing to them, just faces on the road that they wished good day to and passed by. So I did not take much notice of the sound of hoofs that came up from behind till I looked up and saw riders either side of us. One was the horseman who had passed us earlier and looked back.

'You had better stop, sirrah,' he said to Tom.

'Happen I will,' said Tom, 'and then happen I won't. It all depends how I am asked.' He reined in the horse nonetheless.

The gentleman ignored him and pointed at me. 'What is your name?' he said.

I tried to look calm. 'Susan,' I said, 'Susan

Birch.'

'No,' he said, 'it isn't. I note you perjure yourself without compunction. It fits. You had better come along with me. Make no fuss and I shall let your companions carry on their business, or at least I'll let the miller go. This one,' he pointed at Jacob, 'I'm told is needed.'

'On whose authority?' asked Tom, turning to him, red faced.

The rider laughed. 'Saucy fellow, are you? On the authority of my sword. But since you ask, there is a warrant out for her. The bishop has come to terms with Sir William and her neck is part of the bargain. That, and a deal of trees. There's a whiff of Rome about Sir William and a deal of washing to be done. It'll be no small service to him and the bishop, too, to deliver the girl.'

Tom glanced round. The flanking riders looked hastily mounted and carried only staves, but there were four of them. I saw where his thoughts were headed. 'No,' I said, 'please, Tom, you are more use to everyone free and hale.'

I got down as quickly as my back and my ankle would let me. Jacob stepped in front of me, one hand on the knife at his side. I leaned up towards his ear. 'If you let yourself be killed I'll fashion the noose myself,' I said, 'and it'll be you who will have killed me.'

'That's right,' said the gentleman, dismounting, 'no cock of the walk prancing, young man. See –' with a fling of his arm he drew his sword, and pointed it at Jacob's belly – 'I could run you through. You are chaff. I doubt even the miller would bother to pick up your body. Still, you may come in handy.' He nodded to the fellow next to Jacob. 'Tie his arms – it's best.' Then he turned to me. 'I am glad you have a head on your shoulders. None of your cursing, mind, or it'll go hard on you, and harder on the old woman.'

I turned to Tom in alarm. He spread his hands before him, and shrugged. 'What good would it have done you to know?' he said. 'When you weren't at the house they took Ruth. Took her cat, too. Dragged the poor woman off, with old Ben weeping on her skirts. They've penned her in that room above the stables where you learned the boys their letters.'

'Let them take us, Tom, and go on to Worcester,' I said, 'and if you would help us, seek out if there are any learned men in the city who might come to our aid.'

41

BACK IN THE SCHOOLROOM

It was strange to find myself so reduced in the only place I had felt power. A corner of it, at any rate. They had made a kind of cell with a dusty school bench along one wall and a load of straw. There was light enough, from the gaps beneath the eaves. Ruth sat huddled as though trying to press herself into the walls. Her face was full of shock, and she was slowly wagging her head and mumbling. I do not think that at first she knew me, but then her face broke into a smile, which turned into a little cry.

'I prayed that you had got away, child.'

I kneeled down in front of her and took her hands in mine. 'I am so sorry, Ruth,' I said. 'Your kindness has brought you misery and torment. It is all on my account, all of it.'

'Enough of that. You did not command me. I couldn't leave you to be torn to bits. Don't speak of that again. I am old enough and foolish enough to make choices for myself, Martha. Oh, but I fret about Ben. This will not go easy on him.'

Rough hangings cut us off from the rest of the room and a guard sat beyond them, though there was little need for him; neither of us could have done much to escape. He must have been one of the bishop's men. He was not local. He seemed mightily nervous of me, and shrank back when I approached, till he picked up a hazel stick to keep me at a distance.

I did not know what they had done with Jacob. At first I thought he was simply at the other end of the room and I called out to him, but there was no reply and the guard came forward and struck me with his hazel stick and bade me keep quiet if I did not want more stripes. And so it was for hours.

No one came near us. Outside we heard the noises of the stables and the farm: horses coming and going, shouts from the men. Mice ran freely through the straw and a rat or two loped along the far wall. Ruth's cat, Comfrey, was in a nailed crate and couldn't get at them; she mewled pitifully.

I sat on the floor before Ruth and she combed my hair with her fingers over and over and then she plaited it. She had a fine voice for one so old and knew a great many songs and she sang them softly, so as not to annoy the guard. We thought he couldn't hear, but at one point, when she had fallen silent, he growled that she might sing that one again, the one that began 'In Worcester city there lived a maiden'.

I was not happy – I could not say that – for I knew well enough what awaited us, and more, that I had drawn the few people I cared about in all the world into mortal danger. My back stung and however I sat I could not be comfortable. Almost worse, they had taken my white dove from my pocket, 'a better bit of evidence they couldn't have wished for' and like a fool I'd cried to keep it, saying it was my mother's, which made it all the better for them, of course. Yet an odd kind of peace had taken root in me, and I looked back at the way I had fallen into despair with astonishment. I knew in my heart at last that I was not an evil thing to be cast out as the body works up a splinter to the surface and expels it. I had a place here as much as they, and there were people who loved me. I did not want to die. It was fierce and new, this feeling. I felt it even to the tips of my fingers.

One night Ruth had been taken to a barn to be questioned. Father Paul had appeared like a moth, she said, in his flapping cassock, though he bore the light himself. For an hour he had paced around her, exhorting and cajoling. If she confessed, he said, the Lord in His unspeakable mercy would save her soul; even now He would save it.

'I tell you, Martha,' she said, 'he leaned his long face into mine with such supplication, such passion in the Lord's great love that I was moved to weep; had he continued I think I must have succumbed for he seemed to be speaking in the voice of Christ Himself, full up of suffering and pain in His love for me and all I had to do was relent and release myself unto Him.'

'I've felt it myself,' I said. 'It's as though his gaze could see into my heart and find what I myself was not aware of, as though I could be washed clean and new, if only I would unstopper myself and flow into forgiveness.' Father Paul's hands, I remembered, smelled of lavender, and his nails were always clean. Sometimes, as he leaned towards me calling me to repent, his whole body had trembled in his love for Christ. 'What did you do, Ruth? You must not confess to wickedness you were never guilty of.'

'Well, he fell to threatening and then I was safe.' She smiled grimly and her voice shook. 'I might be pardoned, he said, if I confessed to your being a witch. Oh, Martha, it does not take much, after all, for neighbours to turn on one another. To be safe from sin is hard enough, but to be safe from your neighbours! He says there's those come forward who swear that Comfrey over there is my familiar, that these marks on my forehead are where he has sucked my blood, that I caused Joan

Nesbitt's cow to sicken – though that's not such a wonder: she's been against us since Ben caught her boy in the kitchen garden. Goody Reynolds swears that at Mass she has heard me say my prayers in Latin, because Satan forbids the English. He says – oh, Martha, I am sorry, but it is better that you know – that I was confederate with your mother in her youth and she a proven witch.'

'Did you know my mother, Ruth?'

'No, child. I heard about her, of course, and pitied her. Your father in his sickness dwelled on the part Jane Reynolds played, how she was supposed to help your mother's case, but had vented poison on her. I pieced the story from fragments: Jane hoped to gain favour with the mistress; her mind had been so worked on that she saw salvation in sending Bessie Gould to the rope. She's a weak-minded thing. She's going about now with a tale that you are not your father's child, but got upon your mother by a Saracen sailor and dedicated to the devil from your birth.'

'Father Paul told you this?'

'Yes, and more. He was seized with joy, and said so, in the devil being unmasked and the evil purged from the land. He says your blood is rank. You caused the very bones of the land to fester and collapse. For the parish to be whole again all the rot must be cut out. Then the sick would be made whole. Oh, Martha, I think we must pray for a miracle, for the evidence against you is terrible and if I didn't know you and love you I should think you an abomination.'

'Please, tell me all. It's better I hear it from you. It will come out. Chiefly, it is the pulling down of God's holy chapel and bewitching Owen, is it not? And no doubt they are saying that Jacob, too, has been enchanted.'

'Yes, but it's the young boy, above all. Everything turns on him, especially after the baby died.'

* * *

Some time in the afternoon there was a great noise of furniture being dragged up into the space outside our cell.

'Last time I was here she made Jacob Spicer sit down on one of them benches and he turned it over,' Ben Ladding's voice said. 'There weren't no love lost then, I can tell you. Reckon she must have worked on him good and proper if she's got him silly for her.'

'Not just the devil has laid with her, then,' said another I did not recognise. 'Fancy a bit yourself at all?'

Ruth squeezed my hand.

'Set them down and get out,' the guard barked.

When they'd left he ducked into our cell. He leered at me. 'The Father's bringing your love-shaked boy here for a talking. Wants you to hear how he turns on you. He's not to know you're here, not till the Father chooses, at any rate. D'you hear? Any sound from you, either of you, and I'll thrash you. Then I'll call one or two of the lads in so he can flip you on your back to find what the devil thinks so tasty. They're not very particular – might even do the same to granny here.'

I heard Jacob's footsteps first: he was shuffling. Had they beaten him? I looked at Ruth and she pointed. There was a burn hole in the hanging; if I stood up tall I could see through it. The room had been swept clean and a table with a chair behind it had been set out. Jacob was standing before the table, his hands tied in front of him. It was almost more than I could do to stay silent. Just a few feet! His head was bowed, but he looked up when Father Paul entered, and I saw that his left eye was swollen. Ruth had come to stand next to me and she put her finger to my lips and wiped my face. I had not noticed I was weeping. I was like the thrush surprised from the nest with all her perfect dappled eggs exposed, and what thick grubby fingers might come nesting? What hope had Jacob against Father Paul?

'There are those,' Father Paul said at last, after simply staring for a long while, till Jacob shuffled on his shackled feet, 'who assert that you have been an accomplice to the witch since before the catastrophe – I will not call it a Wonder – and that you found the boy because you were in league with her. And then there are others who declare you are a good son and a true Christian who has been worked on cruelly, so that you have abandoned a pretty sweetheart and an honest home to follow after this lame Jezebel. Which is it, Jacob? Which is it?'

Jacob said nothing.

'Because,' the Father went on, 'I am of the latter party. Why would a good, strong lad, affianced to a beauty, loyal son to a worthy mother, abandon all to a tawny shrew unless he were bewitched? Listen, can you hear it? A host of peewits came this morning to cluster on the field outside. Why is that, do you think, Jacob? "Bewitched" – they cry it out for you, "bewitched".'

'She is not a witch.' Jacob spoke so low and hoarse I could barely hear the words. 'She is not a witch and I have married her. She is my wife.'

'Oh, she's a witch, all right, and Ruth Tranter's another, and any marriage conducted by witches cannot be allowed to stand. She lay with Satan long before she lay with you. Those lips you kissed were greasy with filth from the fiend himself.'

I was fearful of the effect of these words, but I saw Jacob throw his head back and look at the priest through half-closed lids. Father Paul got up and walked around the table and his voice grew soft, though he made sure that it was strong enough to carry.

'You could walk free. You are the victim, not the malefactor. Do you think she cares about you? No, no. Recollect. I have heard how she scorned you when you sought to learn how to read God's holy word. She knew you were destined for Agnes Simons, that both families desired it. She is made of envy and of lust. Women are all appetite – the ancients tell us this. The womb is hungry for seed. It must be kept in check. And in one who has forsaken her God and her faith, what limits are there on her desires?'

Jacob glanced away then. I could not see if he reddened, but he looked confused. Oh my darling, I thought, do not weaken.

Father Paul put a hand on his shoulder. 'Ecclesiastes 7:26 tells us: *a woman like that is bitterer than death, she has cast her heart abroad as a net men fish with and her hands are chains. The man who pleases God will escape her but the sinner will be taken with her.* She told you she loved you and no end of pretty words – we all know she is clever. Such cleverness in a woman is dangerous, unnatural. When a woman thinks alone, she thinks evil. A woman is a liar by nature and she stings whilst she delights. Unless they are ruled by faith they cannot help but deceive. I say a liar by nature – I have cause. Wasn't Eve fashioned from a bent rib? There was a crookedness in her from the beginning. Think how the Lord sought to remind you of this by striking the witch a cripple.'

He had begun walking around Jacob slowly, talking gently, occasionally pausing to put an arm on his shoulder. And occasionally, as he did so, he would glance towards us and smile his long-lipped smile, so that I pulled my eye away, convinced that he could see it, though surely it was not possible.

'It is scarcely your fault – she is as wily as the serpent. How can you be surprised, for her mother was a witch before her and fornicated with the devil? From this coupling she was conceived. Her father had none of her, though he damned himself on his own account – and how could he not, living with women such as that? It is written that it is better for a man to dwell with a lion and a dragon than to keep house with a wicked woman. Think, son, the lion and the dragon are her bedfellows.

She waked a dragon under the earth and pulled down God's house. What else is a woman but a foe to friendship, an unescapable punishment, an evil of nature, painted with fair colours? All wickedness is but little to the wickedness of a woman.'

Still Jacob said nothing, but his eyes followed Father Paul as he circled as far as he could without shifting his feet and then he tilted his head back, but whether in scorn or confusion now I could not tell.

'Do you fear God and damnation?'

'I fear God and damnation.'

'You are a simple man and she has subtle arts. This longing you feel for her, it is worked upon you. Think of the Lord Jesus, who died on the cross, for your sins. And think of the fires of hell. I am the keeper of your soul in this parish. Just as your beasts look to you to guide them, let me guide you.'

'I don't know,' he said at last, swaying a little where he stood; his voice a rough whisper. 'I love her and I want to love God. You tell me I cannot do both. But there is no wickedness about her.

She trusts in the Lord Jesus just as I do. I think she does. I am sure of it.'

'Can you be sure? Can you? You've heard of the mermaid, Jacob, that sings in the sea and lures poor fishermen to their deaths? You are like one of those sailors, Jacob, who has listened too long. She has twined her voice around your soul and now you are drowning. Open your ears to God.' Father Paul almost cooed in Jacob's ear. Then louder, 'Cast out the serpent,' and then in a shout, 'Begone!' so that Jacob recoiled in surprise. 'Get thee gone, Satan.' He grasped Jacob's shoulders and clasped him close. 'Sweet Lord Jesus, welcome this lost sheep back to the fold.'

Jacob sank to his knees and began to weep. I could not bear it; I could not bear to watch. Still I heard Father Paul's voice.

'She has confessed. Everything. She told us of the place and how it happened and the charm she used. Look, a carved dove, she had it in her hand when she corrupted you, didn't she? Tell us how she seduced you and you will be free, and your mother will not be brought in as an accomplice and you will not lose your house and your goods, and I will give you water.'

I returned to the peephole. Jacob was still on his knees but he had recovered himself and he was not weeping. Father Paul had resumed his seat behind the table and was furiously writing. Jacob cast his eyes around the room; his gaze drifted vaguely towards us. I did not dare speak, but I pressed my whole body against the hanging and he must have seen for he started and glanced quickly at the priest and the guard, then turned again to me. 'Wait a little,' he said, getting to his feet.

Father Paul looked up. 'No, no, it must be now. I have everything ready. This is the true testimony of Jacob Spicer, stable-hand. Go on...'

'Please,' Jacob said, standing, 'I must pray. I lost my way, almost. I was almost lost, but my good angel strengthens me. I must pray to learn how best to tell you.'

'I can help you with the words. I am the Lord's vassal here.'

'My head swims. I am dizzy. I feel a great need of prayer, sir. I swear to you that I am a God-fearing man and have never served any master but the Lord Jesus and Sir William.'

Father Paul looked at Jacob for a long time, then walked round and stood behind him. 'Do not provoke His anger,' he said softly. 'Cast out Satan or we will drive him hence by force. Till tomorrow, then.'

42

BARGAINS: THE WITCH'S MARK

The next morning the guard roused us, though we had already been wakened by the clatter of the horses.

'You'd best make yourselves ready, you've a visitor.'

We wondered who it could be, for we knew Ben was not permitted, though Ruth longed to hear from him. I had certainly not expected Agnes.

We both stood there, staring, till Ruth took a hand from each of us and placed them together palm on palm and although Agnes pulled it away she did not step back.

I hung my head. 'Aggie, Agnes, I have not done the things they accuse me of, but I have wronged you and for that I am sorry.'

'You can't undo it,' she said sharply.

'No,' I said, 'and I wouldn't if I could. I am sorry for the hurt I caused you. I should not have deceived you. I don't think he did – deceive you, I mean – not for long or perhaps at all. He did not understand himself.'

'You saw to that, they say.'

'No, truly, unless my wishing made it so. I used no herbs or charms, Agnes.' I paused. 'Do you love him very much?'

She looked at me a moment, then shrugged and sat down on the bench. 'I don't know. It was always to be. He's the best-looking boy around here and he's a good heart.' She looked pensive a while. 'I think I loved him, though in my heart I knew I might do better,' and without thinking she patted her hair and I knew I had not lost her utterly. I sat down next to her and leaned my head on her shoulder, and this time, though she winced a little, she let me. I would have hugged her if my hands had not been bound.

'They told me about your back, Martha. What my father and the others did. Let me see it.'

It was scabbing up now, but it made her gasp. 'He was wrong to do that,' she whispered. 'Listen,' she said, as she helped me back on with my robe. 'I know about Owen. Mother could not keep it from me and nor should she, his own sister. My father would see, too, if he were not blinded with rage. My mother is afraid we will lose him again if things go badly for you, but he is too frail to face my father, let alone the courts. And after what happened to Ruth and Jacob, she is afraid of his being taken alongside you, for all he's just a child. But she said to tell you she would do what she could for you.'

I thought of Owen coming to his senses, with the world gone mad around him. Perhaps after treating me so ill, Miss Elizabeth would seek to salve her soul by helping him, and if she did it was I who would have made it possible. The thought comforted me. As though reading the direction of my thoughts Agnes nodded. 'I was let in because Miss Elizabeth sent me.'

I stood up and turned away for I saw again in

my mind the face at the window and the gloved hand on the glass. She loved to wear pearls, stitched in her bodice and threaded in her hair, for the pearl of great price, who was the Christ Child. They spoke of faithfulness and purity, and I had thought her lustrous with them.

'She says she would not have barred the door against you, that she was not told you had come begging, but indeed, whilst she would do what she could it was the Queen's justice and the Lord's mercy you must turn to now.'

'By which I am to know I must never presume to use her name,' I commented bitterly. 'Never trust the rich, Aggie. They will use you and pamper you, then grind you under their satin slippers for you will always be dirt to them.'

Aggie raised her eyebrows at me. 'Who can I trust, pray? Neither my friends nor my family have shown much faith in me of late. But you must hear me out. The next bit you will like even less, I think. Miss Elizabeth wishes me to tell you that, for her part and her father's, they forgive the gross abuse you have made of their time and patronage, but your practising against children she cannot forgive, though she will pray for your deliverance from the evil into which you have strayed.'

I spat on the floor. 'Tell her I don't give a fart for her or her prayers and may she stink in hell as she stinks here on earth. Tell her that, Aggie. No wait...' I stopped myself and thought. 'Tell her I know my father built priest holes in the Hall, that I know where they are and who was lately hid in them, and that if Ruth is not presently released, and Jacob too, I will dig up my father's drawings and rant in open court about Nicholas Craddock. Nay, more, that I will write to the Queen's attorney.'

Aggie's eyes opened wide. 'And why should she believe you will keep your word?'

'Because I am going to die and do not wish to ruin those I leave behind. And Owen must have his scholarship if he recovers – she must declare it publicly – say that too.'

* * *

In the afternoon Ruth was taken to a different

place and I saw no one for the rest of the day, but one or other of the guards. The next morning Agnes visited me again, flustered and red faced. I could not but see that she was happy, though she tried not to show it. She was barely before me than she began talking.

'I am grown quite brazen with the gentry. I have seen her and she was very gracious and said that whilst all you alleged was false, it was the devil's greatest joy to tickle idle tongues. She was confident she could help Ruth. Indeed, she had acted on this already. Jacob would be freed when he confessed and that was expected shortly. As for Owen's scholarship, she declared this was her own idea entirely. She had thought of it long before, but had held off because it might seem, now it was impossible, to taunt my parents with what they'd lost. However, she now believed it might give them heart and would honour what he had once been. Her father had already agreed to announce it after the service on Sunday.

'I was about to leave, Martha, when she called me back, caressing me and saying what a fine girl I was to seek to aid the friend who had used me so cruelly. It only served to show, she said, that she was right in the faith she had felt in me and therefore if I was agreeable I was to take up the position we'd talked of next week, to be trained as a lady's maid to Lady Letitia Swanson. Oh, Martha, it is as I'd hoped. She is newly married and not old at all. Miss Elizabeth says she is known at court.'

'I'm glad for you, Agnes, only be careful, especially of the gentlemen, for they will lick you up like honey and then spit you out. Tell her Jacob must be freed, whether he confesses or no.' I sat down, inexpressibly weary. Ruth would be saved. Perhaps Jacob, too, but very soon I would be hanging, like my mother, from a gallows tree. 'I have played my only card and now I have nothing left,' I said. 'Kiss Owen for me.'

Agnes did not come again. The hours unspooled slowly one by one and outside the world carried on with the bustle of spring. The days went by. I grew filthier and the stench in the cell thicker and more rank, for they scarcely bothered to empty the bucket except when Father Paul came. Night after night he appeared in the early evening as the light through the eaves faltered and the shadows grew and the rats began to grow emboldened. He loathed me, that was plain enough. His body was tense with disgust – the very sight of me appalled him – but still his faith demanded that he worked for my soul to wrest it from damnation.

Most of the time I remained numb to his exhortations; he was a great black fly, with all his buzzing and his hankering for dirt. I could not understand, now, how I had been moved to see myself through his eyes or felt his voice wind itself around my heart. I had my faith and he was apart from it, or only attached as shit is to a wheel. But his words could still bite.

'I expect you would like to hear about Jacob Spicer. He has testified against you, you know. It did not take long for him to turn to the light of Jesus. He reviles you and Satan and all his works. He is at home for now, tended by his mother, poor thing, though it does not look good for him. She has called for me once already in the thick of the night, although the Good Lord did not see fit to take him at that time.'

'He is ill?'

'Oh, yes, very. And he damns you for his ruin.'

If he dies, I thought, I will gnaw through my own wrist as a rat does in a trap, but I did not know how far to believe the Father. Perhaps Jacob *had* testified – I half hoped so, for he would be safer then – yet I was sure Father Paul would not have been able to resist the delight of exhibiting the document.

On the last evening he brought a young man, an officer of the court. They were to inspect my body for the witch's mark, for where I had given suck to my familiars. He untied me and ordered me to strip. The officer looked away, but Father Paul surveyed me steadily. One by one I peeled each wretched garment off, even the bandages, until I felt my nakedness in every pore. The young man gasped when he saw my back and made many notes on the parchment he held, though it was barely light enough to see. Had I eaten, he asked. He would fetch me food. After he had gone Father Paul stepped up close and ran his nail lightly along the scabs, to check, he said, if they were scabs or no. Then he turned me around and about, sniffing and stroking to check for the devil's script. I am wood, I told myself, I am a block of wood. I feel nothing. He paused at a mole on my belly, circling a fingertip around and around it. And then he stepped close and placed his right hand on my head as though blessing me like a papist, but his left hand he drew down my body to my secret places and his long fingers searched me there, while he stared into my face without blinking and his fingers rubbed back and forth, back and forth, and his breath grew short.

'Lust,' he said to the footsteps approaching through the curtain, his mouth so close the sour spittle flecked my lips, 'she brims with it.'

'There was no nipple?' the young man asked.

'Look, this mole, here on her belly – look how the skin puckers around it. It is a witch's mark. You may go. I will stay and pray a little for her.' Whilst I dressed he dropped to his knees, lifted his hands in prayer and bent his head. But as he prayed he sniffed his fingers, and then he licked them one by one. It was only when the young man reappeared, awkwardly looking for his quill, that Father Paul roused himself and left.

43

A MIRACLE

I slept in my boots for fear of the rats, and so when they came for me the next morning and bade me come with them, I had nothing to do but stand up and leave. There was the young officer of the court who had accompanied Father Paul the night before, but the others I did not know. The young man told me his name was Pugh and the men were Hereford constables. I was being taken to the city gaol, for now. Father Paul, he told me, eyeing me closely, was gone ahead this morning. He hoped I was not too shaken by last night's questioning? I said nothing, for I was wood and could feel or say nothing. I had doled out far too many words already. He seemed to want to be friendly, though, Pugh, for he had found me a cloak from somewhere.

'Oh, but you're a poor wretch,' he said, not unkindly, as he fastened it around my shoulders.

I ducked under the lintel and the sun dazzled and kindled me. There was a warmth that spoke to me of summer and I could not help but feel it. A cuckoo called. The golden months were beginning once again. I stood in the yard with the sky above me and closed my eyes a moment to the waiting cart. All would be planting and growing, but like the cuckoo, I might not see the harvest.

Pugh assured me a city constable would ride before the cart; he himself would ride alongside. I should have no fear of a repeat of the savagery that tore my back. I nodded, though just then I scarcely felt present enough to scratch. My mind gusted off till the pain in my joints and a dizzy sickness in my belly recalled me.

We rolled onto the track towards the village, and all above us the wind played softly in the branches while sunlight strained the new veined leaves like church glass. I drank in the clean air. On either side there were lambs in the fields. Only, up on the ridge the great red wound was still open, strewn with the wreckage of trees and hedges. Somewhere in the clay lay the chapel bell and the scattered bodies of the dead. The thought set me shuddering.

Pugh must have been watching me. 'You must not give up hope. There are many men of learning who could tell you how it was weather and not witchcraft caused this slide. I came, you know, after that rent in the road. I met your father. He was a man of sense. You must trust in God. They can only hang you if there is proof you have harmed the boy or the baby who died. It's true the evidence against you is strong and the father is an ardent man. But there's hope for you yet.'

I looked at him properly. He was not so young as I had thought, only his good clothes and his clipped beard made him appear so. 'Tell me,' I said, 'is there news of my husband, Jacob? Father Paul told me he was like to die.'

'It was feared so, indeed, for he took a fever from a wound, but it has broken I hear and it is hoped he will live. Sir William has of late become his advocate. He is determined that Jacob Spicer be a witness only, and not charged along with you.'

'Did he not testify?'

'He declared that he was ready, and I sat down with my parchment and my quill, but his deposition was not to the Father's liking. Much persuasion was used on him, I am afraid. It was little surprise he took ill. Then they swiftly declared him raving and his testimony void, and sent him home. It was his mother, you know, who made the deposition against you, declaring him bewitched, but she is a canny woman. When she saw she might unawares be weaving her son a noose she stepped back a little to think on her words. She would happily see you swing, but she does not wish her malice to leak back and stain her own hearth.'

I was sitting facing back towards the Hall and this was just, for I did not wish to look ahead. I could see only the rutted track I had passed through already. If I bent my eyes very hard on the road then I might keep all in check. Soon we would pass his house. I would be a few feet from where he lay and he would not know. *Husband.* The word lingered on my tongue and it felt strange to me: it belonged to the life I would not have. If he survived all this then in a year – two years, three – he would wed another girl and bring her home, and perhaps, God willing, he would be happy. I tried to imagine it, yet could not bring myself to. In my mind's eye, I pictured him walking alone to the warrens or the stables. When the blackbird sang he would hear the bird that chorused our bridal bed in the wood and he would remember.

I was looking back at the lane so steadily I did not at first register the crowd, though I had ex-pected them. With a jolt I heard Pugh shout, 'Make way, make way, I tell you. I am the Queen's officer and I am about her business. Make way.'

And there they were, on the track before and around the cart: women, men and children. The boys I had taught, their brothers and sisters, the Tuckers, Laddings, Stolleys, Tanners, even the

Clutterbucks come from Putley. There were others, too, that I did not know. And at the front stood Richard Simons, his face set on me in hate and anger; beside him Goody Reynolds, shaking her skinny old fist. Not the Widow, though. I lowered my eyes to the planking in the cart and tried not to hear the jabber. It was only words: things my familiars had done with me, things my neighbours should like to do themselves. I ventured to look and perceived not all were shouting. There were some who looked back at me and nodded, as though I were simply Martha Dynely still, the wheelwright's daughter, who could be gone to for a cure. Will Stolley, Mary Tucker, others too. And there at the back Tom, come back, and by his side a gentleman riding. I tried to smile at Tom, and something in the crowd snapped.

'Look at her grinning like a pig in shit,' someone shouted. A clout of mud hit me and there was a whoop as a man on the bank lifted his smock and waggled his member.

'That's enough! Let us through.' Pugh sounded unsteady. The cart trundled on, but at every step it seemed to me that the shouts grew louder, thicker, though the constables would not let them at me. Richard Simons was beside me, glaring. I made myself stone, but the memory of the scratching jagged at me. Oh, how I wanted my father, wanted Jacob. It was so lonely on the cart. I looked for Aggie but I could not see her. I could hear my breath in my throat, straining. I could barely haul it in. It was heavier than a loaded wagon; I could hear the whine of it. Little Georgie Ladding wriggled through, grinned at me, tossed something at my feet. Oh God! A stinking rat, its eyes pecked out, maggots rippling under the skin. It bounced at my feet.

'There's one of your familiars back for you,' a man cried.

When I saw the rippling belly I fell forward retching and gasping, and I rubbed my wrists against the ropes until the pain loosened my chest. I could hear myself wailing; I was like a pig that knows it's to be stuck and killed, but I could not stop. We were nearing the Simons' house. I could not let Owen hear me like this. I must not. Perhaps Ann was by him, stopping his ears. Somehow, I pushed down on my shrieking breath till I could contain it. The mob had grown quieter to listen to my squealing and they were quite hushed for a moment. From the corner of my eye I saw Richard glance at the door and sign angrily. Ann was there, clutching a handkerchief, silently weeping. As she caught my eye she stretched out an arm to me. A murmur went through the crowd as strangers grasped whose house this was, that the boy lay suffering inside.

'Martha Dynely,' a strong voice rang out, 'confess. His mother points the finger of guilt at you. Her boy lies dying. He saw you cavorting with your Master to bring down the hill.'

Richard Simons broke his silence. 'We don't need her confession. Look at her, twisted in her guilt. Here, here, he lies dumb on the bed!' His voice was broken with pain and the crowd sucked on it and buckled in fury.

The cart stopped. Men had blocked its passage. I saw Pugh's horse begin to prance uneasy, beside me.

'We don't need a trial,' someone shouted.

'Aye, hang her here, on this tree.'

I looked about in horror. The constables had

staves, but there were fifty in the road at the least. Pugh glanced in panic at Tom and the gentleman beside him. I could see they were trying to push through, and others with them, but what could they do against such odds? An egg broke and spattered on my cloak. Then the air was thick with all the grit and shit and loose mud of the lane. A stone hit Pugh's horse and it reared and whinnied.

'In the Queen's name, I command you,' he was shouting, but nobody heard him. I hid my head in my arms. Pugh's voice rang out again, 'In the Queen's name, I tell you...'

I peered through the crook of my arms through the hail of stones and filth. Pugh was forcing his horse through the rabble, slashing the air around the cart to prevent men climbing on.

'There will be justice,' he cried. 'I tell you there will be... Oh, by the Lord Jesus, look!'

A gasp went through the crowd. The fury of the tumult died away all at once, just as a wind can drop and draw in silence in its stead. Even the birds stopped singing. 'Angel,' someone whispered low, and the word went from mouth to mouth. 'Angel...' There, at the door, in a long nightgown, his hand in his mother's, Owen had appeared. The crowd parted for him. I had not noticed how his hair had turned white like the snow that had buried him. Richard Simons took a step towards his son, his face knocked open with astonishment. Owen did not see him. He was advancing alone, falteringly, towards the cart, and when he reached it he began to try to pull himself on. Pugh nodded to one of the constables to help him up and there he was, standing in the grime on the planking opposite me. Somewhere, far away, a ewe called. There was no other sound. Owen put out his hand to push away the hair that had fallen in front of my face and I felt a great sob rise and break, and he flung his arms around my neck and was wiping the tears and blood from my cheeks.

'Don't go, Martha,' he said. 'Martha, don't let them take you. Please, Martha, please. Stay here.'

It was only a moment. I looked into his eyes and saw he was all himself again, his gaze as clear as May. It was only a moment, but it was enough. Even as I buried my face in his hair and clung to him I felt how the fury had dropped from the air.

'Be strong, Owen,' I whispered.

Then someone was pulling him free; he was bundled out of the cart and handed back to his mother. I held out my arms to him. The crowd was a silent congregation that parted without a word. We rolled on. Long after the cart had turned and the cottage was lost to view I held out my empty arms.

'Who would have thought that the boy should recover so,' Tom said, trotting up alongside me. 'If ever heaven sent a sign! They cannot hang you now, girl. Don't fret for Owen. Miss Elizabeth promised to set him up at school, aye, and Oxford too. Likely she didn't dream she'd be called upon to pay, but pay she will. This is Master Reginald Scot, Martha.' He gestured to the gentleman beside him. 'He's a scholar; he's going to speak for you in the trial at Ludlow.'

I must have looked from one to the other wildly enough, for Pugh took me by the arm. 'Do you understand, Martha', he said, very gently, 'you are being taken to Hereford and from thence to the Court of the Marches – to be tried as a witch?'

We had almost climbed the Cockshoot where

the mangled earth lay in sticky heaps about the road. Below me the crowd was as still as a painting. In a moment we would crest the ridge and the valley would be gone.

I nodded. 'To be tried,' I said.

EPILOGUE

When a partner takes your hands and swings you in the dance there is only his own face keen and clear. All else around you is a blear; be it barn or field, it swirls like pictures in water, although in truth it does not move. In those days and weeks after leaving the village I felt myself spinning. Everything further than my hand was like the streak of a bird in flight. I could not grasp it, so I let it go, until there was only the moment and the spaces where the moment happened.

Before I fell and was buried I had loved to dance; or to run so fast it was like letting go of the earth, tumbling through air as a swallow does –

but now I had had too much of giddiness. I needed to hold close to what pieces of a self were left.

It was not that I was in any kind of dream. No, I was acutely aware of each moment. I felt the high kee-kee-kee of a kestrel at Marden on the journey from Hereford to Ludlow and the newly warm sun on my neck; I saw how the light picked out each luminous leaf of a linden tree. Yet I did not understand Pugh's talk of law and the Court of the Marches. I noted he thought it good to be gone from Hereford, and let his explanations skitter off.

At first they put me in a hole with a dozen other women who one by one were taken out as their cases were heard. There were always more. None took kindly to sharing with a witch. Pugh had me moved to another cell with a woman who stank of death and rambled for two days and nights, with her voice going up and down as though scaling a ladder; the same phrases over and over.

'A groat, he said, and I'll bed you. Can't hang you if you're bagged, can they? And so I said, here's your money and he took it and spat. Go to, you rank middencunt, he says. I en't about to mell with you...'

When I tried to approach she scuttled into a corner, but didn't pause in her mumblings. – 'I won't let you down, Nell. A promise is a promise. A good strong pull, that's all. Three farthings and he'll let me do it straight. A good strong pull, clean and quick. It en't a sin, seeing as you're on your way already. Clean and quick, that's the way.'

At last she fell silent and soon after they took her away, whether to be hanged or not I didn't dare ask. Her words lingered through the dark. Had my father done that for my mother? Had he walked forwards and grasped her legs and pulled until she dangled limp and white like a throttled bird?

'When they hang me,' I said to Pugh as he sat one morning, quill in hand, to finish clerking my testimony. 'When they hang me, would you pull at my legs so I go off cleanly? I have a strong neck. I'm so afraid of the time it will take.'

He shook his head. 'I am a clerk of the court,

Martha. I can't do that. But if it should come to it, I promise I'll pay for another to do it.'

'I shouldn't want a stranger. I've no kin and have no friends to ask, unless Tom might come. Could you ask Tom?'

He put his quill down then and smiled. 'He'll not need to do it, Martha. Owen is growing stronger by the day. I have seen him. Richard Simons' anger abates. Owen's mother hopes to speak for you herself in court. You will be acquitted of malfeasance against the family, I'm sure of it.'

They seemed so far off; out somewhere in the world of fields and clouds, it was as though I could hardly remember their faces. All I could see, all I could bear to see, was the stone of my cell and Pugh's writing room. Beyond that was too much pain.

'Jacob?' I had not said his name for days. Not to Pugh, barely to myself.

'He is too ill to attend. That charge persists, but have hope. Do you remember the gentleman accompanying Tom when you were set upon? You are very fortunate – he is taking a special interest in your case. Such a remarkable man, highly talked of. Witchcraft, superstition, it is all delusion – it seeks to usurp the rightful place of God. Even if Goody Reynolds and the Widow testify...'

'He is too ill, then?'

'Yes, I am afraid so. I won't lie to you, Martha. I tried to speak to him but I was prevented. He – he did not wish to, they told me – they could not risk strangers. His word, even just a paper would make all the difference. The case would fall, I'm sure of it. His illness is against you. But don't despair. As it is, even if the charge against him is upheld, you will be released in a year or two. Perhaps then...'

So he was dying quickly; my death would be more slow. I thought of the mad woman in the cell, the sores on her face, the stink of her rotting body and all the ill usage that awaited me. I had heard what girls were made to do in the gaol and how it made them fester like flyblown fruit.

'He loved me.' I had not meant it to sound so much like a challenge, nor so hopeless.

Pugh looked a little flustered and bent his head down to the papers on his desk. 'We must put our trust in God,' he said. 'It will not be long now. The hearing begins tomorrow.'

I nodded vaguely. What cot did he lie in, I wondered. Perhaps they had moved already into my father's house and he lay dying in my bed. They would draw the shutters against the summer. I caught at his image to bury my thoughts in the feel and smell of him, but it hurt too much and my mind let go. There was only the stone and the high slit windows in the walls where the flies buzzed in.

'Martha, listen to me,' Pugh said. I tried to focus. 'You must cease giving the rats crumbs or you'll find they are cited as familiars. You are watched, you know.'

And so the trial began. Speechifying and outrage streamed round me. A great many people discovered me a witch. Some I had known and lived with since a child; some I had never met. Their faces, their voices, their angry pointing fingers were a noisy smear. I stood and looked at the floor or my hands; I thought of the walk from the gaol and the roses I'd glimpsed through a garden door, and, little by little, thinking slantwise, so I could stand it, I tried to picture Jacob.

Tom's gentleman strode up and down, cutting witnesses to pieces with his university talk. Then Ann came, and pleaded for me and wept, looking into my eyes with such affection I would have howled if I had let myself look back; if I hadn't willed myself as dried up as the polished wooden floor.

Tom's gentleman asked them to dismiss the case, then, but the justice said no, there was one more day allotted, to hear the other charge. Or perhaps a morning. It should only take a morning.

Pugh came himself early, long before I was needed. I had been awake most of the night, listening to the rain gutter down. I liked the sound, the loosening it seemed to speak of.

He carried a package, a bundle tied up in sacking under one arm. Behind him stood the guard with a pail of water.

'Tom sent this,' he said, thrusting the bundle towards me. 'It's a gown of his sister's. It might go better for you if you look a little less ragged. Clean yourself up as best you can, Martha, for the sentencing. All rests on how you are believed. You know they are to be called first thing.'

'The Widow is come too, then?'

'Yes, they arrived last night. She says he remains at the gates of death, that only her desire to serve the Lord Jesus and defeat the Devil could have brought her from his side. I warrant there'll be much weeping and wailing, can you bear it?'

'I think I can withstand any amount of railing. Her words are not so sharp as her nails.'

'I fear they may be. She is his mother, after all. She will paint his suffering and her own plight as bold as a pageant. The court can – or rather, it will – do nothing to gainsay her. It has refused to wait on his recovery. There is too much other business to be got through. The sentencing must be today. I'm sorry. I'll stand a little way off while you dress. Call me when you are done.'

My gaoler undid the shackles but he did not have Master Pugh's delicacy. I turned my back on him and untied the parcel. They were finer clothes than any I had ever worn. A white petticoat and a modest kirtle of bright blue. There was a comb, too, and I did what I could with it, after I had scrubbed myself, and used it to pin up my hair. They could call me a slut, but I would not look like one. The dress was a fair fit. I patted the skirts as though I were a lady and I felt the rumple of paper. Tom's sister had been careless not to check the pocket, but it was not my business, so I let it be and turned and called for Pugh.

There was no answer and so the gaoler, having nothing further to watch, shuffled off to find him. I waited. Outside the rain was giving way to a faltering brightness. Gently, a finger of light reached into my cell, making the dust motes dance. Perhaps, I thought, I should read the paper. It could be a prayer, perhaps. Even a list of goods or accounts would be welcome – it had been long enough since I'd read anything at all.

I drew it out. It was not a prayer, nor a list. The outside of the paper bore my name; it was a letter.

Martha, I write this by a friend. I was bedridden, then too weak to force the lock. I heard the man Pugh come but they held me down and gave out I could not speak. Enough of that, I must be quick. Take courage. My mother sets out tomorrow and I a heartbeat after. *Whither thou goest I will go.* You are my only kin now, I will swear it.

Footsteps approached and the door of the cell jerked open.

'Why,' said Pugh, 'you look well. The blue becomes you. If you look down prettily before the bench you may not get above a year.'

'Master Pugh', I asked, 'if Jacob were to come— '

'He could have saved you with a word. I'm sorry. Don't dwell on that. It's time.'

Sounds of the morning filtered from the street outside. I gripped the letter in my palm and stepped out of the cell.

HISTORICAL NOTE

If you walk up from Kynaston towards Woolhope
Cockshoot the Wonder is still clearly visible – the
hillside (now planted with blackcurrants), shelves
away and at the bottom of a sunken lane, its roots
exposed, is the Kynaston Chapel yew. The place is
marked on OS Map 189 as 'The Wonder (Landslip)'. Nothing remains of Kynaston Chapel and it
was never rebuilt. An entry in the *Transactions of
the Woolhope Naturalists' Field Club* of 1899 reports
the farmer at Hall End Farm's recollections of his
father using some of the scattered blocks of stone
for farm buildings. The Chapel bell however, was
unearthed, and by the end of the eighteenth or

beginning of the nineteenth century had found its way to Homme House in Much Marcle, where it hung till the 1960s in the Tower Wing, calling and dismissing workmen from the park and ringing out the curfew.

Camden describes the slip as an instance of 'brasmatia' a kind of earthquake that, according to Aristotle, was accompanied by a violent shaking. His evocative account (published first in Latin in 1586), which I have used as an epigraph, made the Wonder famous. Successive early chroniclers, beginning with John Speed in his *Historie of Great Britaine* (1611), returned to it; Sir Richard Baker, in his *Chronicle of the Kings of England* (1643) noted it began at 'On February 17th at six o' clock p.m. in the 13th year of Elizabeth'; Gideon Harvey in his *Archeologia Philosophia Nova* (1663) writes that 'the hole which this eruption made was at least 40 foot wide, and 80 yards long, lasting from Saturday in the Evening untill Munday at noon.' Samuel Butler gave it a mention in his celebrated Restoration poem *Hudibras*:

Inchant the king's and church's lands
T'obey and follow your commands;

And settle on a new freehold
As Marcly-hill had done of old.

In Elizabethan England phenomena had meaning - they were a warning, a sign, or a foul disruption of divine order (open therefore, to different readings). On stage the elements echoed Lear's madness, and Caesar's murder was heralded by disturbances in nature – because the 'heavens themselves blaze forth the death of princes.' Although as early as 1662 J. Childrey explained the landslip geologically, noting the 'fat and clammy soil,' early commentators emphasised wondrous, possibly divine causes. In America the Wonder as witchcraft resurfaced in 1684 when it was cited by Increase Mather, father of Cotton Mather and defender of the Salem witch trials, in his work *Remarkable Providences*, which sought to persuade that witches and witchcraft were real.

It was not witchcraft of course which caused the slip, but the rain percolating through the beds of clay and limestone that form the ridge. With the burgeoning interest in local history and antiquities in the late eighteenth and nineteenth centuries the Wonder continued to attract visitors – a regular stop for naturalists, geologists and antiquarians. The topography and relics sustained public interest – in 1893 for example the fate of the Kynaston bell prompted a lively and extended debate in the letters pages of the *Hereford Journal*.

BOOK CLUB QUESTIONS

- What do you think of Walter Dynely –
  how much sympathy do you have
  for him?
- What is Martha's relationship to the
  village and the place she comes from?
  Does it change, do you think?
- As I write this, Herefordshire is still
  suffering from appalling floods. Do
  you think there are any parallels in the
  way our society today is responding to
  the climate catastrophe and the way
  people respond to the landslip in the
  novel?

- I was drawn to the way magic and superstition and religion were intertwined for Elizabethan people – how different are we now?
- Do you think Father Paul is sincere?
- The historian Eamon Duffy describes the tracts of the Reformation as 'a relentless torrent carrying away the landmarks of a thousand years' – how are the social and religious tensions of the Reformation played out in the novel?
- How much agency do women have in the world of the novel?
- Martha's grandmother warned her not to trust the gentry – 'We go on foot and they ride,' she'd say, 'and no matter how good they are they won't have us riding along with them; they'll leave us in the dirt sooner than slip out of the saddle.' How socially fixed is social class in the world of the novel?
- Although the story itself is fictional the places in the novel are real and the

Wonder itself is a historical event. How important do you think it is for historical fiction to try to be accurate? How much liberty with the facts is too much?

- Following on from that – why do you think we like to try to enter the worldview of people who died so long ago?
- What do you think will happen to Martha next – what will she do?

ACKNOWLEDGMENTS

Thank you first to people: to Chris Xia for letting Martha live with us so long; to Joe and Lily my next best readers; to Tilda for pulling me back to the present; to wonderful Peter Buckman my agent, for championing my work; to Amanda Ridout for falling for Martha and, with the fabulous team at Boldwood, looking after her and me so well; to fellow Scribblers Olivia Levez, Mike Woods, Cathy Knights, Tim Reeves and Mel Dufty, for so much patient critiquing; to all my lovely friends for their support, particularly Kathleen Cattle and Clare Mockridge for their careful reading of an early draft and Jane Greenwood,

Louise Collinge and Miriam Farbey for their generous advice; to John Porter and Sarah Eisner for their enthusiasm and help; to Sarah Porter for ideas and weekends; to my parents who took me on the hills and showed me the Wonder and who have given and continue to give me so much.

Next a thank you to books (and maps): OS Map 189 was my constant companion (the Wonder is still marked on it); I'm indebted to Keith Thomas's seminal *Religion and the Decline of Magic*; to Eamon Duffy's *The Voices of Morebath* and *The Stripping of the Altars*; to *Witchcraft in Europe* ed. Alan Kors and Edward Peters, particularly for the *Malleus Malleficarum*; to Robert MacFarlane's wordhoard *Landmarks*; to William Camden's *Britannia*, Ella Leather's *The Folklore of Herefordshire*. All my many mistakes, of course, are my own.

MORE FROM ELEANOR PORTER

We hope you enjoyed reading *The Wheelwright's Daughter*. If you did, please leave a review.

If you'd like to gift a copy, this book is also available as an ebook, digital audio download and audiobook CD.

Sign up to Eleanor Porter's mailing list for news, competitions and updates on future books.

http://bit.ly/EleanorPorterNewsletter

ABOUT THE AUTHOR

Eleanor Porter has lectured at Universities in England and Hong Kong and her poetry and short fiction has been published in magazines. *The Wheelwright's Daughter* is her first novel.

Follow Eleanor on social media:

facebook.com/ellie_porter_author

twitter.com/elporterauthor

instagram.com/eleanorporterauthor

ABOUT BOLDWOOD BOOKS

Boldwood Books is a fiction publishing company seeking out the best stories from around the world.

Find out more at www.boldwoodbooks.com

Sign up to the Book and Tonic newsletter for news, offers and competitions from Boldwood Books!

http://www.bit.ly/bookandtonic

We'd love to hear from you, follow us on social media:

facebook.com/BookandTonic

twitter.com/BoldwoodBooks

instagram.com/BookandTonic

Lightning Source UK Ltd.
Milton Keynes UK
UKHW042342030921
389811UK00005B/537